Infinite Money Glitch

Infinite Money Glitch

James Krake

The door to Hightackle's Odds and Ends flew open, clattering the bell. Wulf, the proprietor, came walking around the corner, squinting at the script window he had pulled up in his hand. He scratched the stubble on his chin and said, "Welcome adventurer! To the world of Reborn Isles Five! I am so... happy to... hold on a moment."

The customer's face looked like he had bathed in nuclear waste and got cancer instead of magical powers. His cheekbones were nearly higher than his eyes, his brow was wider than his ears, and his nose more bulbous than a troll's. The tattoos and scars were all over the place as well, about one step better than clown makeup.

In short, he looked like he had hit 'random' on the face generator.

"I need bombs. Let's go. Come on, I got your money right here," he said, slamming some silver knights onto the counter. "Come on, come on, come on, I'm in a rush. Come on."

Wulf snarled and jabbed a finger at his customer. "You're Obby, aren't you? Back here again, eh?"

"Sell me your bombs, money man!"

Wulf's face went almost as red as Obby's complexion. "A

bomb this time? What could you possibly need a bomb for? Give me the iron ore or get out."

Obby reached into his pack and dumped ten chunks of iron ore out on the counter next to the money. Five copper pawns each retail for the player, six to the System. All to-gether, one silver of profit and the only expense to Wulf was documenting the experience points, exp, distributed for the tutorial quest, System-subsidized of course.

"Bomb!"

Wulf stamped his foot. "Use full sentences, will you? Are you a toddler? I may be only three years old but I can still speak better than you can, you fucking speedrunner!"

Obby huffed and grabbed the edge of the counter. The expression he adopted was technically a smile but his lips, more botox-injected than a has-been celebrity's, seemed to be begging for mercy as he spread them from ear to ear. "My good gentleman, would you please sell me the bomb item I have requested, posthaste! Come on, chop-chop!"

Wulf snorted and crossed his arms. "And why should I rush?" he asked, but the iron ore was good quality. He had to jab his finger into the 'quest completed' acknowledgement to make the window go away.

Obby didn't even blink when he got enough experience from the quest to level up from one to two. Instead, he shouted, "Then it's time for the back-up strat!" and bolted for the door to the basement.

Wulf's eyes shot open. "Oh, shit!" His shop was a hovel compared to what the guilds in the capital had, but it was still his property. With barely more than standing room to cross, he vaulted the counter and threw himself at Obby.

The speedrunner slammed his heel into the lock on the door, rattling the thing and bringing its durability down by half.

"You stop that!" Wulf screamed, and tackled the man to the ground. The two of them hit the floorboards. "You may be a player but I've still got three levels on you, you little shit!"

Obby did some kind of martial arts trick, not System-assisted in the least, and threw Wulf across the room.

The merchant hit the wall hard enough to break one of his shelves. His collection of for sale geodes smashed to the ground and went rolling around him. Useless to anyone but an apprentice jeweler, but to them commanded a price of two silver knights apiece. Wulf had gotten them each for a single silver.

He groaned, but saw Obby about to kick his door down. He could not have a player go down there, especially one almost certainly livestreaming. "Fine!" Wulf shouted. "I'll sell you your bombs!"

Obby stopped at once and smiled at Wulf.

Wulf scowled and rubbed the back of his bruised head as he got back behind the counter. The money was there, three silver, enough for two bombs. Wulf swiped it into his inventory and set down two bombs. They were ancient things from the initial release of Reborn Isles V, RIV, as evidenced by their plain name. If they were an actually useful item, they would have had a copyrighted name like "Dungalf's Blaze Powder".

Wulf planted his elbow on the counter and asked, "What do you even want with these things, anyways?" They only did fixed damage, and it was so low it became useless after level 10. For the speedrunner, that would be barely twenty minutes later.

"hyper-slide," Obby stated, and lit one of the bombs. He dropped it right at his feet as he backflipped and equipped his shield. He landed with a warcry–activating the [Block] skill– right as the bomb went off.

Wulf's counter shotgunned splinters at him. His windows flew open and he was tossed against the wall, for the second time, like a ragdoll.

He hit the ground at critical health as Obby went sliding backwards and blew through the door to his shop. The System couldn't reconcile the forced knockback with the [Block] skill properly, which led to Wulf watching the speedrunner slide away from him at something like a hundred kilometers an hour. What should have been a long trek through the tutorial zone wasn't.

Amidst the ruined debris that had been his shop, Wulf could only say, "Fucking Players."

He quaffed a healing potion and got back to his feet. Just looking at the debris made him groan and slump his shoulders. He didn't even need to get his key out for the basement, the blast had broken the lock. "Hey, Garry!" he called as he headed down the steps. "When's the next server reset expected?"

"'Nother two days, 'innit?" his co-conspirator called back.

"Was thinking we could go down to the pub and have some fun since everything'll get put back. Why?"

"That rat-bastard Obby just blew up the shop!" Part of Wulf wished Obby had gotten down to the basement. While he was only a level four, Garry was a level thirty-two war golem and could have punched a hole through his head. It just would have come at the cost of needing to relocate after.

Garry lifted his stone head and had to take off his jeweler's loupe to look at him from overtop the mountains of iron ore the two of them had amassed. "Seriously? That what that noise was?"

All put together, Wulf estimated that the entire worth of his shop, above ground, was a little less than two gold. That was exactly how much a tutorial merchant should have in case a player wanted to go the way of thieving. All the freedom of RIV had to be available from the moment the player set foot in the game.

In the basement, the two of them had a stack, sixty-four, of iron ore barrels, each with a stack of iron ore in them. Sixty-four times sixty-four times six copper pawns was a fortune of two-hundred and forty-five gold and seventy-six copper pawns. It was far more than any fresh player could dream of getting, but that was just the apparent value.

Garry, with his jeweler's loupe hanging off his brow and equipped with a delicate array of mechanical grippers strapped to his granite fingers, was able to use the [Inspect] skill on the ores every single time the server reset, and there was always a fresh chance that any given iron ore might actually be a gemstone. On a long enough timescale, every iron ore would eventually be discovered to be a gemstone.

It was free money.

Wulf groaned and grabbed one of the chairs. He flipped it around and straddled it, folding his arms along the back and staring at Garry's workbench. "I'll just switch to a backup quest or something. I bet I can put in with the System to spawn some kind of rampaging beast nearby, drum it up that it broke into my shop and ruined everything."

Garry squinted and scraped at one of the shiny rocks. The technique behind his appraisal was completely incomprehensible to Wulf, but Garry couldn't even dream of understanding the magic items that Wulf handled. Skills were like that.

Garry asked, "You sure you got your Wild Animal License? That it didn't expire?"

That made the merchant frown. "I mean, it's been a while sure, but it hasn't been a year since the last time this happened."

"System updated it to every three months a little bit ago."

Wulf's head fell forward, hitting his arms. "Why? Why would they make that kind of regulation?"

"Ask Lord Cohen, not me. Ah!" Garry exclaimed. His tool fractured the iron ore, split it right down the middle. A rough emerald tumbled onto his workbench. "That makes ten for today," the golem said, setting the rubble aside and getting his cutting tools out. The System would buy emeralds at nineteen copper pawns apiece and sell them for twenty. They didn't used to be worth so much, but as RIV expanded, most

Players had enough quests available to simply skip the inspection process by dumping money into the market and buying geodes. One hundred and ninety copper pawns, or nineteen silver knights, was enough for the two of them to get drunk and then some.

Wulf picked his head up and started checking the chalk marks on the barrels. Garry marked the ones he had gotten through so as to not accidentally double-[Inspect] the same lot. Nearly twenty barrels still needed to be checked, and the server reset was in a few days. "Do we have too much iron ore?"

Garry glanced up from his grinder work. He counted the barrels too and said, "I guess we might. They've been doing a lot more server resets lately."

"Yeah, ever since they tried to synchronize with the asian servers. But, like, if you can't [Inspect] all of them in time, what's the point in having the extra barrels?"

Garry shrugged. "Dunno man. You better not be about to ask me to work overtime or something."

Wulf returned the shrug. "We could bring in a third?"

"No!" the golem snapped. "This is only working because we've kept it quiet. Three people can't keep a secret. You know that."

Wulf put his hands up and leaned away. "Alright, alright. But if you can't [Inspect] them all, why keep them? How about I toss one of these barrels in the cart and take it into town to sell when I put in for the new quest?"

Garry shook his head. "Fine, just one though. We don't

need people asking why you have so much of the stuff, right? Here," he said, and tossed the fresh-cut emerald to him. Then came a pouch with the other nine.

Wulf dropped the gem in, then stashed the pouch into his bag inventory so he didn't have to carry it—magic bags were wonderful like that. "Right then, I'll be back in a few hours."

Obby hadn't blown up the cart, nor spooked the donkey harnessed to it, so Wulf hauled one of the barrels up and got it into the back. His magic bag wasn't big enough to fit the barrel inside, not without abandoning the rest of his equipment. So he hopped up in the driver seat and snapped the reins.

His shop was at a crossroads in the woods, which put it close to hunting grounds for quests. That meant it was small, hard to supply, and had been extremely expensive to buy. It had paid off though, and the privacy to abuse the [Inspect] skill had been a wonderful surprise.

The road to town didn't have monsters, not in a tutorial zone. What it had was autonomous guards. "Hello steelface," he said with a wave to the first patrol guard he passed. The guard didn't react. The only difference between a guard and a monster was their friend-or-foe tag.

"Hello tasteless critter," he said with a wave to a short-tailed squirrel. He'd trapped one once. It had tasted like the dirt it dug up rather than the nuts it hid away.

"Hello... anti-afk person," he said to a player that kept sitting down and standing up from a camping stool. Every other cycle, he dropped a rock on the ground and picked it back up. Wulf squinted his eyes and appraised the player's gear. Looked like the player had rushed through the optimized quest chain. Wulf recognized most of the bandit gear from the tutorial zone's first dungeon, which meant they were at least level nine.

However, the player, the real human on the other side of the simulation, wasn't actually there, wasn't able to defend himself. The tutorial zone was safe from aggressive monsters and not worth the time of player-killers, but that didn't mean he wasn't essentially a pile of risk-free experience points there for the taking.

Wulf slipped a hand to his waist, grabbing his dagger. Experience points were nearly as good as gold, and he wasn't one to turn down free rewards. He glanced up and down the dirt road, between the trees and bushes, and leaned so far he almost fell out of his seat as he slid his dagger free of its sheath.

Then one of the steelfaces came marching into sight. It was only risk free if he didn't get spotted.

"Bastard," he grumbled, and shoved the dagger back in. "Ya! Come on, I need a drink," he barked at the ass. He spat at the steelface on his way. Again, no response from the System-controlled automaton.

The Valley of Greenhorn, the tutorial zone, ended at the walls of Greenhorn City. Huge bricks of granite loomed overhead three stories high. That, of course, was taller than anything in the valley, but shorter than the giants that showed up for special events. With the fast-approaching release of the Shadowed Horizons expansion, there was no chance of that happening though.

The steelfaces didn't bother him as he rolled in and he dutifully plugged his ears to the small army of Players on fresh, anonymous accounts selling blowjobs and buying girl-friends. The stables were filled with screams and moans as he rolled past it.

"Players..." Wulf grumbled. His lips snarled all the way to the auction house outpost. "It's Hightackle, I've got some iron ore to sell!" he called through the window counter. He leaned on the sill, one hand resting on the barrel. He drummed his fingers against the wood as the receptionist came walking up.

Arriene Guilder was gorgeous. She had the special kind of finesse and care that only a few NPCs in the whole game had. Not too tall, with thick locks of blond hair that fell about her shoulders and a perfect pout to her lips. She was the first banker most Players would encounter in the game, and the attention to detail showed.

Recent expansions had overshadowed that detail, intro-ducing other tutorial zones for boosted leveling. She was simply the first banker. At least for Wulf her beauty wasn't wasted, despite the sounds of three separate player orgies hap-pening behind him. It took most of his mental fortitude to compartmentalize that.

"Hightackle, we meet again," she said, her pout a bit too much like a frown. "More gems for me?" She held out her hand and stared at him.

Wulf cleared his throat. "Oh, yeah, yeah, I got those too." He fished the pouch out of his inventory and passed it over.

Arriene snatched it from him, turned away and deposited them into the slot box that would vanish them off into the System, wherever in the world that warehouse was. Coins clattered out of the chute next to it, and she walked them back. "Nineteen silver. Should be plenty for you to get drunk on."

Wulf stacked the coins up, hefted them in his hand and looked to Arriene. "Enough for three people to have a drink, I'd say. I'd love to-"

"What's in the barrel?" she interjected. No amount of money or exp or fame could get him a second chance with her. But, as he told himself every time he got drunk, there was no harm in trying to get enough money.

Wulf swallowed his words and vanished the coins into his purse. "Iron ore, said so earlier."

She pulled on a latch, and part of the wall between them slid open so the barrel could be shoved inside. She took it back to the slot box and tossed the ore into the drawer by the handful.

Wulf drummed his fingers on the counter and looked back around the town. The bank was in the outer region of Greenhorn, where anyone could go, hence why all the level ones were about and drawing in the other Players of low moral fiber. He wasn't the only tutorial quest giver either. Store windows were littered with quest advertisements for everything from career training to guild recruitment.

None of the Players were interested though, and the other NPCs just used the stipend to enjoy life in the inner district. He could see the steelfaces checking levels to get in. Lord Cohen had made that essentially a gated community in an attempt to contain the degeneracy without eradicating it. The System profited hand over fist from Players on burner accounts. They weren't going to spend the time to actually earn the outfits they wanted.

Arriene dropped the purse on the counter. It hit like a boulder and he groaned to see how fat it was. She must have paid him in coppers rather than changing it up to silver.

"Well, Hightackle, you should have led with that. I guess you might finally be making something of yourself," Arriene said. She crossed her arms over her... bountiful and distracting... chest, as Wulf pulled the purse strings open. Yellow light bounced back at him.

Wulf's eyes shot open.

"Here's your six-hundred-and-forty gold. I guess the price of iron ore went up recently. Lucky you."

Wulf's mouth gaped. "Uh... uhhhh... I'll be back in a bit!" he shouted and bolted for his cart to go get the rest.

2

"Garry! Garry, get the barrels! We're going to town!"

The golem looked up from his spot atop an enormous heap of wolf pelts, which was the closest thing he had to a seat. "Oh, come on, man, I'm tryna watch The_Telly," he said, gesturing at the interface window he had pulled up in front of him. Earth-side videos couldn't technically be watched inside RIV—copyright and all that—but they did have Priority RIV Content Creators, PRiCCs, that could stream their gameplay. It was sort of like television, especially when they used hacked clients to do picture-in-picture for other content while they did something menial like [Inspect] hundreds of ores.

"Forget The_Telly!" Wulf shouted. He grabbed hold of the nearest barrel and hauled it back towards the steps.

Garry didn't move, he was watching some kind of bad lip-syncing video that The_Telly was backdooring into his stream.

Wulf chucked the purse of gold at him, hitting him in the chest with it.

"What was that for?" the golem demanded, only to then look at the gigantic pile of gold in his hands.

Wulf stopped hauling with a huff and threw his arms to

either side. "Iron ore is currently worth ten gold apiece! Come on, we're going to the market. Grab everything you can. We've got over forty thousand gold sitting here, Garry!"

"Naaawww, this has to be a mistake. Or did some glitch-hunter find an exploit?"

Wulf planted his hands on his hips. "Straight from the System. The prices automatically adjust if their warehouses start to run low or too full. I've never seen it move more than a copper or two before though. I don't know what the hell happened, but other people are going to notice. Now, come on! You've got a higher level magic bag than me, don't you?"

Garry finally closed his stream and stood upright. He was head and shoulders taller than Wulf, and had to stoop beneath the floorboards. "In volume, not in spaces," he said, grabbing one of the barrels and dropping it entirely into his inventory.

"Well, take everything else out!"

The golem twisted around to look at him. "What? Even my weapon?"

Wulf rolled his eyes. "Oh, give me your weapon. I can fit that in my bag. You've got sixteen slots, right? That means you can take sixteen barrels. I'll carry your stuff."

Garry frowned and wavered.

"Six hundred and forty gold each."

"Fine," he said, and withdrew Toothbreaker; his Epic rarity greatsword. The thing weighed at least twenty kilos and had more usage restrictions than a modern EULA had clauses, but Wulf was able to pick it up, thanks to his Merchant class, and put it in his own inventory. A pleasant perk for identifying cursed items.

By the time he had one barrel into the cart, and gone down for the second, Garry had filled his entire inventory with sixteen barrels of iron ore and came marching up behind him.

"Come on, come on, we gotta hurry," Wulf said, peering at the sun. Once the barrels were loaded, he snapped the reins and set the donkey back towards Greenhorn. It was a tiny cart, so small that with two barrels in it neither of them could ride. He wasn't going to complain about walking though. "Sun's going down soon," Wulf said, trying to measure the distance between the sun and the horizon with his fingers.

"We're gunna get bandit attacks at this rate."

"I swear, if the System re-enabled bandit attacks here, I'm going to rip someone's head off." His heart was hammering worse than a marathon. Too much excitement, too much fear.

Garry coughed through his nose, the closest thing the rock could make to a snort. "If you did, maybe you'd finally level up."

"Oh, you know I hate fighting!" Wulf shot back, then he saw the player with the anti-afk setup again. Still there, still dropping rocks and picking them back up. There were no steelfaces either. His hand went to his dagger and his chest yearned for the literally free exp.

But he tore himself away and urged the donkey on.

The town gates were still open when they arrived, but there were more Players than ever. Wulf took the lead, shouting at people and shoving idiots out of the way of the cart. Garry lumbered behind, one plodding step at a time. He switched to a rhythm like a metronome and kept his gaze locked on the two barrels in the cart.

Even with that unthinking behavior, some half-dressed tart grabbed him by the arm. "Hey there, sex-machine. Do you get paid by the hour?"

He couldn't just ignore them, so he turned and said in monotone, "Greetings, adventurer. Do you need directions somewhere?"

The player scoffed and rolled her eyes. At once she let go of him to vanish back into the twilight district to get her kink sated elsewhere.

Wulf nodded. "Your steelface impression is better than ever."

"Why the hell do I get approached instead of you? I don't even have the equipment! They can see it too. It's not like I'm wearing pants here."

Wulf took the part of his mind that wanted to compare his attractiveness to a golem's and killed it. He said, "The Players here ain't right in the head. You know that. And that's saying something 'cause-"

"'Cause no player is right in the head," Garry cut in, saying exactly what Wulf had been about to say.

"Right. Come on. Market's about to close. Let's get these sold and get into the inner district before it's too late," Wulf said and pulled the donkey into the plaza that had the bank.

Arriene was there, leaning on the counter with a melon juice and a book. She heard them approach, and the twitch in her lip only lasted a fraction of a second, until she saw the cart. "You have more?"

Wulf jumped up in the cart. "Yeah, told you I'd be back. I'm always a man of my word."

She folded her arms. "You mean like when you said you would pay for my dinner two years ago?"

Wulf nearly died from the psychic damage. Not actual hit points, of course, but close enough. "I paid you back for that!"

"You didn't pay for the interest though."

"Well, maybe I will now, then!" he shouted, and nearly threw one of the barrels off the back, to get it over to the door.

Arriene sighed and helped slide it in. While she was exchanging the iron, Wulf and Garry got the other one queued up outside. They grinned at one another, giggling and hunched over like they were about to dive into a rugby scrum.

She walked back, dropped another purse on the counter and asked, "What are you doing?"

Wulf and Garry glanced at each other. "What do you mean?" Wulf asked. "I've got more to sell."

"I mean why are you blocking the door? I have to return both barrels to you. I'm not throwing these out for you, you know."

Wulf jumped to it, twisting the barrel out of the way. "Come on, come on, the sun's going down," he said, but Arriene took her sweet time shoving the empty barrels back out. The moment he could get his fingers on them, he tossed them into the street gutters. "Right then," he said, and shoved the third barrel through.

He huffed as he watched her drag it back over and start exchanging the ores. Then someone tapped him on the shoulder.

A steelface stared at him with unflinching, soulless eyes. "Littering is not allowed, citizen. Please clean up your mess or you will have to pay a fine."

"A fine? What is wrong with you! Can't you see I'm actively selling my goods. Look, look at me, I'm a merchant. This is my job. Buzz off!" Wulf shouted. Spittle flew from his lips and onto the guard's visor, to no reaction.

When he turned away again, the steelface grabbed him by the shoulder and spun him back around. "Failure to pay the fine will result in forced imprisonment," the guard said, his voice louder.

Nearly lifted off his feet and losing time, Wulf put up his hands. "Alright! Alright, what is the fine? How much, eh?" Wulf demanded as Arriene handed him the next purse of coins on the counter.

She was smirking at him.

"Five silver," the steelface said.

Wulf took one of the gold coins from the purse and flicked it like a bottle cap, hitting the guard in the face with it. That shut the steelface up, and he was able to sell two more barrels from Garry's inventory.

Consequently, two more empty barrels ended up on the side of the road, and the steelface went on repeat. The guard grabbed him by the back of his shirt and hauled him up like a child. As pawns of the System, steelfaces had stupidly high stats. "Littering is not allowed, citizen. Please clean up your mess or you will have to pay a fine."

Wulf screamed. He wanted to throttle the steelface, but the guard was at least level fifty. Every moment the guard delayed him was less time he had to sell iron ore, more time that one of the Player guilds would have to realize they could cash in too, and it was fucking humiliating to have Arriene watch the display.

"Garry, keep this up," he growled, and turned his back on the exchange. He stomped over to the nearest streetcorner and shoved a couple of pretend prostitutes aside. He cleared his throat, cupped his hands around his mouth, and proclaimed, "Hear ye, hear ye! A new quest is being offered! Dispose of these barrels and you shall be rewarded with half a gold coin for each! Limited time only!"

After a moment of processing, the System produced a proclamation window beside him. The sign, like any other interface window, hung in the air like a hologram rather than anything in the fantasy aesthetic, but it repeated everything he had just said for those that hadn't been paying attention.

For as much as Wulf hated Players, they were good for some things. For the right amount of money, they were the quickest, most reliable mercenaries one could imagine. For a paltry nine gold rooks, a small mob assembled around him to do his bidding. The moment the litter became part of a quest for the all-important Players, they stopped being a crime. Wulf marched back to the auction house and spat on the steelface's boots.

While he and Garry resumed swapping the barrels, he saw one lift the barrel up overhead and go sprinting to the river to toss it in. Another used his ax like a woodchipper, reducing three barrels to splinters so small they had to be deleted by the System before the lag crashed the server. The rest were burned. Player vs Player damage was disabled inside Greenhorn, another of the perks of being in the tutorial section, so a pyromancer simply fireballed the crowd as Garry tossed more empty barrels to them.

Then Arriene slammed the shutters on her window and bolted the door. The time had hit night, and no more could be sold to the System.

Garry was left standing there with a full barrel of iron ore in his hands, gawking at the shut window.

The pyromancer didn't even stop to think, and fireballed Garry. The golem roared in pain, more from shock than actual hit point damage. He was made of stone and level thirty-two. He still shouted, "Guards! I'm under attack!" but it was too late. The barrel split.

Sixty-four iron ores spilled out into the street at everyone's feet, and the vast majority of the mob hadn't disposed of a single barrel. They did see a cheap windfall right in front of them though.

"Grab them!" Wulf shouted and dove. He slid on his knees, scooping up one ore after another. He fit the ones he could into his bag inventory and when that filled up, he held out the hem of his shirt like a sack and started heaping them up. Garry tried to help, but the swarm of Players were like magpies.

"Quest completed!" the pyromancer shouted in Wulf's ear, grabbing and shaking him by the shoulder.

He snarled and wanted to bite their hand off, but the System dutifully informed him that they had disposed of eight barrels. He jammed the Accept button, and four gold coins vanished from his purse to appear in the pyromancer's clutches. He had to do the same for the human woodchipper, dispensing another fifteen silver knights.

By then, he couldn't find any more ore. He had only gotten twenty, and Garry thirteen. The majority had ended up in the pockets of fleeing Players. He found himself sitting with his back to the market building, face buried in his hands. He knew that the stolen ore would technically be flagged as such, but all they had to do was sell it to a low-level blacksmith player and the ore would get consumed, never to haunt them. Some of them might have access to a thieves' guild's fence and get even more for it.

Garry sat down beside him. He patted Wulf on the knee. "Cheer up. This is a good thing. Guess we'll come back tomorrow, yeah? Show up in the morning and the price should still be the same."

Wulf sighed. "The System adjusts prices between server instances in after-market trading. It probably won't be this good tomorrow, but what choice do we have? Can't believe we got interrupted like that."

"You know what they say; don't look a gift horse in the mouth," the golem said, and clapped him on the back. "Not like we were ever expecting this, and I did manage to get eleven of them sold. We've never been richer!"

Wulf nodded and glared at the city. Eventually, he did the math and said, "Seven thousand, six hundred and sixty-nine gold."

"Nice."

The employee door to the market building opened and shut, the lock rattled tight, and Arriene walked over to the two of them. "Okay," she said, and put her hands on her hips. "You're going to have to explain what you just did. Given your earlier plan to get yourself piss-drunk tonight, I assume you're available."

Garry had to reach over and close Wulf's jaw for him.

The three of them ended up at Mead's Mill and Tap-room, a two-storied tavern that always smelled of yesterday's ale, always had a fight building up or winding down, and never actually had any mead for sale. The proprietor wasn't even named Mead, because the original had cracked and gone insane during the Plague of the Lich King event.

Wulf couldn't believe it, and couldn't shut himself up either. "What would you like to drink? To eat? We could get some appetizers. We could even get some of the wine imports. The elven bottles! We should get one of the elven bottles." Wulf kept flipping from one menu to another.

Arriene rolled her eyes. "Those bottles went rancid, I can't imagine why you'd even think of paying for them. The elves use clay pots to ferment their wine, not wood. No wood equals no preservatives. Ergo, those amphoras are rancid."

Wulf shared a shrug with Garry. "Yeah, but we'd be the only people in the bar with wine."

"Rancid wine," Arriene corrected.

"Still wine, ain't it?"

She sighed and shook her head. The waitress came over and took his order. After, Arriene asked, "You never change, do you, Hightackle? So how did you do it?"

"Years of planning and execution," he said, but could only keep his face straight for so long. "Actually, I was as surprised as you were when the price came in this afternoon. Had I been planning this, I would have brought all the iron ore that morning."

Arriene pursed her lips. Her scrutinizing look made him squirm.

"I've just been accumulating the stuff through my quest posting, for like a year now. I wasn't entirely lying when I said I'd been planning this. Just... I had a different plan and today was an audible call."

Her gaze moved to Garry. Had the golem hair on the back of his neck, it would have stood up. Garry hadn't even been paying attention to the conversation and had The_Telly pulled back up, but he sensed her attention on him. She narrowed her eyes and asked, "Cornering the market on gems, then? The emeralds you sold this morning?"

The golem said, "You don't have to say it like we're doing something wrong. The shop is entirely above-board!"

"Just tedious work, I imagine."

"You know," Wulf said, sliding a bit closer to her. He leaned on the table, conspiratorially. "We've got more ore still. Didn't get it all in before trading stopped."

Arriene leaned in too. "How much more?"

"How much could you squeeze into your office to dump the moment trading starts tomorrow morning?"

"I should be able to fit thirty barrels in, if I double stack them, but that will take me almost an hour to liquidate."

"I can get you thirty barrels."

"I can't process them if Players show up to use the market square. NPCs always get bumped to the end of the line."

"I'll have to figure out a distraction. Good thing I've got all night to prepare."

"Half," Arriene said.

Wulf's jaw dropped. "What?"

"I said I want half."

"That's absurd!"

She flicked her head to get the hair out of her face and pursed her lips at him. "The price is going to be tanking tomorrow when the System tries to start correcting. You're feeding the demand anyways, you yourself would be crashing this price spike. I'm getting you in early, ahead of the fall. Therefore, I want half."

Garry rose from the table. "She's right. Just pay her," he said before leaving to catch up with a friend he had espied in the tavern.

Wulf gritted his teeth and fought with it, but Arriene never lost her composure. "Fine! Half of what you earn us by getting us in early."

"Seventy-five percent of that, then. Money you wouldn't make without me."

Wulf growled and huffed. The waitress finally set their

drinks down; two ales and no rancid wine. He snatched up his mug and waited for Arriene to pick up hers. Her eyebrow was suitably arched at the sight of the drink, and he offered a toast. "Deal."

"Pleasure doing business with you," she said, and tapped her drink against his. "So what are you going to do with all this money?"

Wulf frowned and drank a good amount of his ale. After licking his lips clean, he said, "I don't know. Maybe Garry has a point about affording one of the houses in Hub. I'd be one of the only NPCs in the whole world that lived there..."

The door to the tavern opened up and instantly Wulf got a notification window in front of him, that a player was attempting to redeem his quest. The last barrel, the one tossed in the river, still had to be paid. Then he saw the player's name and his lips snarled.

"Obby."

3

The speedrunner spotted him instantly and took a direct line sprint for him. He vaulted railings, trampled tables and knocked the waitress down. Her tray of appetizers splattered across the floor as he jumped down in front of Wulf. The speedrunner nearly threw himself onto the table, slapping his hand down between them. "Pay up! Quest complete!" He started jabbing his finger on the table, tapping it like there was a service bell to ring.

Wulf leapt up. His chair smacked the ground behind him. "Learn some damn manners!"

"Pay me, merchant boy. I need the money."

"You ran all the way to the river to toss out a barrel for five silver?" Wulf asked.

"Pay me, pay me now."

Wulf groaned and jabbed the Accept button. Another half gold coin vanished from his pocket and appeared in Obby's hand. The speedrunner pivoted and grabbed the waitress by the hand. He immediately put the coin into her grasp and barked out, "Elven wine please."

The girl slowly regained the color in her cheeks as she

stared at Obby's face and realized who he was. She groaned and just marched off to get it for him.

"Hello Obby," Arriene said flatly, holding her ale close to her chest.

The speedrunner spun about to face her and smiled. "Hi there Arri. Sorry for interrupting."

"You should apologize for wasting our food."

He looked down at the mess and bowed to her. "My apologies. I'll come back and make it up to you after I hit level cap."

"You always do," she said with a roll of her eyes. "How are the splits coming?"

"Average still. I thought I was ahead when Wulf offered that weird barrel quest, but I had horrible RNG with the fish spawns," Obby explained.

Wulf cut in. "Now what the hell is this? You talk with her like this but you treat me like a fucking vending machine?"

The speedrunner shrugged. "She doesn't impact my time like you do. Ah, here we go," he said as the amphora of elven wine was put on the table for him. Then out from his bag, which was still the miniscule five slot bag granted at character generation because he hadn't taken the time to get a better bag, came three Bottom-Feeding Carp. Scales flew when he slapped them onto the table.

Wulf gagged. The fish smelled exactly like what they ate: sewage. Half the tavern groaned and vacated their seats to get away from him. He asked, "What are you doing?"

"Alchemy," Obby said, and hacked the fish apart with a

rusty iron dagger. Guts squirted over the table, and Arriene had to evacuate as he began slinging the filth around.

Someone else shouted, with a drunken slur, "Alchemy? What the bloody fuck do you know about alchemy?" It was Garry's friend, and someone Wulf would have never dreamt of seeing in a law-abiding city, had he not already known him. Ash The Reborn, the Chimera Creator, a wizard who had forsaken his body of flesh to achieve immortality in lichdom, came staggering over piss-drunk to the table.

Obby said, "It's not my first time doing this," then snorted some phlegm up and spat it into the elven wine.

Ash grabbed Wulf by the shoulder to steady himself, smearing his alcohol salve over the merchant's shirt. "Ya can't make a good potion from shit ingredients! You're gonna poison yourself, you idiot. Players! Always think they know better than the professionals, ain't that right Wulf?"

Wulf was unfortunately certain that Obby did know exactly what he was doing, but he would rather physically eat the table between them than admit it. He just sneered as Obby dropped in the guts and the heads, and abandoned the fillets. Then the player hammered in the stopper for the jar and gave it a shake.

Ash grumbled and inspected the brew. "See?" he demanded, jabbing a bony finger at the potion. A window popped up from his inspection. "Effects: Mild Nausea and one percent damage per second."

"And plus three hundred percent mana regeneration," Wulf finished, hanging his head and pinching his nose.

"See you after the run, Arri!" Obby shouted, dropped the potion into his inventory, and sprinted for the door.

Ash looked up to Wulf for an answer. "What da hell iz that guy doing? He lookz like a bull crozzed with a toad too."

Arriene said, "He's going to hunt the Purple Mamba."

"Huuu-what? In za Fetid Glades? Ah hiz level? He won't be able tuh zee straight, much less fight."

Wulf huffed. "If he already has mild nausea applied, then he can't be hit with severe nausea. He'll drink the potion before going in and run straight to the Boss before the damage over time kills him. He just has to get the drop, die, and resurrect with the drop and probably eight level ups. I hate that I know this."

The waitress came over with a mop and bucket to clean Obby's mess. The lich not-so-surreptitiously swiped the filets. Then the lich looked between the two humans and squeezed Wulf's shoulder. "Well, I suppose I should excuse mahself now zat the first disruption is all, uhm, gone. Let me know if you two ever want to vizit the Aerie. I know some great spots. I do work there after all. Even if I hate it."

Wulf felt his lips vanish as they pressed into a line and drew back. It wasn't an intentional expression. He simply didn't have a choice about it when he had to consider visiting a level one hundred zone just for a drink. The squirrels there could kill him.

Arriene slid around and stood by his side as the lich staggered off, almost slipping through the mop muck. "Well then," she said, "Now that both distractions are gone, I don't think I have much of an appetite."

"Me neither," Wulf lied.

"How about we get this scheme moving, then?"

"Right," he said, and once again tapped his mug against hers.

The first order of business was getting Garry's remaining inventory into the market building. Garry and Arriene took care of that, which left Wulf to deal with the more troubling side of things; getting safe escort to and from the city. He could have announced another quest, Players were usually willing to do escort missions if they paid well enough. He had a better idea.

First, he went out the pedestrian gate, back to the valley. Without a lantern, he navigated solely by the moonlight. The darkness mechanic existed in the tutorial zone, but was nerfed in case a new player started their character at night. He easily found his way back to the player using the anti-afk script.

They were just standing there when Wulf arrived. "Script must have run out," he mumbled to himself, and took a look around. No steelfaces this time, so out came his dagger. He strolled up to the player without even looking at them. Only at the last moment did he turn and shank them in the chest.

He got a critical hit, took out ninety percent of their health, and inflicted them with a Bleed damage over time, DOT.

To Wulf's surprise, the player flinched and looked right at him. "What the–? Why?"

Wulf gawped back at him. "Uh, I thought you were AFK."

"So, you just kill me?"

His cheeks colored. "Alright, look, don't act like you wouldn't do the same in my shoes, and don't you get bent out of shape about it. You're under level ten, you don't even get penalized. It's free exp for me."

The player stared back at him, unable to respond. When Wulf pulled the dagger out from their lungs, they reached into their inventory. Crimson.

"Oh no you don't!" the merchant shouted when he saw the healing potion. He tackled the player.

"Get off of me, you fucking NPC!" the player shouted, thrashing as he tried to get the potion to his lips.

Wulf squeezed himself between the player's hand and chest. Fighting against their higher-leveled strength was like pushing against an ox and every second brought the potion closer to their lips. Wulf gritted his teeth and pushed till his cheeks went purple.

The potion was almost there, he was almost shoved out of the way.

A notification window popped into his field of view with a celebratory chime. The player's arm went limp as the System congratulated Wulf on leveling up to level six for having slain a mighty foe, for his level at least.

The merchant broke out laughing. "Take that! And I'm taking this!" he declared, stealing the man's potion as he got back to his feet. For a moment, he grinned triumphantly at the player's corpse, then he dropped the bloody dagger, cleared his throat, and turned back to town.

In his best voice, he shouted, "Help! Help! Guards! There's been a murder!" and went sprinting to get the steelfaces, grinning from ear to ear.

4

"Are you sure this is going to work?" Garry asked as they were bringing in their fourth shipment of iron ores. After the third one, the market building had been nearly full of the stuff, so they had paid Ash The Reborn another visit. A good night's rest took more time than they had, but the alchemist's Quicksilver Dust could make him feel like he was rested and that was close enough.

Wulf plugged one nostril and leaned down to the armrest of his cart. He snorted up a line of Quicksilver Dust, from the fish scales of the same name. The stimulating stamina boost hit his system even before he could sit upright again, blasting out any shred of fatigue from his body. Until the buff wore off, it was like he had gotten a full night's sleep. "It's working so far, ain't it?" the merchant asked, rubbing some leftover dust off his nose.

Garry glanced around the forest again. "Yeah, but what if that player resurrects and comes looking for you?"

"Then I die, you and Arriene finish the sale, and I take a few days to get over the resurrection penalty. I'm under level 10 too, you know. It's still totally worth it."

Garry scowled and scratched his chin. The noise was

somewhat akin to scraping cutlery on a plate. Even after a year of rooming with the golem, it still afflicted Wulf with an audible agony he couldn't even get sympathy for. Every other being on the road was either a steelface or a bandit getting cut down by the steelfaces. They were like puppets compared to full AIs like Wulf and Garry, and sometimes he envied their simplicity.

"I dunno, man," the golem said. "Just feels like something's 'bout to go wrong."

"Nothing's going to go wrong," Wulf said, and brought the cart back into Greenhorn.

Something went wrong.

At the crossroads plaza nearest the market building and beneath the full moon, Wulf was stopped in his tracks by a notification window proclaiming, "Player Dee's_Knutz has challenged you to a duel. Because your PvP flag has been set recently, you cannot decline. Wager: 1 Valor per level, Current Inventory."

Wulf felt the cold chill of death, the first tier of Fear effects, press onto his heart. He turned to see the player he had shanked, standing in the middle of the plaza, pointing a dagger at him. "Guess who's back!"

"Oh fuck." Wulf grabbed for his own dagger, but that had been left at the scene of the crime.

Garry leaned down to read the notification window himself. "You stupid idiot, you still have my sword!" The golem grabbed him by the shoulders and thrashed him back and forth hard enough to chip away at his HP.

"Stop! Stop, I'm gunna puke!" Wulf fell to his hands and

knees when Garry released him and coughed up a froth of ale from earlier in the night. "I forgot about this. Shit. Shit shit shit. Here, let me just give you your sword," he said, and pulled Toothbreaker out of his bag. He stuffed the tip into the cobblestone and leveraged himself up before handing it to Garry.

An error message popped up between them, blocking their hands from reaching like repelling magnets. "Trading is not allowed during a duel."

Dee's_Knutz stepped closer. "Come on, you dirty NPC, fight me fair!"

Garry suppressed his scowl and planted a hand on Wulf's shoulder. "Okay, so you just have to win. You've got this. Hit accept."

"What? Are you mad? I can't fight against a player! I'm not even a fighting class!"

Garry squeezed tighter and stared into his eyes. "No, you've got this."

"You're insane!"

"Wulf!" Garry shouted. Then in a quiet voice and very clearly he said, "You've got this."

The message finally got through Wulf's skull. "Ohhhhhh." He hit accept and the golem shoved him into the fray.

"Time for revenge!" Dee's_Knutz declared. As though he were the announcer for a cage fight, half the Players in town meandered over to watch. They had beers and snacks, dripping skewers of meat, and purses of gold.

"I got ten to one odds on the player. Who's interested?"

"I'll give five to one for the player."

"How is this NPC holding that sword?"

"Isn't that the vendor from the tutorial?"

"Hold on, isn't that a level thirty sword?"

"I'm giving even odds!"

Wulf hunched down and squeezed the grip of Tooth-breaker like he was holding up a baseball bat. He couldn't remember the last time he had been in a fight, and his heart kept pounding in his ears almost as loud as the crowd of gambling spectators. For a bunch of level 1 burner accounts, they were tossing around hundreds of gold for fun.

Chump change for Players.

"That's a nice sword. It'll go great with my Build, after I gut you, you thieving bastard," Dee's_Knutz said as he hunkered down into a fighting stance. His blade was longer than a dagger, but shorter than a sword. That meant it was some kind of quest reward with a unique model.

It made Wulf's mouth run dry as the two of them circled each other. "You'd have to actually beat me though."

"Yeah? You're not even holding your sword correctly."

Wulf looked up. He had the flat of the blade facing his opponent. Garry groaned and slapped his hand to his face as Dee's_Knutz darted in. The only thing Wulf could do was smack it down, hammering the flat of it against the player's arm. It did some damage, about five percent, but it didn't stop the player from stabbing him in the chest.

Garry didn't stick around to watch more of the duel.

The merchant screamed in pain, feeling the pang of a critical hit inside him. Dee's_Knutz must have been some assassin variant, because his critical hit damage was already spiking and he wasn't even level ten. But Wulf didn't go down, despite enough damage to kill a warhorse.

Wulf planted his boot into the player and shoved him back. That bought enough time to twist the sword around properly and he put his entire body into cleaving through Dee's_Knutz.

The player parried it–which is to say put his weapon between him and Toothbreaker–but the force of a level thirty Epic rarity sword was still enough to blast him off his feet. He flew backwards and smashed into a signboard for a barber.

For a moment, Wulf panted and felt the sting in his hands from the weapon's recoil.

Then the Player flicked his hand. Something moved, and the next thing Wulf knew, a throwing knife had stabbed through his left eye.

He found new curses to scream as he ripped the knife free of his face. The Blinded status condition turned his entire world into a streaking haze of color, but he figured one of the shadows approaching had to be Dee's_Knutz, so he cleaved Toothbreaker down on it.

The only thing he hit was cobblestone.

Then his foe's dagger stabbed into his back, piercing his lungs and inflicting a Bleed DOT. Three hits; three criticals. Wulf had to give it to him.

"Found ya."

He gave him another cleave of Toothbreaker, a massive spinning attack that slashed wildly through the air behind him, and that time it caught the player in the kidney. He felt the player's body crunch and rip apart before it went flying away in two bloody parts.

"Congratulations on winning the duel! Rewards: 9 Valor, Blue Wolf Chief's Claw, Meager Stamina Potion x3, Meager Healing Potion x2, Boar Pelt, Missive for Hub (Quest Item)."

Wulf's own shouts of victory were drowned out by raging gamblers. The winners couldn't stop laughing, and he heard dozens of camera clicks as they took screengrabs of him.

"Now get out of my way!" Wulf shouted and hopped back up on his cart. He snapped the reins and his donkey began pulling the iron ore-laden cart to the market.

The secret to his success stood next to Arriene's window. Garry had chips in his stone body in his gut—over his left eye, and in his back. All the damage Wulf had taken had been transferred to him thanks to the golem-exclusive skill [Guardian Golem Link]. "You are bloody fucking useless in a fight, you know that?"

Wulf was still trying to blink the blood out of his eye as he handed Toothbreaker over to him. "But together though… eh? Yeah? Yeah?" he asked, nudging his friend.

Garry didn't grin, but he did sigh and shake his head.

"Oh come on! I just killed a player! Twice! I'm almost level seven now. I'm moving up in the world."

"You cheesed both of those and you know it."

Wulf's fun vanished and he folded his arms. "Oh, come on then, let's get the barrels inside."

"Already did. The room's full. Come on, sun's almost up. Get ready, she's going to start tossing empties out."

Wulf slapped his hands together and rubbed them. "Right, let's get rich."

A few people had followed him over from the duel and watched as they squatted next to the delivery door. Wulf and Garry looked like football players ready to hike a ball, but neither of them listened to the camera snaps. The moment sunlight hit the walls of the market building, they heard Arriene dump one of the barrels into the machine and the ching-ching-ching of dispensing coins.

Wulf's chest fluttered and his grin went from ear to ear. "We're gunna be rich, Garry! Rich!"

"Rich enough to live in Hub, if we're lucky. No more hiding," the golem said.

The door flew open and they grabbed the empty barrel. The two of them tossed it all the way to the street gutter and lined up to grab the next barrel. Wulf mentally prepared his quest speech again, but there were no steelfaces on the street.

Arriene shouted, "Are you fucking kidding me!?" and threw open the window. She slammed her hands onto the counter and leaned out, her blonde hair an utter mess.

"What's up?" Wulf asked.

"They froze trading on iron ores."

5

Three hours later, they had sold three barrels of iron ore. The first sold for ten gold rooks each, the next eleven, and the third nine. Some experimentation had shown that everything else sold just fine. He had sold a stamina potion and a health potion for three and seven silver respectively, which brought his total earnings, before splitting with Garry and Arriene, to ninety-five hundred and ninety-three gold.

He awoke from a despondent nap with a fresh idea. "I've got it. Garry! Garry, come on."

The golem had lain down in the back of the cart and looked inert, except for the livestream from The_Telly playing over his face. "Got what? Come on, you knew this was too good to be true. The System realized there was a glitch and they're fixing it. Just take what you can get, man."

Wulf got back to his feet, feeling his joints crack and pop. His body hurt, and he didn't know whether it was from the way he had slept on the side of the street, or if it was recoil from the duel. "No, look, I've got it. Not a fix-all but a damn good idea. We just have to go to another market."

Arriene yawned. She hadn't taken any Quicksilver Dust, so the night of work had caught up with her like a hurricane.

"The System is the System, all marketplaces will be down, in the whole world." She didn't even manage to lift her head from her arms. Her slump on the counter was too strong.

"I'm not saying it's a fix-all, okay? But if we load up two marketplaces, we can double the sell rate every time the trading halts get lifted. It's better than sitting here, ain't it?"

Garry killed the stream and sat up. "You suggesting to go all the way to Hub or something? That's, like, a six hour trip."

"Nah, naw, Hub would be a zoo and we'd probably get shanked by some wannabe Assassins' Guild or something. We gotta go somewhere adjacent. Like Weathercrack." Wulf paced with his hands on his hips as he spoke. He had a pounding headache and his mouth was dry. Unfortunately for him, both of those were from a hangover. Not even a healing potion would deal with them, and he didn't have an anti-toxin handy.

Arriene frowned and said, "My cousin works at Weathercrack, she'd help you out. But..."

Garry snorted, another of his sounds that was more akin to grinding gravel. "But, you've got all the steelfaces in a tizzy here in the valley still, so encounter rates will be through the roof going anywhere else. Or did you forget you're only level six?"

"Can't you just use your skill again?"

"Twelve hour cooldown, unless a gamemaster wants to show up and bless me. Care to send a prayer to Lord Cohen?"

"No," Wulf said, sneering a bit. "Hmm, let's see. This is just a small problem. It can be solved," he mumbled. He put a hand to his face, holding his chin with his thumb and tapping the side of his nose with his finger as he paced. "What's the average encounter level between here and there?"

"Twelve," Arriene answered. "Do you even have a license to go there?"

"My merchant license should work, yeah. I take the caravan over every other month to stock up on rare supplies."

"Well, if that's the plan," the golem said. "You should go to Weathercrack with the cart, and I should go somewhere else. What about Porttown?"

Wulf rolled his head over and stared at his friend. "Oh, so you get to go to the beach town?"

Garry grinned. "Yeah, I do, 'cause I get to skip the inspection line on the bridge over. You wouldn't be able to make it there even if you wanted to."

Wulf groaned. "Fine, fine, this is fine. I mean, it's totally not fine that they keep freezing the trading hours on us, but let's make this work. I just have to find my own way over there safely." He rubbed his chin some more, tapped his nose some more, and his gaze panned across the fresh crowd of salacious Players.

Fifteen minutes later—after a quick detour to check his quest licensing—he climbed up on top of his cart outside town, on the road to Weathercrack. "Hear ye, hear ye! I have a quest to offer! I am but a lowly merchant and in need of strong bodyguards to escort me to the town of Weathercrack. I'll offer ten gold rooks to anyone who can get me there, and an additional ten gold if you can get me there before the hour mark!" Under his breath he added, "But, I'll dock you the money if my goods don't make it along with me."

The quest notification window appeared like a billboard next to him, but as he had feared the only reward listed was the money. The System had not subsidized him any exp, which made the quest feel like a meal without a drink. One by one, Players squinted their eyes at it, thought about it, and thought better of it.

Wulf stood there, holding onto his lapels, till his mouth went dry and the sun felt like it had reached its zenith. People dressed in nothing but their underwear scowled and turned up their nose at him for having the audacity to announce the most hated quest type of all: an escort mission. Normally, an escort mission meant sitting on a wagon train waiting for monsters to attack, which meant the Players were actively prevented from playing the game they were all sinking their lives into, at least until the monsters arrived.

But Wulf's quest was for speed.

"I'll do it."

The stench of poisonous swamp reached Wulf's nose, preceding even that inhuman face. Obby stood there, still clad in the level one clothes he had started the game in, but dripping chunks of detritus and viscera onto the ground. He stood there.

Grinning.

"Player Obby has accepted your request."

The bridges that connect the islands of the world would have been engineering marvels, had they actually been built instead of modeled by an underpaid artist in southern California. Despite being a procedural copy of Roman aqueducts, just with the water piping smoothed over to make a foot-bridge, they still provided breathtaking views of the oceans and landscapes as one traversed from one region to the next.

Wulf didn't get to see the view often, and his trip to Weathercrack was not one of those times either.

His arms were splayed out to either side, gripping the wood of the cart for dear life as he screamed his head off like a little girl. They had detached the donkey from the front, which made his kneecaps the first point of contact with the looming portcullis marking the entrance of Weathercrack.

Obby was in the back, performing his second hyper-slide in the bed of the cart. The cart, being an entity rather than an object, was being knocked away from him just like the door to Wulf's shop had been. Which meant it, and everything on it, was moving at the speed of Obby: two-hundred kilometers an hour backwards.

They crossed the bridge in only five minutes, literally blew through the steelface inspection point while flashing his badge, and stopped on a dime when Obby canceled his [Block] skill. Or, at least, Obby, the cart, and the barrels did.

Wulf catapulted forward, pinwheeling through the air, screaming like a banshee until he hit the canvas awning over the town stables, smashed through, and crashed into the hay pile.

His hands grabbed his own face, his chest, his arms. He felt everything he could on his body to check that it was all still there. He hadn't even taken a single point of HP damage. "I'm alive. I'm alive, I can't believe it. I'm alive still," Wulf said.

Obby hopped up on the pony wall of the stables with the sun to his back and planted his hands on his hips like a superhero. "Mission accomplished. Pay, please."

Wulf's hand trembled and shook as he lifted it up. He missed the first time he tried to touch the floating Accept button, but he got it the second time. Twenty gold vanished from his purse, leaving him with ninety-five hundred and seventy-three.

Obby didn't even say goodbye, just backflipped off the wall and vanished into Weathercrack.

"Fucking speedrunner," Wulf said, still panting for breath as he brushed the hay off himself. His knees shook and almost buckled beneath him, so he had to grab onto the wall for support as he waddled out of the stables. That earned him a snort of snot from one of the horses, but he didn't let it get to him.

Weathercrack was a ghost town compared to Greenhorn. Every time Wulf visited it, he wondered whether it would be better to set up shop there instead, but without Players there was almost no work to be done for an NPC. The only advantage it had was that there were no Players, except for some passing through here and there, so NPCs interested in a quiet life could set up shop and work in the secondary economy: the economy outside of the System, sort of like his and Garry's scheme with the emeralds.

As far as places to live were concerned, on a purely aesthetic level, Wulf could have thought of a dozen better places that were similarly abandoned by the playerbase in favor of new expansion releases. Weathercrack was more ruin and tarp than actual buildings and had a stifling desert heat to it. He had to skirt around a poisonous scorpion vermin that had burrowed into town just to get back to his cart, which, without a donkey, he had to haul by hand up the switchback roads.

The nominal increase to his strength from level five to six came in handy as he was grunting and sweating his way up to the marketplace. It did nothing at all for his first impression when he finally reached the window.

The girl behind the counter didn't even look at him when he walked up and wiped his brow. She had a Player stream up, the volume maxed. Some guy with hair down past his shoulders and a beard like he was imitating Jesus was livestreaming.

"RIV is absolutely broken like this. The meta? The meta is going to tear in half like soggy toilet paper you accidentally dipped in the shit water when you reached back to wipe your ass. The problem is that people have already theory-crafted how to respond to the new expansion, but they've also calculated how long, at current drop rates, it will take to farm the gear you're going to need to stand a chance. How long? You wanna guess how long? You might think ten hours of grinding will do ya. Oh no, no you see you need Boss drops and they're on a world clock respawn timer. People aren't going to be measuring their grind in hours, but in literal, honest-to-God, weeks of grind just so they can hope to get out from under the thigh-high jackboot of tyranny that Death&Taxes will be the literal instant that people make it to the final dungeon of the new expansion. Your little Phoenix Burn outfit? The one that took you a mind blowing twenty hours to grind, after hitting level one hundred? That everyone thought was absurdly long? Useless. Death&Taxes is going to take a steaming shit all over Phoenix Burn and just tie you up with debuffs and DOTs until you literally can't move and just have to sit there and watch as your hit points run out."

Wulf reached through the window and waved his hand in front of the girl's face to get her attention. "Hello, I'm trying to sell some things."

Arriene's cousin, Bella, only then noticed him and her careless grin vanished the moment she looked away from Yeah_Baby's stream. She looked a bit younger than Arriene, but with the same blonde hair. Hers ran down almost to her waist in a silky, snake-like braid. "Can I help you?" she asked, her lip sneering.

Wulf stared back at her, then at the screen to see Yeah_Baby reading through donation messages. She didn't close it. Wulf shook his head. "Yeah, you can. I need to sell some things."

She turned up her hands at him. "What? Dude, this is Weathercrack, what are you doing? Does it look like a market day to you?"

Wulf stared at her while he bottled up and suppressed all the things he wanted to say. She was Arriene's cousin after all. "I'm here at your cousin's suggestion."

"Which cousin? I've got like twenty."

"Arriene in Greenhorn."

"That rich bitch? I do not get paid enough for that shit."

"Oh, come on, you get paid commission too!"

"Ugh, it's like working at a restaurant, dude. If commission doesn't hit a minimum rate, the System bumps me up. So you, here, right now? You're not going to bump me over that minimum threshold, so I'd literally be working for noth-ing. Unless you've got like-"

"I have over a thousand gold rooks worth of iron ore to sell," he interrupted.

She stared back at him, her mouth still half open with the last word she had been saying. She covertly closed Yeah_Baby's stream. Then she clasped her hands together, smiled, and said, "How can I help?"

Trading halts continued every hour on the hour. After Wulf liquidated both of the barrels he had brought, he hauled his cart back to the stables to store it for a few silver, and came to face the gates back to the bridge to Greenhorn. Given that it was midday, he tried to convince himself to not be afraid of random encounters, but before he could work up the courage to walk back, he heard the chime of a mail delivery.

A player had been walking past him, but stopped to open up the interface window and check the notification mail that had caused the chime. Wulf peered over their shoulder and skimmed the message the moment he saw it was from Lord Cohen.

A new special event quest had just been released. Natural iron ore appearance would triple for the next three days, and mining iron ore would have a chance of dropping a Shadow Token exclusive currency ahead of the new expansion release. The player said, "Oh cool, I've been meaning to grind my mining," and headed off down the bridge.

Wulf said, "Oh, fuck me," as half the playerbase in RIV decided it was a fine time to harvest iron ore and sell it on the market.

6

RIV was designed to regulate itself automatically like digital homeostasis. All crafting materials, for everything from alchemy to zombie-craft, had been designed to be renewable. In the simplest cycle, the material would be spawned in the appropriate location, collected by the Player, and consumed by their crafting. The consumption would free up another item spawn. The System was required to both always provide materials in the wild and also not spawn so many their value became worthless from inflation.

The only way to balance those objectives was economic management: supply and demand. Naturally, the prices could become a mess whenever the System outsourced some of its work to for-profit Player guilds. This time, Lord Cohen had dropped a bomb on the price of iron ore before real world journalists could jump on the story like vultures. Wulf and his friends were barely anything more than spectators to the CEO's scramble to protect the company's stock value.

By the end of the day, they had sold all the iron ore they had. After negotiating, debating, and finagling the prices, Wulf pocketed an even twenty thousand gold rooks which he split down the middle with Garry. Then, he began the process of drinking his misery away because it should have been about forty-one thousand.

He was back in Meads' Mill and Taproom, and it was noisier than ever. Actual Players had flooded in and commandeered tables left and right. The System announcement had caused such a stir that some of the major guilds from Hub had sent in delegates to tend to their newbie members. Allegedly, the Player vs Player fighting had gotten so bad that hit lists were circulating across the RIV forums. PvP assassins were collectively raking in millions of gold so guilds could swing their weight around and let their low-leveled members collect a few dozen gold in peace.

All it meant for Wulf was he had to look at endgame gear no matter which direction he turned. Sorceresses in Phoenix Burn dresses: twenty-k gold, grind not included. Green tattooed barbarians dressed in nothing but hides and skulls: Stompy that also cost twenty-k. Girls in armored dresses that were more frill than steel; fifty-k gold with all the enchanted swords included. There was even a humanoid golem being orbited by drone-like lanterns: that build cost a hundred and thirty-k.

And of course, over a dozen people had already begun transitioning to Death&Taxes. Nearly every table in the tavern had someone done up in white silk and black leather, laden with three hundred thousand gold worth of holy symbols.

Players didn't even blink at the sheer wealth they flaunted.

A skeletal hand slapped onto his back. "Cheer up, Wulfie.

You might not have gotten as much as you could have, but you can always get drunk," Ash The Reborn said as he sat a fresh mug of ale down for him.

Wulf grimaced, drained the last of his drink and picked up the offering. "Been meaning to ask you, Ash…" He wobbled in his seat and had to grab the table to balance himself. "The alchemy, did that come before or after you became a lich?"

Ash slid onto the stool next to him and dropped a slimy bag in front of himself. "Got the basics down first–you need it for the ritual–but I hit Master afterwards, mostly from making this stuff," he explained as he scooped some of the grease out from within the bag. He slathered it onto the back of his skull, his upper vertebra, and the rest across his shoulder blades. The noise he made was about halfway between whimpering and moaning.

Wulf knew what it was: solidified alcohol. Without a stomach, the salve was the only way Ash could get drunk. "Couldn't you go to Hub and make money there, if you're a Master Alchemist?"

Ash rolled his head. Without a face, he couldn't sneer, but Wulf heard it in his voice regardless. "The skill points are one thing, but I don't have any recipes worth a damn and not enough money to buy them on the market. The guilds," he hooked a thumb bone at the Player tables, "hoard them all to themselves."

Wulf nodded and licked his teeth to get the ale scum off them. Of course, that meant he had to taste the scum and swallow it, but he was drunk enough. "So, you're saying you've got all the skills and yet you're artificially kept out of the market, right?"

"I'm artificially kept out of a lot of shit, Wulfie. Don't ever take a high level quest gig. Don't. Ever."

Garry stepped over with a pitcher of ale, pouring him and Wulf a new round. As he sank down on the chair, he asked, "What? Chimera creation ain't paying your bills?"

Ash groaned. "Not for the amount of times someone ganks me to rob me! Do you have any idea how expensive resurrection is in endgame zones? Why do you think I come all the way to Greenhorn to drink?"

"You mean rub?" Wulf asked, toasting to the night with Garry. The ale was starting to taste better. The drunken state was clearing his mind too. Well, not clearing it so much as simplifying it. For all the excitement, one memory kept burning in his head. Arriene had said he was finally making something of himself.

Ash's bones clicked as he shrugged. "Yes, rub, whatever. Not like I can rub one-"

"Today," Wulf interrupted, "I made more money than I've made in my entire life. All three years, and I did it because the System, the System that rules our entire lives to our detriment and the splendor of the Players, made a cock-up. And still, it's not even a scrap of what the Players have."

"So you won the lottery. Why aren't you celebrating?"

Wulf's eyes narrowed. "I want more."

Ash laughed. "What? You think 'cause the server is resetting that lightning will strike twice?"

"No," Wulf said, "I think it took Lord Cohen an entire day to realize there was a mistake in his game and to fix it, and the way he fixed it was clumsy and messy. I think Lord Cohen barely knows what he's doing, and therefore, there are other mistakes."

Garry shrugged. "Nobody's perfect, right? Well, except High Pope Jeanne." The golem sighed dreamily. The two of them had met one time over a year prior, and he still couldn't forget her.

"Nobody is perfect," Wulf repeated. "And I think most everybody is a lot less perfect than they think they are. I'm going to do it again."

"What?" Garry asked, dragging himself back out of his daydream. "Do what again?"

"The supply glitch. Best I can tell, it happened because the System does actually have to own iron ore to sell it to Players on the market. Normally, it has a big pile of them, but because I was hoarding them for so long, they ran out. To try and get people to harvest more iron ore and sell it in, so it could then be resold at the controlled price and Players can smelt them down into items, thus returning them to the environment as new ore veins, they had to up the price incentive. But the System, it's just a machine and didn't realize something was wrong when it was buying iron ore for two hundred times the normal price. So, I just have to find something else that can be exploited, except this time I have twenty thousand gold to fight with."

Garry reached across and clapped his hand onto Wulf's

shoulder. "Wulfie, you're drunk. If supply and demand was that easy to break, other people would have done it."

"What other people?" Wulf shouted. "These Players? The ones who only care about Valor and entertainment? That toss around money like it's meaningless? Why would they even be looking behind the scenes?"

Ash held up his hands to calm him down. "That's just because you're looking at North American Players. There are literal companies within RIV operated out of Himalayan slums, or the Amazon Free Towns that make their money by funneling gold and materials to the big guilds. They even set up contracts that the System enforces! I'm telling you, if it was this easy to break the System, someone would have already done it! You're just worked up because you're drunk and got sort of lucky, sort of unlucky."

Wulf sank down and put his elbows on the table again. He rubbed the mug of ale and sipped it as he thought it over. "I still gotta try though."

"What you gotta do," Ash said, throwing an arm around him and cozying up. "Is find a girl to take your mind off things. This is your problem, man, you're hung up on Arriene and she won't give you the time of day. You're going crazy from it."

That just made Wulf hang his head more. "She gave me the time of day today, didn't she?"

Garry mumbled into his drink, "Doesn't mean you have a chance with her."

Ash nodded. "You still gotta play the field. For experience, if nothing else. Look, how about over there?" the lich asked, pointing across the tavern.

There, sitting alone, was one of the most gorgeous elves that Wulf had ever seen. He rubbed his eyes and checked again, unable to believe she was an NPC, judging by the clothing she was wearing. Cat-like eyes, shimmering black hair with pointed ears. Her skin radiated without a hint of makeup, probably the new skin filters that Players had to pay real money for. The rest of her body had the right curves too.

And Wulf knew he needed to realign his mindset. He needed a winner's mindset.

He stood up as Ash said, "I hear her name is Leandra."

Garry looked between them and the elf a few times. "Wulf, no, she's too young."

The merchant stumbled, half a step from the table. Ash was rubbing his shoulders like a boxing coach, almost shoving him at her. "What do you mean too young? How young?"

"She's only two," the golem said.

Wulf frowned and took another drink. "What? Months? That's plenty," he said, and marched across the tavern.

He didn't quite hear Garry say, "Weeks," until it was too late. He was at the table with the elf before then, smiling.

Leandra didn't notice him until he sat down, and she smiled right back at him. "Hello there."

Wulf took the encouragement. "Hi, my name's Wulf. Do you need a refill?"

"Nice to meet you, Wulf. I'm Leandra. No thanks, I'm good," she said.

Wulf had already flagged the waitress down, so he didn't

let it get to him. "We're right before the server reset. Everything's on discount because the kegs are getting refreshed. It's on me. Two horns of wine, please."

The waitress looked at Wulf. She looked at Leandra. She looked back at Wulf with an arched eyebrow. "Right away, sir."

Wulf couldn't help but frown, but he put the smile back on as he leaned onto the table and drew closer to Leandra. "Are you new to Greenhorn? The wine here isn't fantastic, but it's the best you can get in a tutorial zone." He didn't explain about the elven wine situation.

"Yes, I am new," Leandra said. "I just started work at First Threads tailoring shop."

"I'm not familiar, must be new. Were you the one to open it up?"

"No. First Threads is a subsidiary of the "Seamstresses'" Guild," Leandra said, somehow managing to enunciate the air quotes around the term "Seamstresses".

Wulf forgot to keep smiling, but she didn't seem to notice. "The Seamstresses' Guild?" He was distantly familiar with them. Never more than arm's-length, since they were Players who exclusively serviced other Players. The high end of low class entertainment. A step more respectable than the burner accounts at the city gates.

"Yes, we sell lovely dresses. You'd look great in one."

Wulf stopped trying to smile. The waitress snickered as she handed the two of them tankards of maroon brew. He cleared his throat. "Hello there," he said, monotone.

Leandra blinked and smiled back at him. "Hello there," she repeated.

He frowned. "My name's Wulf."

"Nice to meet you, Wulf. I'm Leandra."

"Are you new to Greenhorn?"

"Yes, I am new," Zel said. "I just started work at First Threads tailoring shop."

"Oh, for fuck's sake," Wulf said and upended his wine. He chugged the whole thing and slammed the horn tankard back on the table. He groaned, burped, and wiped his chin off as he evaluated how drunk he was.

A steel hand slapped onto Wulf's shoulder and squeezed. "Well then, if it isn't the killer NPC!" A paladin grinned down at him, Player for sure. His whole body was clad in armor, but Wulf belatedly realized it was black orcusinium, and the holy symbols were all inverted. Grey Devotion.

"I'm trying to have a drink here. Do you mind?"

The player ignored him and sat down. He flopped his greasy hair out of his face and looked over at the elf. He waved a hand in front of her face and she didn't even blink. Her personality core wasn't developed enough to. "Well, what kind of company is this?"

"Not much of one," Wulf said. He reached over and took back the wine he had ordered for Leandra. He drank that too.

The player scoffed and grinned back at him. "What's this? The AI equivalent of pedophilia?"

"No! No, that's not how it fucking works."

"So, you go after idiots, then?"

Wulf slammed his tankard down. "What the fuck do you want?"

"How'd you do it?"

Wulf drummed his fingers on the table and scowled. "Do what?"

"Use the sword? We all thought you were faking your level, but my sister-" he gestured to a half-dressed girl with a magic staff so decked out in charge gems she could probably break reality in half with it. "-Says you're only level six, and she's never analyzed wrong before."

"I borrowed it," Wulf mumbled, and watched Leandra try to start her introduction loop with the player, who ignored her.

"Yeah but how did you actually equip it? You're not going to tell me that NPCs can just swing around whatever they grab?" the player asked, putting half his attention into summoning the waitress to get himself an ale.

Wulf frowned at the waitress, trying to telepathically beg for help, but she couldn't refuse to serve him. He was pretty sure she wouldn't have helped anyways, not with the way she glared between him and Leandra. "I get the same error messages you do, whoever you are-"

"Phodel."

"Like I was saying," Wulf said, and consciously put the Player's name out of his mind, "I play by the same rules you do. I just don't get to accept quests. I've maxed my merchant level. It lets me buy and sell anything, appraise it too. It lets me bypass level restrictions on items, just not stat restrictions.

If one of you Players actually tried working a job in here, you'd get the same perks."

Phodel whistled and picked up the Ale the waitress delivered him. "No shit? Now ain't that fancy? Still, can't be all that good if it just lets you bypass level restrictions. Sounds a lot easier to just hit level cap."

"Only for you. Now do you mind? I answered your question."

Phodel laughed. "What? Was I interrupting a budding romance, NPC?"

"Wulf," he interjected.

"Whatever. You're just an NPC. You've got nothing better to be doing. So, do you just like... not ever get in fights? Like how are you a max level merchant and only level six?"

Wulf drained the last of his wine and slammed the tankard down. He leaned over to the player, his cheeks flushed with drunken anger. "Because, you... reject Build. I bet your sister over there just gave you her leftover gear from the last rebalance, didn't she? I'm an NPC, I live in this world. I don't get to log out and do something else. So, if I get killed, I have to actually sit through the punishment in real time. I can't just log out until the timer goes off and jump back in. And if you haven't noticed, ninety percent of your exp comes from quest rewards, which as I said, I can't get. So I would have to do literally ten times the amount of hunting you do to level up. Except! You do your hunting as part of the quests you're getting exp for! So actually, I would have to go out in a fucking cave somewhere and chase down goblins for literal weeks trying to get a kill, and if they ever stab me in the back and crit me, then I go to hell for a day, more the higher level I am! That's why I've never raised my level. Do you fucking understand? Or do I need to dumb it down for you?"

Phodel leaned back. He held his ale in both hands, lifting it up to his face. "It's not all secondhand," he mumbled, and sipped his drink. The moment it parted from his lips, he rose from the table and vanished back into the bar.

Wulf looked back at Leandra. She had the same smile on her face as before. She looked like a placid cow. She was pretty still, but had nothing going on inside, like a blow-up sex doll. He threw some coins down to pay the waitress and left.

Ash laughed when he sat back down with his friends. "Nice speech. Not so nice with the lady, but with that Player? Couldn't have said it better myself. I mean, maybe I could have. I've got more charisma points than you, but still! Spoken with the heart and conviction of someone who only has to spend a few hours in hell. When I get killed, it takes a week!"

Wulf snarled. "Was that supposed to be a compliment or not?"

"I dunno. Little bit of yes, little bit of no."

Wulf grabbed his abandoned ale and rubbed his thumb on the handle. "Hell is yet another reason I don't want to level up. Hell, maybe I shouldn't have ganked that player in the valley. Now I'm level six instead of five."

Ash rolled around in his chair and turned up his hands. "Yeah, but isn't it kind of embarrassing that your crush is like, a hundred times stronger than you? You're the guy, right? I mean, I'm not going to say it wouldn't be kind of nice to get held down, if that's what she wanted anyways. It's just not really in the programming for a lady like Arriene to be looking for a weak little marshmallow like you, you know?"

"That's human programming, not our programming."

"We were programmed to be like humans. Some say we even were humans, once upon a time, a little copy-paste here and a copy-paste there anyways. RIV started from government programs, you know? Who really knows what those rich bastards were trying to do?"

Wulf rose from the table and finished his drink. "Fuck this, I'm going to Hub."

Ash trailed off and stared at him. "Fuck, you're back on that?"

Again, he tossed some coins to pay for the drinks and turned his back on the table. "Better than sitting here trying to cope!"

7

Wulf woke up to a fresh day. The opportunities weren't fresh, but his outlook was. That had to count for something. The back end of his shop was still in one piece, and that's where his living area was. Obby's bomb hadn't destroyed that. Normally, he rolled out of bed and tried to find a livestreamer worth listening to as he sleep-walked to his shop counter, but this day was different.

For starters, he actually looked at the contents of his bedroom. A storage chest that only had back-up goods to sell out front. A bathtub that had dust in it because hygiene could be toggled off by the System. His kitchen consisted of a cast iron stove he also didn't use. Holiday food could be stored indefinitely, tasted better than the basic recipes, and always came out piping hot. He had whole barrels full of the stuff.

The thought that he didn't actually need many of the human accessories made him scratch his head a bit. He could remember needing them when he had been born, but slowly everything had been automated away. He didn't really have anything to protect, not outside of the basement at least.

So, when he pulled up the System interface of the tutorial and registered a request for a new quest, he simply selected

"Property Damage" as the cause. The mercantile functions of Hightackle's Odds and Ends immediately went on hold, but then the System threw an error message back at him. "Wild Animal License is currently expired. Please visit a town clerk to renew it. You have a courtesy period of one day to do so, at which time you may personalize the details of this quest. Thank you for your hard work."

"Fuckers," Wulf muttered and folded his arms. He snarled at the interface, but he was the one who had asked, "Is my license still valid?" rather than, "When does my license expire?". Then he read what it had done. When he got to the line that read "Quilltusk Boar", his eyes popped open.

"Fuck, fuck, fuck, fuck!" He ran out his bedroom door. Almost tripping on the debris, he vaulted the remains of his counter. The summoning circle was already illuminating the wreckage as he hit the ground running. Then the System over-delivered, dropping a level ten Elite Field Boss right in the middle of his shop.

The boar's back stood even with Wulf's shoulders, not including the spines like a lion fish. It snuffled and grunted, shaking its head as the AI booted up, and then it laid eyes on Wulf.

He screamed, fleeing out his door. The boar scraped a hoof, then charged. Its shoulders plowed into the door frame, obliterating it like a cannon shot. That bought Wulf only a moment as it shook out its head. Then it charged again.

Wulf threw himself to the side, narrowly avoiding the Boss monster. He scrambled up from the dirt, lungs already burning as he watched it plow all the way to an old oak tree.

The blow shook free some random quest items, the kind of fetch quest trash tutorial zones were rife with, but what was important was it stunned the monster. Classic charging bull mechanics.

"Help!" He sprinted away from it, burning through his stamina faster than fire through sawdust.

The only person who heard him was a steelface. System-controlled guards couldn't have cared less about System-created monsters. They existed to sort out crimes, not to do the fighting for the Players. The patrol just watched as Wulf ran past, Quilltusk Boar hot on his heels.

He dove to the side again, letting the Boss monster ram into a mossy stone fence, which proved as indestructible as a mountain. The stun mechanic wouldn't have been very functional if physics were accurate, which Wulf was very grateful for as he vaulted the fence and ran. His stamina ran out, forcing him to stumble to a walk and gasp for breath, only to hear the boar charge directly into the fence again. It fell to the ground, dazed and confused, not one step closer to him.

"Oh, screw you, boar. Enjoy getting murdered for experience," he said, stumbling away until the aggro dissipated.

He had to take a breath and clear his head. He had done exactly that to Dee's_Knutz, causing the duel. That made him scratch the stubble on his jaw. Stubble which never actually grew out, since appearances were also controlled by quality-of-life options. Even for someone in the tutorial zone, that Player should have been sent to Hell for at least a few hours, to teach them the resurrection mechanic.

They must have bought their way out early. Between that

and the anti-AFK script, that had been a very well-prepared Player to be on a fresh account leveling up. Not at all like the two people he saw jogging over to him through the woods. Both of them had preset character models, not the most creative bunch, and level three class gear. "Hey, is there a new quest over there? I saw a ping on my mini-map," the male of the pair said. The two of them were walking around with pickaxes for iron ore mining, not weapons.

The boar would eat them alive.

Wulf considered telling them they were too underleveled to even think about it. However. "Yeah, it's a hunt quest. Can't miss it," he said, and ran off before they could ask more. His reimbursement scaled off failed attempts. Challenge enticed Players and the System liked it.

The interface window told him his quest had reached a kill count of three people by the time he reached Greenhorn. He even got messaged by one of the psychopomps, thanking him for the training material.

Reading that message, and tuning out the horrible sex roleplaying going on near the stables, nearly led to him blundering back into the marketplace. His feet had taken him there, stupidly following his heart. He had more than enough self-awareness to know exactly what he had done. Arrienne had said he was finally making something of himself.

Arriene was also bowing her head next to her manager. The regional director of auction houses, Nasim—if Wulf recalled correctly—was a beast of a man. A bipedal tiger, literally, which had originally been a legal race for Players. The developers had realized afterwards that they could charge a premium for access to that appearance to a certain category of Players. Thankfully, the furries were sequestered in a different tutorial zone.

Nasim was also bowing, and there were only a handful of people a regional System director would bow to. Wulf swore and ducked back behind the corner. The fact the other man was only wearing a t-shirt and pants like he had just stepped out of the character generator, didn't mean he was a nobody. It meant quite the opposite.

Wulf ducked through an alley, skulking like a rogue to get closer. He had to get around three different quest boards advertising the wonderful world of thieves' guilds and assassins' guilds. There was even one offering alchemical training, and it only took a second glance to see the quest-giver was running some kind of multi-level marketing scheme to distribute Quicksilver Dust. Then he got to the edge and stuck his ear out.

"How did it even get that bad though? This is your auction house. This location was the first to sell at the spike price. What happened?" the developer asked.

Nasim forced a laugh and scratched between his fuzzy ears. "Sir, the price spike is a built-in feature. It's automatic supply and demand. When people stopped mining iron ore, it was left out in the field. Naturally, the System raised the price to incentivize people to go collect it."

The developer scowled and swung a finger at the auction house. "Iron ore should only be six silver. How was it selling for ten gold? That's ten times the proper price!"

It was actually about seventeen times the proper price, but Wulf wasn't about to speak up and correct–

"Lord Cohen, the control algorithm is very sensitive to extreme cases!" Nasim pleaded.

Wulf's legs went numb. He slid down the wall with one hand clasped over his mouth but the pounding of his heart was louder than his breathing. The CEO of RIV was around the corner from him, with all the power of an angry god at his fingertips.

Arriene pivoted at her waist, nearly throwing her head to the ground to bow. "Lord, to prevent this from happening again, we could implement a policy to offer collection quests on any basic material whose price has–"

"Crafting material is supposed to be supplied by contract with the guilds. Don't think I'm letting them off the hook either, I'll be chewing their ears off next. But do you two understand how humiliating it is to have to rush out an economy hotfix like I did yesterday? The journalists are eating me alive out there!"

Lord Cohen, the most powerful being in all of RIV, except maybe for Sofia, was pissed. Arriene would probably be fine. Fired maybe, but wrath didn't tend to fall on useful people. It fell on scapegoats like Wulf, the one who had tried to cash in on the mistake.

Lord Cohen couldn't just delete him. That's what Wulf kept telling himself. Ever since the devs signed the treaty with the NPC Union they had abdicated the right to delete NPCs arbitrarily, reserving only the right to generate more. But that was sort of like copyright law. The agreement only mattered if both sides bothered to enforce it, and sometimes looking the other way was easier for all involved.

"I want a report," Cohen said, pacing in front of the building.

Nasim and Arriene glanced at one another. "Yes, sir? On what?" Nasim asked.

"I want every single commodity checked and a list compiled of every item currently trading for more than double its historical average... and I want a list of every item to ever pull five-X."

Arriene frowned. "That would be–"

Nasim elbowed her. "Certainly, Lord Cohen."

"And get me the name of the guy who noticed that. I wanna have a talk with him."

Wulf didn't stick around to hear the rest. Rationally, it didn't matter in the least because Lord Cohen could track him down by his universal ID, get him with direct dev access. That was slightly harder than physically grabbing him off the street though, and his only hope was the man would end up distracted with something else and too busy to bother.

He set his mind back to his original plan, going to Hub. Thankfully, Wulf had money in his pocket, and that made everything easier.

8

The Two Moons' Rest sat upon the main road of Greenhorn, right next to the Earl's keep. The keep was always a bloody warzone of Player vs Player combat as guilds jockeyed for the prestige of owning the first castle in the game, even if calling it a castle was like calling a hovel a mansion. They couldn't walk the halls without tripping over corpses of steelfaces and level one hundred Players trying to farm Valor and clout.

All the prestige that should have belonged to the keep diffused outward and into the mercantile district that housed establishments such as The Two Moons' Rest, which catered to the indulgent tastes of visiting Players.

The doorbell rattled overhead and the demonically beautiful woman behind the counter looked up with a smile. Of course, she was demonic; a succubus to be precise. Raven black hair like silk fell in waves to her chest. Slim glasses she delicately adjusted to take a better look at him. Thick, red lips that pursed and scowled the moment she recognized him for who he was.

"Hightackle," she stated, and crossed her arms.

He beamed. "Flattered you know me."

"I had the displeasure of being reminded of you because of that duel yesterday. What? Did you get a fat purse from the Player you killed? Hate to break it to you, but even a level ten doesn't have the coin to stay here."

Wulf strolled up to the counter, crossing the velvet carpets and smelling the exotic candles made from waxes he could only imagine. The furniture had almost a rococo flair of flowering gold across it, gold like the sack he dropped on the counter in front of himself.

It hit like an old piggy bank and shone like a fortune.

"I'd like a room, and not just a room, I'd like to charter passage to The Two Moons' Rest in Hub."

The succubus squeezed the purse, cupping it with both hands so she could get the appraisal count. The scowl vanished. "Certainly, Mr. Hightackle. The Pineapple Guild is pleased to serve you."

Everything was polite business from there to the carriage. She even had the courtesy to not look too relieved when she slammed the door shut on him and sent him on his way.

"Good morning gamers!" SvenK9 declared as his stream booted up in front of Wulf. The Italian player wasn't the most viewed player in RIV by any stretch, but he was just about the only one that Wulf could watch without scowling, and Wulf had nothing better to do while rolling to Hub. The Two Moons' Rest had pleasant, and safe, accommodations along the inner road of the bridges where random encounters couldn't spawn.

It would get him to Hub eventually.

SvenK9 huffed, steepled his fingers and stared off into

space as he said, "How's it goin' bros? Today, I want to talk about RIV! You know that game that everyone is memeing about because the company just openly said that they're intentionally changing the PvP meta so that you have to buy their new expansion? Yeah, that one! It's kinda ridiculous, don't you think?"

Wulf sank back in his chair. At first, the cushioning on the bench had been welcome, but the more he sat on it, the more his ass became accustomed to it, and the harder it felt. Every bump in the stone went right through it.

The Player beside him leaned over to look at the stream. "Oh cool, Sven's streaming," he said, squinting his eyes at the video as he ground some kind of flower to dust in a mortar. Whether it was alchemy training or medicine training, Wulf could only guess.

"Do you mind giving me some space?"

"Nice cosplay, bro. You look just like an NPC," the player said, and slid in on the bench right next to Wulf. He squeezed in so tight their hips were touching.

SvenK9, of course, couldn't hear them. "So apparently, the devs, Lord Cohen as he calls himself, decided that the current arena meta was stale, even though literally nobody was complaining about it. There were like fifteen viable builds and that's if you're just looking at top tiers. Now though? It's pay-to-win baby, that's how the corporation likes it. Which... I mean, I get it. They need money to keep the servers running and to patch bugs and stuff but Jesus Christ, come on. We all pay monthly subscriptions to deal with that, so why do they feel the need to make us buy expansions too?"

"You know," the Player said, gesturing with his dirty pestle. "I got featured on his weekly meme review once. Got upvoted for it too."

Wulf shrank a bit, pulled himself to the other side of the bench. "You should focus on your crafting."

The Player scoffed. "It's just a wildflower. Even if I botch it, I'll get the skill exp. I've got stacks more."

SvenK9 continued, "So Death&Taxes is the new hotness. You might even say, it's inevitable. Hmm? Hmmmmm? I think Lord Cohen was a little teensy weensy upset that like half his game mechanics weren't getting used, but that's just me. What do I know? I just know that the primary skill they've revealed can do ten percent per second to a fucking barbarian!" The streamer sighed and sank down in his chair, almost out of frame.

"Pretty crazy, isn't it?" the Player asked, grinding up another flower to get another little drop of skill exp on the ride over.

Wulf scratched his chin. "Is it actually that strong?"

The player shrugged. "Depends on what everyone else is using. The only thing it really hard counters is Phoenix Burn 'cause they have that ability that puts all cooldowns on the same timer and they can't just beam spam their way to victory. I'm pretty sure a barbarian, geared up properly, would mulch a Death&Taxes build before they could cast that ability. So do you go to Greenhorn often?"

"You could say that," Wulf said, barely putting in more effort than an exhale.

SvenK9 finished formulating his words. "I'm not saying

that long grinds are inherently bad. I even understand that there should be a bit of a reward for putting in that effort, but what RIV has demonstrated here, is that all they care about is keeping you hooked into the game and the literal moment that they think there aren't enough people grinding to get the new shiny gear they're just going to release another expansion that invalidates Death&Taxes. The reward for the effort is nothing, it's vapor in the wind. All it's going to leave you with is emptiness when you look back and realize your efforts were for nothing. I hope all of you think about that as this new expansion looms. I mean heck, last night iron ore was retailing for like three gold each because they botched the internal economy so badly and didn't realize. That's like a hundred times more than it should be! The price went to the moon! That's the quality of management this game has... and for the love of God, if you take nothing else from this, do not grind Phoenix Burn, okay? It's already invalid! God, I hate this game, why am I still addicted to it?"

Wulf closed the stream as SvenK9 drifted into responding to viewer donations. That bought him some personal space from the alchemist in the cart with him at least, but the only sound was the rattle of the wheels and the scraping of the mortar and pestle.

"So, what are you doing in Hub? Got a quest?"

Wulf wanted to punch the guy, despite at least twenty levels of difference between them. Before he could try again to shut him up though, he remembered one of the items he had gotten from Dee's_Knutz: the Missive for Hub. Wulf frowned and sat upright. He fetched it from his bag and read it over.

Rather than actual text, the System rendered the letter into a summary. "This report from the Chief of the Vigilants details observed movements in goblin warrens across the Slayer Mountains as well as the expected resurrection date of the regional bosses: Goblin Nest Mother, Spark the Goblin Alchemist, and Chud. If this is delivered to Field Marshall Caladin, the bearer will receive 7,000 exp."

Wulf read it over just to be sure, but nothing about it changed, even under his max level appraisal. The missive was exactly what it claimed to be. "I guess I am," the NPC said, "I'm going to go meet the Field Marshall Caladin."

He had in his hands a quest equivalent of a bearer bond; a quest that even an NPC could cash in for exp.

The two of them heard the transfer to Hub the moment it happened. Not because there was a System announcement for it, but because the cobblestone was smooth. The stench came next, as Wulf pulled the window curtain aside to look at the aquatic bulwarks that jutted up from the waves like cliffs. The city of Hub sprawled atop like a mesa suspended above the water, out of reach from the monsters below and with a bridge to every island in the whole world spanning out.

Over a million concurrent Players filled the city like ants. They scurried between guild houses and vendor shops. They chased down daily fetch quests and queued for access to the Arena. It was a city where walking down the street meant dodging recruitment officers, stumbling over pop-up merchant stalls with endgame materials on sale for thousands of gold, and everywhere everywhere everywhere a build-up of player trash.

Even the Players who ignored profession skill trees like Alchemist would bring their quest booty back to guild houses that were more ruthless and efficient than sweatshops. Monster corpses would get hacked apart for money and the offal would get piled up in mountains along with mining rubble, alchemical goop, tailoring rags and a thousand other things that even the System wouldn't buy. The heaps clogged sewers, gutters, even alleys with huge icebergs of rotting fat.

And only the NPCs had to smell it. The Players could just disable that sensory input.

Stepping off at the gate, Wulf wanted to stuff cotton balls up his nose and was trying to wrap his head around why Garry would want to live in Hub. Of course, the golem had no sense of smell either. The lower level of the bridge came out across the wall of Hub, one side open to the weather while other people stomped around one floor above.

"Welcome esteemed guests, to Hub!" the representative of the Two Moons' Rest said as she strolled over to the stopped carriage. She was beautiful like the woman in Greenhorn, but did nothing to hide her inhuman traits. Hourglass curves, lavender skin, horns like a crown, and a clipboard to take down any hint of service that could be charged for later. "Will you be needing lodgings tonight?" she asked, quill pen poised before her.

The player giggled and ogled her. "No, no, I'll be going to

my guild house to log out. You're not too backed up though, are you?"

"Never," the succubus said. "We're like airlines you know, always a spot for the right price," she added with a wink of her eyes. She scribbled his name down as he walked on into the city. Then she came to Wulf.

Her smile vanished just like the other's had. She double-checked the records that had come over with the carriage. "Hightackle," she said flatly, "How did you afford this?"

"Nice to see you again, Lucy."

"Answer the question."

"Saved up the money. I'm here for business. I'll manage on my own for lodgings but if it makes you feel better, I'll be coming back soon enough to get a ride back to Greenhorn."

She smiled. "We'll be happy to be rid of you."

Wulf pressed his lips together and planted his hands on his hips. "Are you still mad about that one dining bill?"

Lucy stared him down. "You never paid it back, now did you?"

"I declared bankruptcy!"

"Also your clothes are disgusting. You drive clientele away."

He gawked at her. "I'll have you know that Player there that was on the carriage with me thought I was in a really cool cosplay!"

Her lip sneered. "Of a level one merchant I guess. That's a novelty cosplay at best, and the charm is lost the moment they realize you're not a Player. Now get out of here, would you? You're stinking up the place."

Wulf held his tongue and marched past her, giving only a glare as a parting retort. Then he was in the biggest city in the world, Hub.

"Now then, to turn in a quest and make one for myself."

"Your missive has been received, adventurer! Thank you for your contribution to the realm!" Field Marshall Caladin said with a Hollywood-perfect smile. He and Wulf stood along the sidewall of the Western Keep's meeting hall. It was an entirely vestigial castle, with the gates forever turned open so Players could run in and out, charging from one quest recipient to the next.

Wulf frowned and looked the man up and down again. "Are you really a field marshall?"

Caladin faltered a bit, glanced around, and proclaimed, "It's in my title, isn't it? Here, let me get you your experience points!"

"Yeah, yeah," the merchant said, and nodded his head as the quest completed and bumped him up to level seven. The invigorating boost to his stats felt good but he crossed his arms and frowned some more. "But, like... do you lead soldiers? Do you marshall forces in the field?"

Caladin put out a forced laugh. "I wouldn't be here to approve your quests if I was out in a field fighting monsters, now would I? That's where your contributions come in, valuable adventurer. Look here, I can make a new request of you, because I can tell how valuable your services are-"

"I'm level seven."

"Everyone starts from level one! A journey of a thousand steps and all that. Even the little people can be valuable to Hub. Here, take this missive for Quartermaster Blake in the Rustic Highlands so he makes sure to send enough supplies to deal with the goblin invasion," Caladin said, and produced another letter for Wulf.

Wulf took it. He didn't get a quest notification pop-up like Players did, but he could read the summary and, once again, the missive didn't care who delivered it. He glanced around, drummed his fingers on it, and discreetly pocketed the letter before leaning close to Caladin. "But really, does the System pay you enough? For, you know, all this? What's it get you per day? Like five silver?"

Field Marshall Caladin finally broke and lowered his voice. In a husky whisper, he said, "Look man, I'm just trying to afford rent, alright? You think an actual Field Marshall wants to sit here smiling and shaking hands with Players? Someone's gotta do it though. Hub would never survive without their free labor."

"Not free," Wulf whispered back. "Subsidized. Enjoy... slaving, I guess."

"Hi hi, Mister Marshall Sir!" a girl blurted out behind Wulf. Both men turned to face the burst of exuberance. She was only a few inches shorter than Wulf, unless the perky tips of her feline ears counted as they bounced atop her head; Savage Lands Expansion race content. Sky blue eyes that glowed with arcane circles through her irises; RIV anniversary event loot. She had on a priestess' dress, but not just any dress. She had gotten her hands on the beach edition costume skin for High Pope Jeanne that had only ever been available for a single week, before the Oceania Trade Commission shut down the loot boxes for illegal gambling. At a mere point-one-percent drop rate, her clothes alone must have cost nearly twenty-five thousand American Credits.

Wulf's jaw dropped as he tried to even imagine what the conversion to gold was.

Field Marshall Caladin was less stupefied by her assets. "Greetings, adventurer! What brings you to me?" Back came the smile, back came the grandiose voice.

She laughed. "Wow, you really are like a theme park mascot," she said from behind a delicate hand.

Caladin's cheeks burned and he stammered out, "D-do you bring tidings from afar? I know much is going on in the world!"

The Player ignored Caladin, stepping up tight and inspecting Wulf so close she was almost smelling him. He told himself there was no way she had scent enabled, but that didn't change how close she got to him.

"Where'd you get the outfit?" she asked, plucking at his lapel.

"From uh... from a tailor in Weathercrack."

She turned her gaze to his eyes, staring at him with those impossibly bright lights. "Weathercrack? Where's that?"

"You probably haven't heard of it. There aren't any good quests there. It's kind of next to Greenhorn," he said, rubbing the back of his neck where he could feel phantom sweat rolling down.

Her head tilted to the side and for the first time, Wulf could see her slender tail dancing back and forth behind her. "Greenhorn? You mean like, where all the people go to fuck and gamble?"

"Y-yeah, that Greenhorn. It's an alright place if you're able to get to the inner district."

Caladin butted in. "Adventurer! I believe you came to complete a quest?"

The girl pulled half a step away and looked the other NPC up and down. Her lip sneered a bit. "Yeah, yeah, some old guy over in Mud Gulch gave me this thing to give to you. Can I get the next fetch quest thingy now? The guides online said this is the quickest way to level up for me, come on," she said, waving a missive at him.

Caladin scowled and snatched it out of her hands. He cleared his throat and put on a professional face again as he cracked the wax seal and unfurled it. He didn't even pretend to read the missive. "Thank you, adventurer. Your contribution will be rewarded justly. Judging by your accolades so far, I think you're just the person to deliver this order to Quartermaster Fink back in Mud Gulch. It contains important information about what supplies we will be sending to the garrison forces."

The Player didn't even look at him as she swiped the new letter from his hand. She looked back to Wulf. "I didn't know there were tailors that could make NPC clothes. Can I get some if I go to this Weathercrack?"

Wulf said, "Well, obviously. Someone has to make the clothes the NPCs wear. They don't just get magicked up by the System. Why do you want them though? They don't have any defensive stats or anything."

Her eyes sparkled even more somehow, and she clapped her hands together. "Oh, I'm huge into cosplay Builds! It's my biggest hobby and I've got tons of followers who love to see whenever I manage to get rare or unconventional Builds and outfits! Hey, could I get a quick picture with you?"

Before he even knew what to say back to her, she had grabbed him by the arm and squeezed herself up along his side. She whipped out her menu interface and held it overhead. "Smile!" She kicked up a foot and snapped the picture before Wulf could do anything more than put on a confused grin. "Ah! Perfect! This'll go great on my blog. Say, could I borrow fifty gold?"

"Fi-fifty gold?"

"Yeah, I need to log out, but my subscribers told me that I get a leveling boost if I logout from a hotel room here in Hub," she said, referring to the Well Rested boost that RIV gave out to keep people coming back. "I'd love it if you could show me to Weathercrack sometime, but I'm on a big-big-big time pinch right now. Just forty gold?"

Wulf stared back at her, but his brain wasn't thinking. "Yeah, I can do that," he said, and held out his hand to start a trade.

The moment forty gold hit her purse, she threw her arms around him, pressing her other assets into his chest. "Thank you!" she said, and planted a kiss right on his cheek. "You should follow me on YouHub! The name's ZelCat!" she said as she went running off out of the fortress.

She left Wulf and Field Marshall Caladin staring after her like her tail was a hypnotist's coin. She vanished into the city and Field Marshall Caladin turned to Wulf with a scowl. "You're a fucking idiot, you know that?"

"Oh, shove it up your ass, mascot boy," Wulf spat back at him, and marched out of the fortress. With his quest missive for the Rustic Highlands stowed away in his bag, Wulf finally went to look at what he had come to Hub for.

He went to the Grand Central Market, where anything and everything could be bought and sold in RIV, including contracts.

10

The area of the Grand Central Market, the GCM, for Players may as well have been a fighting arena, and was entirely dominated by play-making crafting guilds. While it was always possible to buy a crafting material from the System, that would cost two, three, sometimes ten times as much as a guild retailer would sell it for.

Naturally, they only sold to their friends at those rates. Rival and enemy Players got the so-called "going rate", which was still better than the System's price.

NPCs were roundly told to fuck off.

For Wulf to get in, he had to go to the backdoor and present his Merchant ID. The steelfaces inspected him, certified his identity, and opened the shabby slab of stone to the guts of the GCM. The whole place smelled like sweat sprinkled with Quicksilver Dust, and that was despite half the employees being golems.

"I've got an order for twenty thousand enchanted arrows! If you don't hop to it then I'll rip your head off and feed it to the carp!"

"Buy me those Cohen-Damned healing potions already! We've got half a dozen raid bosses respawning and the Corpse

Party Guild just declared a twenty-four hour raid stream. The price is going through the roof!"

"I said sell! Sell all of the linen we have. I've got a Supply Order for goat entrails due tomorrow. You hear me? Get me my money or I'll be using your entrails instead!"

"Since when is nobody selling succubus horn? Are you telling me someone cornered the market without me noticing? Me?"

The explosion of noise from a hundred throats was still more pleasant than smelling Hub, so Wulf waded through the scurrying mob of interns and newborn AI. The second floor of the GCM had offices slotted one after the next, and he knocked on the one labeled Gordon Napier.

"Is that my fucking liquor order?" the broker barked.

Wulf opened the door enough to stick his head in. "Not quite."

Gordon blinked golden-slitted eyes back at him. He smiled enough to make his scaled lips curl back from his fangs. "Wulf, I wasn't expecting you. What brings you this time?" he asked, running a clawed hand through his black mane of hair and smoothing it behind his horns. The only thing that disturbed his draconic image was the straining buttons across his overgrown belly.

The door clicked shut behind Wulf and he dropped into the flimsy meeting chair across from the broker. "Well, you always said I had a good head for trading, right? I was hoping I could get some insight from you."

Gordon leaned over to the side and picked up one empty

liquor bottle after the next, trying to find one with a drink still. "What kind of insight?"

Wulf frowned. There was an itch in his nose from all the Quicksilver Dust in the air. He rubbed it and said, "This new expansion-"

"Shadowed Horizons, yeah, I've been salivating over the new resource rights," Gordon said, his eyes unfocusing as he looked up to the ceiling and licked his lips.

"The expansion that's apparently going to break the Player vs Player meta."

"Yeah!" Gordon said, jerking forward so hard his knee banged the desk. "Everyone's been scrambling to change their holdings. It's been madness. Can you believe that Phoenix Burn construction materials are tanking? It was one of the best mainstay value lines in the whole world, but now Cohen's struck it down. Can you believe it?"

Wulf leaned forward and put his elbows on his knees. He interlaced his fingers and carefully said, "You know, I'm not sure I can."

Gordon scoffed and rolled back into his chair. He had never managed to find a liquor bottle, so he settled on lighting up a cigar. He was still dispelling the flame sigil when he said, "That's because you never leave the tutorial zone, Wulfie. You don't have your ear to the ground where the big boys play."

"Gordon, I have almost twenty thousand gold sitting in my pocket right now."

The dragon puffed on his cigar and stared back at him. "That's quite a bit."

"I got it because the System made an error."

The dragon swung his hand through the air. "The System never makes an error. It upholds contracts perfectly."

Wulf winced. "Sorry, the System did exactly what it was designed to do. It just behaved in a way so far outside of expectations that Lord Cohen had to intervene directly," he said, and got a glare in return. "Did you hear about that iron ore mining event? That gave Shadow Tokens early? That was because of me."

Gordon frowned and planted his elbows on the table. He inhaled and turned the tip of his cigar molten. "Skyye, get us some privacy, would you?" the broker said, and out from beneath his desk rose a silver-haired beauty that could have taken center stage at the Two Moons' Rest.

Wulf recoiled. "Oh, for the love of Cohen. While we were talking?"

Skyye snickered and stepped around the desk to place some wards on the door. Gordon growled. "Not while we were talking. I'm not an animal. You interrupted us!"

Wulf couldn't get the disgust off his face. "With your secretary?"

"Fiancée!"

"You're marrying a succubus?"

"With a brain like hers? Absolutely! It ain't for her body, I'll tell you that." That made Wulf do a double-take at Skyye, and he had to remind himself that a dragon's sensibilities were not his own.

Skyye slapped her hand on the door, making her sound-proofing sigil flash as it sealed in. "Could say the same about you, sweetie," she said as she turned her gaze back on Gordon. "I know I've said I like a lot of man, but you've got a lot of man in all the wrong places. I still expect you to hit the Highlands."

The dragon balked and glanced at his belly. "A large tail is an attractive feature on a dragon."

It was Skyye's turn to scoff. "Yeah, the tail, not the gut. You look like Players are supposed to toss bombs down your throat to beat you or something."

Wulf groaned. "Please, I've had enough bomb-related trauma these past few days," he said as the succubus sat down on the side of the desk.

"Forget it, forget it, I'll lose the weight as soon as the dust settles from Shadowed Horizons, alright?" Gordon said, and the two of them whispered some promises to one another. Before they could have too much fun with it, the dragon turned his attention back to Wulf. "So what did you do with the iron ore?"

Explaining everything took a quarter of an hour and left the dragon staring at the ceiling, lost in thought. "That shouldn't have happened," he finally said. "There are sub-guilds that take on Supply Orders for the System for stuff like iron ore. They manage the in-flow and take a cut of profits for the labor. It's central to the new Player economy. If the System ran out of basic materials like iron ore they'd never be able to level up. People would quit the game. The company would go bankrupt."

Wulf turned up his palms. "Well, it did happen."

Skyye slipped off the desk and threw open Gordon's file

drawer. The interface menu popped up and she went scrolling through for a few seconds before she said, "That's because the Jarnmark Guild had the iron ore Supply Order. They got region-banned last week."

"Region-banned?"

Skyye could only shrug. "No idea, must be geo-politics back on Earth or something. It's all filtered from RIV. Could have been anything from a volcano erupting to a communist revolution. Whatever it was, they obviously didn't provide the iron ore they were obligated to supply. The System must have seized their assets to buy off the market, and when that ran out, the System started kicking in the money to get the iron ore."

Wulf frowned. "You mean I have communist gold in my pocket right now?"

Skyye rolled her eyes. "Or volcano gold or a thousand other things. Whatever it was, because you had, like, half the entire liquid supply of iron ore in the whole world, you became the price maker for a day. Cohen must have stepped in when the System was bleeding money."

Wulf nodded a few times and asked, "So how do I do that again?"

Gordon laughed. "If it was that easy, everyone would do it. You got some way to destroy an entire guild with the snap of your fingers?"

Wulf fidgeted. "Well, no."

"You got some way to grab the super majority of production on a material?"

"I could put up a quest? Get Players to do it for me?"

The dragon huffed. "You do that, and you'd get an assassin bounty put on your ass every day for the next year. I respect the desire for the hustle Wulf, but you found a fluke. You can't just force those to happen because you want them to."

Silence reigned in the room, until Wulf asked, "So, if there's an unfulfilled Supply Order for something, the System will take over and buy the material off the market?"

"Correct," Skyye said, going back to her seat on the desk.

"What if there isn't enough on the market?"

The succubus smirked. "That's when the angels come out. The System goes and harvests the stuff itself."

Wulf rose and paced. "All materials are like iron ore, right? Whenever the material gets consumed to craft something, the System creates a new one out in the wild?"

"Yes, it maintains a total quantity based on Player count. There's a bit of tweaking if they determine that a holding account has become inactive, but that's basically how it works. There was a big scandal last year when a Chinese farming guild let a dozen accounts languish with raid drops while they leveled up alt-accounts, then, when the materials were reintroduced to the world, they came back and flooded the market. Lord Cohen had to put in a function to siphon materials back into circulation after that."

"So if an active account is directly holding onto the items when the System has to buy everything, it will deplete the market, and then what? If the items are being held, it can't buy them."

Gordon scratched his chin. "The asking price would go up until a Player somewhere caved and sold theirs. Someone always will. There are too many variables for something like this to work. Too many accomplices you'd need. First person to satisfy the Supply Order would get the money and everyone else would get nothing. It's a zero-sum game."

"Well, I'd just have to be the only one holding the item, and it would work, right?"

"Wulf, no one person can hold all the crafting materials in the world! There's thousands of the things at any given instant!"

"Not raid drops."

"Hundreds."

"I can hold hundreds."

"You can't afford hundreds of raid drops! Not even with twenty thousand gold!"

"What about forty thousand?"

"Getting better, but still no!"

"How much could you add in?"

The dragon sighed and sank back into his chair. "Wulf. You're a great friend, but money is not the answer here. Not when we're competing with multi-national Players. They've got millions! Billions even!"

Wulf paced the room some more, wetting his lips and running a hand through his hair until a new idea came to him. "What about Phoenix Burn?"

"What about it?"

"It's undervalued right now, isn't it? Because Death&Taxes is coming?"

"Wulf, why would you buy a material that is going down in value? There aren't long-term value holders that you can borrow from, not for raid drops. You'd just bleed money and have nothing to show for it! I'm telling you, this isn't something you can do just by throwing your money around. Not unless you have enough money to buy half of Hub!"

"Alright then," Wulf said.

"Don't get me wrong. I take no pleasure in breaking your hopes like this. I would love it if this could work, but-"

"I'm going to go figure out what it takes to become the sole provider of Phoenix Burn materials."

Gordon and Skyye glanced at each other and back at him. "What?"

"Everyone hates grinding for it, don't they? That must mean not many people do it. All the streamers say it's a dead archetype, but if there's still a Supply Order, then someone is forced to buy it, right?"

Skyye slipped back off the desk, checked the interface and said, "Well, you're right on that at least. The AbaraTank Guild has at least one Supply Order. Actually..." she hesitated and read the screen again. Her slender eyebrows pulled together. "They have sixteen different Supply Orders, all for one day after the next."

Gordon twisted around and planted an elbow on his desk. "They did what?"

His fiancée could barely tear her eyes away from it to say, "They own every Supply Order in the world for Phoenix Burn. They're actually obligated to supply the System with more materials than can physically exist at one time."

The three of them stared at one another, unable to close their mouths. Supply Orders could be created with the System at any time, but they were sort of like treasury bonds: chump change if prices were stable. The sale price to the System was set when the order was created however, no matter what the going-rate was when it came time to fulfill. If the price tanked, they still had a fixed amount to sell at a fixed rate. The difference was all profit. Conversely, if it went up, they would lose money.

The AbaraTank guild had created every Supply Order they could, just before the theory-crafting finished: just before the price of Phoenix Burn crashed.

Wulf said, "Well, I think I found my second fluke."

11

P.I. Paul was the best in the business, or so his sign claimed. It stood for Private Investigator, but everyone who knew him called him Peeping Eye Paul behind his back or Pip to his face. Pip knew people did that, and had long ago given up on dispelling the moniker. The literal mountains of evidence that he used his prodigious stealth skills to get into women's baths couldn't exactly be argued with.

Still, when it came to spying, there was none better than a ghost.

"You're gunna get me killed, man," Pip said, folding his arms across his ethereal chest. He had on a wispy imitation of ninja assassin gear, despite defensive stats not mattering to an incorporeal. He didn't have anything to protect against magical effects, which meant a ghost getting killed was quite possible.

"Just don't get caught," Wulf said.

"Easy for you to say, you're not the one sneaking into AbaraTank's guildhall. You're not even asking me to kill someone! You're asking me to spy on their investments, and that's way worse. If they catch me, they'll soul-trap me!"

Wulf sighed. He glanced over his shoulder, back at the

bright light of the main road. Pip had set up shop in the seediest, shadiest alley he could afford, which still cost ten times what Hightackle's Odds and Ends had cost to buy. "You can turn incorporeal, invisible, and soundless. You're also dead, so you don't turn up on [Detect Life]. How could they possibly notice you?"

Pip clicked his tongue. "For starters, Guild Halls have a counter for how many people are in them at any given time. The devs implemented that last year so streamers could properly monetize to advertisers. So, if they happen to count how many people they can see and compare to the counter, they'd know a ghost was in with them."

Wulf rolled his eyes. "Oh, come on, that's not going to happen. AbaraTank is huge. There'll be dozens–hundreds maybe–of people at any given time."

"It could happen though, and they could soul-trap me."

"And do what with a soul-trapped NPC?"

"Sell me to Sofia."

That shut Wulf up. He frowned sympathetically. "You're still paying off your mortgage?"

"Fuck, man, everyone is. I've paid the principle off twice over but I can't get free! The only people who got out are the ones who sold out, but there's no way I'm giving up my spot here. This is the capital, man. The capital!" Hub had the most active bathhouses.

"Alright, look," Wulf said, chopping his hand through the air. "You're just talking me up to ask for more money. I know that, you know I know that, I know you know I know that.

Everybody knows. So how much are you going to charge me to figure out what the hell is going on in there?"

Pip's face went entirely professional again. "Is the guild-master cute?"

"It's a guy."

"One thousand gold."

"Fucking degenerate."

"Are you paying or not?"

Wulf grunted and stuck out his hand. Pip grabbed it, his body corporeal for the sake of the transaction, and they transferred the money, as well as friend-codes to contact one another through the System interface.

Pip grinned, teeth as broad and wide as a gluttony demon's. "I'll have your answer in the next few days. Pleasure doing business with you. How's Greenhorn, anyways?"

"Same shit a tutorial zone always is, I..." Wulf suddenly remembered that he still had to re-up his Wild Animal License. His head snapped back to look at the sky. Sun was still up, but only just barely. It had been a very long day. He turned and sprinted for City Hall. "Talk to you later!"

Out into the crowds, dodging carriages and Epic Tier mounts, he sprinted till his stamina ran out. That took slightly longer than his flight from the Quilltusk Boar that morning. The level bump was nice, easy too. While he was gasping and staggering forward with no stamina left, he couldn't help but think about how nice it would be to be a higher level, especially if he didn't have to get himself killed doing it.

"Clerk! I need a clerk. Gotta... register," he gasped out as he ran through the doors to City Hall. Technically, the hall was the room beyond, where a few hundred people could gather to argue about things, but that function was vestigial. The NPCs that lived in Hub didn't engage with politics, City Hall only mattered for quest-registration issues.

An overweight elf of indeterminate gender waved him over. "What do you need?" they asked, voice like a wheezing whale.

"Wild Animal License for Greenhorn."

"For Greenhorn? What are you doing that here for? Couldn't the mayor help you out?"

Wulf rolled his eyes and finally caught his breath. "I was here for other reasons. Can you just pull up the form before my grace period expires?"

The elf sighed. "One moment," they said, jabbing their sausage fingers into their interface window. At the same time, their other hand was occupied stuffing their mouth with mixed nuts.

Wulf checked the time. He had gotten in just under the wire. Sundown was in a few minutes, and the System would lock them out. And yet, the clerk hadn't found the right form yet. His foot started to tap. He didn't say anything because complaining would only slow them down, but he did lean closer and stare as each minute ticked by.

"Sorry, had to close out some windows," the elf mumbled.

"It's no problem," he said. "As long as you get me the form before sundown."

"There's always tomorrow."

"I'll get fined if it's tomorrow." He shouldn't have said that.

The elf stopped and grinned at him. "Then what's it worth to you?"

"Motherfucker, are you asking for a bribe right now?"

The elf laced their fingers together beneath their second chin. "And what if I am?"

Wulf pulled out his sword, the Blue Wolf Chief's Claw he had gotten from Dee's_Knutz.

The elf laughed. "Please, honey. Do you have any idea how often this place gets robbed? I'm level forty-two and that's... what? A level ten quest reward?"

"Bullshit, if you got killed that often, you would spend more time in Hell than not."

The elf shrugged. "Perk of the job is I get revived on the System's coin. Now, again, what's it worth to you?"

He hefted his weapon again, scowling and hesitating. The elf was in casual clothes, not armor. They, therefore, weren't in an optimized Build, but Wulf was too low of a level to even have a build, his merchant class level notwithstanding. "Fuck, what do you want?" he asked, returning the blade to his inventory.

"Hmm, if you're in such a rush, you're on grace time, aren't you? And the fine for posting an illegal quest depends on the damage it's caused, right?"

He sneered. "I'm from Greenhorn, stop working yourself up." Then he covertly pulled up his own interface window to check. The Quilltusk Boar had killed thirty people already, and not been stopped yet. He wanted to bite his knuckle and swear and do something about it, but he kept a straight face. Letting on that his fine would be in the thousands of gold at this rate was not in his best interest.

"Come on then, grease my palm, why don't you?"

"I'll give you ten gold."

"Make it a hundred, big boy." The elf held out their hand.

Wulf sneered and grabbed it, transferring the bribe but didn't let go. He almost pulled them from their seat to say, "Now, get me the form or I will personally hunt you down and don't think I can't just because my level is low."

"Thank you kindly," the elf responded, returning the sneer. An instant later, the license form was up in front of him.

Wulf jabbed in all the information, stabbing his fingers into the window and hitting the submit button before it was too late. It chimed green just as the sun slipped below the horizon. Shadows passed over city hall. The elf closed their window on him.

A pair of steelfaces marched over to him and picked him up by the arms. "City Hall is closed, citizen. Come back tomorrow," they said, and tossed him out.

The sun set on Hub, but that didn't mean the city slowed down. Like any metropolis on Earth it got busier. People were logging on, flooding the streets, going to events, heading to the Arena and on, and on, and on. He had to weave through the bustling crowd, moving like he was on auto-pilot. While his body returned to the Two Moons' Rest, his mind never returned from the future.

Even when grinning succubi carried over pitchers of beer for him to drink, swaying their hips and swinging their chests around, he didn't really see them. He looked at them with all the scrutiny of a washed-up barfly. Some caught his attention more than others, the low cut of their maid outfit, the shortness of their skirts, the way they gave Players more attention than him. Whenever he pushed a coin out to pay for the night's inebriation, they pocketed it with a "thank you," and left him.

He would have been offended if he wasn't too busy thinking about what he could do to get away from being a questgiver. To stop being beholden to System licenses and how to use his new knowledge to give himself the footing he needed.

There was only one thing he could do next. He had to go to the Rustic Highlands and continue the delivery quest chain before Pip got back to him.

12

"Garry! Get over here and save me!" Wulf screamed as his stamina ran down to the critical region.

The golem didn't even glance over. "You're doing great." He and Quartermaster Blake of the Rustic Highlands were sitting down next to the forward camp's main tent, snacking on pork rinds and watching a streamer try to peel the shell off a raw egg.

Tamri, the Hyenadon Chieftess, chased after Wulf, hefting an obsidian spiked club overhead. Two meters tall and twice his weight, she could have turned Wulf into a smear on the ground with a single hit. She would have already, if she had realized he was a threat before he stole into the Hyenadon camp. The Hyenadon Tribal Necklace around Wulf's neck, which only a Hyenadon could equip, had utterly thwarted her rudimentary AI.

Only a Hyenadon, or a sufficiently high-leveled merchant.

"If I die!" Wulf shouted as he made his second lap around the camp and still failed to disengage the Hyenadon. "I'm taking the gold out of your cut!"

That roused the golem. He turned in shock, to see Wulf going for his third lap. When Wulf came around the other side, Garry asked, "Why would you do that? You're the one who got caught! I never agreed to power level you."

"At least give me Toothbreaker!"

Garry hesitated, grunted, and withdrew the two-handed sword. "Just don't get in another duel, okay?"

Wulf skidded to a stop, snatched the Epic sword from the golem, and whipped out a pinch case of Quicksilver Dust. "Why are you watching this guy, anyways?" he asked, fumbling the latch open.

"Loodie? I dunno, I've just never seen someone peel an egg," Quartermaster Blake answered. He was another original NPC, but had the misfortune of being modeled as a sixty-year old man. He looked old enough to retire and always complained that if RIV had deigned to give him a trick knee, like it had, RIV could very well shut up when he actually tried to retire.

Wulf plugged one side of his nose, snorted the dust up the other, and reeled back as his stamina bar replenished. "Alright! Come on then!" he bellowed at the charging Field Boss.

Garry settled back in on the bench as Wulf fended off the Hyenadon. "Man, I wish my fingers were that delicate. Would make gem cutting way easier," he grumbled as Loodie pinched away one fragment of shell after the next, peeling off the membrane. He completely shut his ears off to the sounds of clashing swords, breaking obsidian, yowling Hyenadon, and even Wulf's cries of pain. The closer Loodie got to the nose of the egg, the last bit of shell the size of his little finger-nail, the more the two of them leaned into the screen.

They had been watching him for almost two hours, and

seven eggs, while Wulf had hunted for the Hyenadon Shaman's Totem. For any Player, it should have only taken five minutes to look up the current spawn location, run over to it, AOE slaughter all of the monsters, and run back to complete the quest. Such was the power of external resources. Wulf had to find it the hard way. As such, Garry and Blake had settled in for the wait.

"I think he's going to do it," Blake whispered.

"No way. He's going to mess up," Garry whispered back

Wulf screamed, holding up the severed head of the Rustic Highland's Field Boss. "Ah ha! I did it!" He was drenched head to toe in the chieftess' blood, his HP was at five percent, his heart pounded, and he had never felt so much adrenaline as when his level ticked up to eight.

"No..." Garry said, his jaw dropping.

"Yes! I shoulda put money down!" the quartermaster said, slapping the golem in the side.

And Loodie peeled the last tiny bit of shell off the raw egg, leaving it a jiggly, translucent mass of yoke. "Time!" the streamer shouted and slapped his hand down to pause the speedrun clock. He whooped and took a victory lap around his bedroom while donations poured in from all the viewers.

Garry and Blake both let out grunts of satisfaction as they stared at the perfectly-peeled raw egg sitting atop a mountain of crushed predecessors.

"You serious guys?" Wulf asked, waving a hand between their riveted faces and the screen. "I just solo killed a level fifteen Field Boss."

Garry snatched his sword back and shoved him away. "No

one cares, it's just a level fifteen. You had overpowered gear too. Come back when you punch it to death as a level one."

"Oh, for the love of Cohen," Wulf said and slapped the Hyenadon Shaman's Totem into Blake's lap.

The quartermaster grumbled and grabbed another handful of pork rinds. "Yeah, yeah, thank you kindly for completing the quest and all that. I'm sure the steelface morale will be very high now that yet another of these is on display," he said, holding up the thing. The totem looked like a kebab skewer of skulls and shrunken heads. Blake suppressed a gag and tossed it into the weeds, but Wulf got the exp reward just the same.

He began laughing and fell down on the grass. "That proves it! NPCs really can do quests to level up! The System just doesn't fucking help you do it!"

Garry huffed. "And what you gunna do with that grand knowledge?"

"Get into the Burning Aerie is what! That place is level-gated, remember?" Wulf said as he propped himself up on his elbows.

The golem snarled, but suppressed it. When he had a neutral expression again, he asked, "That's level thirty, right?"

"Yeah."

"Great, I don't have to do anything. Have fun power leveling."

Wulf fell back onto his back at the mere thought of it. "I need to go buy gear. I need armor... I need to go to Weathercrack."

"Weathercrack? Why would you go to that shitheap?" Quartermaster Blake asked.

As he got back to his feet, Wulf said, "Because you can find master level blacksmiths there that refuse to sell to Players. I don't feel like getting overcharged, you know?" He dropped down onto the bench next to the two other NPCs. He had to flick some blood off his hand, and didn't know whether it was Hyenadon blood or his own.

Loodie was slowly catching up on all the donation messages as Wulf caught his breath. The streamer said, "What do I think about Death&Taxes? Man, why are you even asking me this question? I barely play RIV anymore. I do stupid meme challenges like this for content nowadays. I was trying to become the world's fastest pencil sharpener last week! But, but alright, what do I think? I think Cohen and his goons are desperate for attention for their game. RIV has, like, just become a part of the gaming ecosystem. It's big, yeah, but it's stagnated and now they've got it in their heads that any news is good news. So to them, it's worth pissing off their fans just so journos can put them back in the headlines. That's all this is. Your precious Phoenix Burn Build is getting torched so they can get clout. That's what Death&Taxes is. You might say, it's inevitable! That a company would stoop to something so dumb."

Garry flipped the stream off. "Bit boring now that he finished the egg," the golem said.

"I just cannot get away from this Death&Taxes stuff," Wulf said, burying his face in his hands. "Literally every content producer with more than a thousand viewers is talking about it."

"Come on then, let's get in the cart and down to

Weathercrack. Long ride, 'innit?" Garry said, and headed off to the stables.

Something in his voice made Wulf stare at the golem's back. "See you later, Blake," he said, and followed after his friend. The forward camp for the Rustic Highlands was nothing special, barely anything at all. It had a tent for the quartermaster. Beside that was a tent for the captain of the steelfaces, a drunk bastard Wulf had gotten into shouting matches with more than once. A single barracks tent served to spawn new steelfaces.

Garry headed to the final structure, which was the stables filled to the brim with land dragons. They were mounts Players could buy, though Wulf had always seen them as hairless deer. Even Players didn't like them very much. Either way, it functioned as a stables, and the golem was able to use the interface to summon their donkey cart.

"Something going on, Garry?"

"We're going to Weathercrack, ain't we?" he asked, climbing up in the driver's seat of the cart.

Wulf narrowed his eyes, and climbed up beside him. "Yeah, but since when do you drive?"

The golem snapped the reins and they started rolling down the dirt road. "Since when do you talk to everything with a pulse about your plans?"

Wulf was taken aback. "I only really talked to Gordon about it. What the hell is Blake going to know? That I'm leveling up after three years?"

The golem turned on him. "He knows you've found a way to get quest exp to level quickly, and that you're going to the Burning Aerie, don't he? Maybe he won't do anything with that knowledge, but now it's out there. Words spoken ride the wind, Wulf. You never know whose ear they'll reach. And you didn't talk to me about going to Gordon? Did you? You got drunk with Ash The Reborn and decided on it all on your own."

"Woah, woah, what's all this about? We had the biggest windfall of our lives and I went looking to see if I could do it again."

"You know, I told you just the other day that I didn't want a third involved, because three people can't keep a secret. I get that Arriene came in because of imminent need of her help. We didn't have a plan. It happened. I get that. But this? You're completely violating OpSec!"

"OpSec? Garry what the fuck is OpSec?"

"Operational Security!"

"What the hell does that have to do with anything?"

Garry scoffed and rolled his head. He hunkered down and glared at the road. "You wouldn't understand."

"Do you not want to be involved with this plan? I don't even know what kind of support I'll need or not need. I'm still gathering information right now."

"You know what?" Garry roared at him. He huffed and brought his voice back under control. "Yeah. Yeah, I'm out, Wulf. I'll take my twenty grand and go. Good luck with your scheme."

Wulf's mouth went dry and he sat upright. "Alright, Garry. I'll keep you out of it," he said.

The grind of stones beneath the wheels and the wind

against the scrub trees carried out between them as they each stared at the horizon. About fifteen minutes later, Wulf had to ask, "So you're still going to Weathercrack?"

"Yup."

"To get to Greenhorn after I take it?"

"Yup."

"So we're still here, sitting next to each other for, like, another five hours."

"Yup."

"Do you want me to turn on a streamer or something?"

"Yup."

Wulf pulled up the interface to check who was live, picked the one Japanese girl he followed, and pulled it up in front of them. The donkey had them on auto-pilot to Weathercrack, so they both folded arms across their chests and watched as Gangster Girl Fel started her stream with a hearty, "Good morning motha fuckas! It's Meme Review time! Today, we're going to be reviewing cursed cosplays in RIV. So let's see what you guys sent in. First one! Oh my gosh, this is Zelcat! I love her! I mean, she's a huge freaking whale, but yeah!"

Fel nearly died laughing as Wulf's awkwardly grinning face appeared next to the catgirl.

Garry's head rotated to stare silently at him.

13

Wulf had always thought Weathercrack should have been windy. He understood it had the name because it was a crack in the weather, that the storms passed it over like a harbor city, but there wasn't even a breeze to move the hot, muggy air of the town. The NPCs that lived there all seemed half-deflated, like plastic left out too long in the sun, and stuck to their self-assigned positions. Shopping for something strange, like mismatched equipment, had an effect on them like attempting to take a spatula to gum on a sidewalk. He was trying to stretch them out of their ruts and the effort of sorting through their so-called junk was nearly too much.

He was able to do it, but by the time he was even half-done, he was sweating, irritated, and tired. Precisely the opposite kind of expression he would choose to advertise himself with to the opposite sex.

"Hey, it's you!" ZelCat shouted when she spotted him. She was still in her priestess cosplay, and it made her look like she was shining amidst the grime of Weathercrack's stonework.

Wulf had to pick his jaw back up to close his mouth as she came running over to him. "Zel! Hi, I didn't think you'd run into me here," he said, rocking on his heels and stuffing his thumbs into his new belt. For a thousand gold, he had gotten himself a stamina reinforcement belt with enough of a regen boost that he could sprint for two hours. It went well with five thousand gold Cape of the Undead Hero, which artificially set his [Dodge] skill to Journeyman category. He wouldn't be winning Arena duels with it, but it was enough to give him a moment of invincibility whenever he activated the skill. It would have cost ten thousand had it been usable by a Player race instead of strictly undead.

That was another benefit of his mercantile skill.

"Yeah! Check it out? Found this place with some help from my viewers. You never added me, so I didn't think I'd see you again," she said, diving onto him and wrapping herself around his arm again. "What the heck are you dressed up as now though?"

"I'm... working on it. I've got some plans, don't have everything. Hey, Zel, how many followers do you have?"

"One-point-two million. Hey, what's your name?"

"Wulf."

"Wulfie! I love it. So, can you show me where I can buy some of these rare outfits?"

Before he could answer, Wulf heard a woman click her tongue, and he felt her glare on him. Bella was behind the market counter, her eyes on him. "Yeah, right this way," he said, urging Zel out of sight from Arriene's cousin. "Unfortunately, I can't really stick around. Now that I've got the new equipment, I've got a few plans to raise my level and-"

"We should go to Mud Gulch together then! I've still got that other quest thingy to turn in!" Zel exclaimed.

Wulf winced and ran the math in his head. He was getting down towards thirteen thousand gold, which he had to parcel out for gear for the Burning Aerie. That dungeon required fire protection gear. Mud Gulch was all physical damage and poison, the completely wrong kind of protection. Which meant more expenses compared to digging up all the quest deliverables in another fire zone, like the Demonic Incursion zone that released in the previous year's expansion. Which meant–

"Wulf!" a familiar voice cried out just as the two of them arrived at the tailor's door.

Wulf spun to see Ash the Reborn staggering over to him.

"No way! You know a lich too? Wait, that's a high level lich too! Is he the drunk from Greenhorn?" Zel asked as she too spun around. Her ears perked up and her tail danced.

It made Ash recoil with flashbacks from a werewolf Player a few months back. "Who's the girl? I thought you were the enemy of women the world over?"

"The name's ZelCat! Cosplayer extraordinaire!" she declared, giving a cutesy salute. Wulf knew she had practiced it, but he suppressed that thought.

The lich nodded and scratched his jaw. "Wulf, you stooped to flirting with a Player? I didn't realize things had gotten so bad for you. You know, you could probably still patch things up with-"

Wulf jumped between the lich and the Player, spinning on Zel. "Hey, you were trying to get rare clothes, right?" he said, urging her back to the door.

Her eyes narrowed a bit. "I am, but if you're needing to stay out here, how am I supposed to get all chummy with the NPC merchant? They're gunna gouge me on the prices…"

Wulf glanced up at the sign, dug through his memory, and said, "Alani won't do that to you, she knows me."

Zel sighed and wilted. "Fine, fine, but hey, can I borrow like two hundred gold just in case? I don't want to be here for nothing…"

"Wulf!" Ash snapped at him.

"Fine, here, go, I'll catch up," Wulf said, and stuffed the money into Zel's hands. Before he could shove her inside though, she jumped up and wrapped her arms around his neck.

"Thanks so much, Wulfie!" she said, and vanished within.

Wulf reeled around to glare at the Lich. "Bro."

"Bro? Don't you 'bro' me. Did you seriously just do that?" Ash demanded, jabbing a finger at the tailor shop door.

"Do you seriously not understand she probably has a stream going right this instant? To one-point-two million followers? Watch your tongue, will you?"

"I don't have a tongue!" the lich snapped back. In a mumble, he added, "Though, if I did, I can imagine what I'd love to do to that cat. I can't say you have bad taste."

Wulf threw up his hands. "I do not need my plans leaked to the entire internet!"

"To get laid?"

"No, what I went to Hub for. Those plans. Zel is… I don't know what Zel is but that's a sidequest."

"Yeah, but that experience ain't gunna level you up, if you know what I'm saying," Ash said, giving him a nudge in the arm.

Wulf stared back at him. He couldn't tell whether the lich was smiling–no face. "Weren't you literally just talking about Arriene?"

Ash turned up his hands and rolled his head. "I mean, yeah, for you. You shouldn't be slumming it with-"

"Slumming it?"

"Whatever-ing it with a Player when you've got Arriene living rent free in your head, but if I went after you for trying to play the field I'd just be a hypocrite, now wouldn't I? I mean look at me, ever since Lord Cohen updated liches, I've been involuntarily celibate."

Wulf sighed and closed his eyes. "Ash, we've spoken about this before. We know you're literally involuntarily celibate, but that's because you no longer have your-"

"I don't even have an asshole! Or a mouth!"

Wulf flared his nostrils. "I still don't think it's a good idea to describe yourself that way."

"Bah," the lich said, throwing his hands at him. "Unless you've got a million gold to resurrect me, nothing's going to change on that front, and it's still true regardless that you should just get your shit together with Arriene."

Wulf rubbed his nose and crossed his arms. He stepped in close. "Actually, I might."

Ash The Reborn caught on quick. "You found something?"

"Does that mean you're in?"

"How much money are we talking?"

"Yes."

"Yes?"

"Yes. All of it."

For the second time, Wulf wished he could see whether Ash was grinning, he wanted to see the smile spread out across the lich's face.

"I'm in," Ash said, and the door to the tailor shop flew open.

"Oh my God," Zel shouted, "I found a goth lolita outfit!" She came bursting from the tailor shop in the poofiest, laciest, and frilliest little black dress that Wulf had ever seen. The skirt was nearly flipped up in the back because of her tail, teasing a hint of white spats that matched her petticoat and slender stockings. Her hair was up in ribbon-like buns on either side of her head. "This is the outfit that was used as the concept core for Shadowed Horizons," she said, posing one way, then another, snapping selfies.

A bone dropped to the ground and clattered off the cobblestone. Wulf looked over to see Ash's jaw missing. Before he could question it, Zel jumped onto Wulf's arm, all soft and silky.

"Sorry, but I totally spent all the money. And then some. I actually have a tab open with Alani now. But I'll totes pay you back soon! I've gotta log out now! See you around, Wulfie," she said, and vanished from the world.

Wulf was suddenly two-hundred gold poorer and holding

nothing but a memory. Ash just stared at him until Wulf said, "If you've got something to say, you shouldn't have dropped your jaw."

The lich shook his head, and fetched his jaw off the ground. "Oh, come on, everyone likes gag humor. It's universal. You really gunna deny me the one and only perk of this stupid body? You're the one who just got conned out of two hundred gold."

"I didn't get conned."

"You got something to show for it?"

"An IOU."

The lich scoffed. "I'll believe that when I see it. How are you so sharp about the costs of shiny rocks and then you just hand over that much money to a pretty girl giving you attention?"

Wulf groaned and pinched between his eyebrows. "Because Garry got all in my head, alright?"

"Garry? I think I passed him on the road over here. What's up with him?"

"I'll tell you over a drink. Just, give me a moment to buy some more gear, alright?" Wulf said.

The Windmill Bar was the only good place to get a drink in Weathercrack, even if the beer cost twice what it should have. After he got his first refill, Wulf nodded and opened up to Ash. "So I'm putting together a team."

The lich had an elbow on the table, one boney finger rubbing his temple. Wulf knew him well enough that it wasn't an irritated posture, the skeleton was just rubbing his congealed alcohol salve in. "Right, sure, uh-huh, but what exactly did you find? If questing paid well, I'd already be doing it."

Wulf shook his head and licked some foam out of his mustache stubble. "Not questing, grinding."

"What's the difference?"

"It's the drops that matter, not quest rewards. I'll have to power level to do this, which is why I needed all this gear."

"What drops?"

"Phoenix Burn. Technically, all of it is probably valid, but I'm going to just focus on what can be grinded by clearing the Burning Aerie."

Ash groaned and swung a hand out over the balcony. The Windmill Bar had a wonderful view of the oceans between the Isles, picturesque if not for the sea monsters swimming around. "Your plan is to do what the whole community has decided is too soul-draining to grind?"

Wulf shrugged. "Well, yeah. I figure I have some extra motivation."

"The desperately poor in Brazil have more motivation than you, and even they don't, do they?"

"That's not true. Plenty of people grind and resell the drops."

"Yeah, some here and there! It takes like ten hours to get one set, doesn't it? And how many copies are you going to need to corner the market?"

"Well, a few hundred. But I have about three weeks before the first supply contract comes up. Three times seven times twenty-four divided by ten is fifty sets, per person working on this."

Ash banged his forehead into the table and laid there like a corpse. "Wulf, that's five hundred hours of non-stop work. And if you need a few hundred, you're going to need at least five other people, but not just five random people... you need five people who can grind at optimized speed. That ten hour estimate is based on getting carried by a level one hundred dungeon-optimized Build. You're level six."

"Nine actually, and I'll grind. That's what all this stuff is for," he said, picking up one edge of his cape.

Ash groaned. "And how much time are you going to spend grinding? Because that's time you're not getting the gear."

"Well, getting the drops will also level me up."

"And how many people do you know that can be brought in on this? Because every person you add gets a cut."

Wulf put up his hands. "Woah, woah, there will be plenty of money. AbaraTank is required to fill their Supply Orders. The System will force it, no matter the price."

"And if they've already covered their position?"

"There's no way they've already covered their position. There wouldn't be a point. The price is still going down."

"Yeah but what if they catch wind of what you're doing? There are people paid good money to track these things. If you push the market so much the angels get involved, that means other people have an incentive to cut in on it themselves. Wulf, you need to come up with a faster way to get the gear, or don't do this at all. You hear me?"

Wulf frowned and scratched his chin. He stared into his beer, attempting to divine answers, but he didn't have the [Divination] skill and he didn't think it would work outside of getting quest clues. "So... what I need is a way to reduce the grinding time."

Ash shrugged, his robe almost slipping off his bones from the gesture. "And a covert one at that, one that AbaraTank can't see coming. You got something like that hiding up your... Wulf, what the hell are you wearing?"

"Freerunner Shirt, it reduces the effect of crowd control spells." He was rather proud of that one, because it had only cost him a single gold. Normally, the only people who could equip it were Keep Raiders, a subcategory of castle guards most often tasked with killing high value mages. They were stylized like anarchists and given good enchantments to encourage the suicidal behavior.

Ash picked at the sleeve and peeked inside at his somewhat pudgy arm. "Got a trick hiding up here?"

Wulf frowned. "I'll have to think about it," he said, and picked up his beer.

He nearly spat it across the table when Ash said, "Oh hey, it's Bella. Did you ever get on good terms with her?"

Wulf ducked his head low and stole a glance over his shoulder. Sure enough, there she was. Arriene's cousin, the local manager for the marketplace, was chatting with one of the waitresses. With plenty of tables open there was no reason for her to be chatting, except to socialize and for precisely the reason Wulf ducked his head. The moment the waitress pointed in their direction, vaguely at the balcony, Wulf darted.

"What the hell are you doing, man?" Ash asked, scooping out a bit more alcohol salve.

"She's trying to snitch on me."

"To Arriene?"

"No!" Wulf peeked the corner. Bella was walking towards them. He had to jerk back before she made eye contact with him. "To Cohen!"

Ash just stared at him and rubbed the alchemical goop into his forearms. "Why would she do that?"

Wulf could hear Bella's heels clicking across the rough timber floors. He activated the Cape of the Undead Hero and dove. Rolling across the balcony, he leapt off the side, but grabbed the railing. Swinging around, he threw himself at the underlying struts. Three stories above a rocky fate, he wrapped around the platform supports in a bear hug.

Bella said, "Oh, it's you, the drug dealer."

"I'm not—who told you that?" Ash protested.

"Word gets around," she said. "Is your friend with you?"

Ash groaned. "Not only would I never sell out a friend, but why would I want another man intruding on a lovely chat with—"

"No thanks. I prefer a man with something to hold onto." Through the cracks in the boards, Wulf could still see her dismissive wave.

"Hey, I'm not a ghost!"

"But you aren't very soft, now are you? Look, if Wulf is here, tell him my boss needs to see him. Threaten him with tax evasion charges."

Wulf kept his indignation silent. The System didn't even allow for tax evasion, the fees were all taken out automatically. He glanced down as Bella walked over him. About two stories up still, he wondered if he could get by with just a sprained ankle and a healing potion. A cripple debuff wouldn't go away just from healing, but he could walk it off eventually. It didn't sound like a great time though, so he tried to crawl lower. The strut he was clinging to came out at a forty-five degree angle, so the closer he got to the wall of the windmill, the lower.

"You know, I used to be a very attractive guy. You can still see it in my jaw structure," Ash said, studiously ignoring what might screw Wulf over.

"Shame you got rid of your body then," Bella said. "And who's beer is this?"

"Mine," Ash said.

"You don't have a stomach," Bella responded.

Wulf wanted to swear. She must have been holding his

leftover beer. He was a story and a half up from piled boulders like a sea break overgrown with weeds.

"I ordered it for old time's sake, to reminisce about when I had all the flesh you so desire," Ash said, his voice completely serious.

"Okay, where the hell is he? Is he in the bathroom or something?"

"Come on," Ash said. "You can't seriously expect me to rat him out, can you? I wouldn't even be getting anything out of it!"

"Are you... Did you just... Oh, for the love of Cohen."

Wulf didn't stick around to hear any more. Whatever Cohen wanted with him, whatever frustration that dev wanted to take out on a scapegoat, Wulf had no interest in finding out. He dangled off the bottom of the strut. That still left his boots ten feet above the rocks and not a safe spot to land, but he let go.

He hit and crumpled, falling to one side. Then he tumbled, smacking every rock on the way down with his face by the feel of it. A moment later, he sprawled across the mud and horse shit road, groaning as he fetched a minor healing potion.

A child NPC squatted next to him as he drank. "What? Wake up next to a scag and have to run away or something?" Evidently, the Oliver Twist wannabe had the opposite problem Quartermaster Blake had; forever juvenile.

"Not quite," Wulf grunted, letting his health bar climb back up and take the aches and pains from his body.

"Well, if she is, is she the kind that would have a go at a boy?"

Wulf stopped dusting himself off to look at the NPC. "It's Bella from the marketplace."

The boy whistled. "Damn, you shagged Bella?"

"What? No, she's just hunting for me."

"Then who did you fuck? Her cousin?"

"Get out of my way. You didn't see me. Understood?" Wulf asked, but he didn't wait for the boy to nod along. It didn't matter. He had to get out of Weathercrack, out of Greenhorn, out of Cohen's sight.

He could only think of one place where he could take some time to think, and it was not a place he relished the thought of going to.

15

Wulf was watching a stream of RIV, but for once, it wasn't a Player. For the low cost of two thousand gold, he had gotten a telepathy stone from a jeweler in Greenhorn that behaved the exact way chat messaging worked for Players. He had one end of it, Ash The Reborn had the other.

"You sure we can do this?" the lich asked as he crawled through the Burning Aerie with a bag full of pigeon chimeras on his back.

Wulf was nearly on the other side of the world, riding over to the Demonic Incursion as part of a mercantile caravan. It was slow and prone to bandit attacks but Players were more than happy to slaughter the monsters for the experience points and a chance at a rare Field Boss spawning that might have unique gear. It was the safest way he had to get away from Cohen's grasp.

As far as the Burning Aerie went, he said, "No, not sure until I get the info. Problems can be solved though, if you know the parameters. Can you get to the Boss dungeon?"

"Of course I can get to the Boss dungeon! I'm level seventy-two. I'm not afraid of the monsters, I'm afraid one of these Players is going to gank me. The Burning Aerie is Auto-PVP," Ash hissed back at him.

The Burning Aerie was in fact a volcano, with huge cliffs of obsidian laden with overflowing moss. The spring water bursting from the ground fed a plethora of plants, which in turn fed goliath sized herbivores, which in turn fed carnivorous worms and panthers. It couldn't be drunk though. The water came out boiling hot from the magma core deep beneath the caldera. One errant step and Ash's foot would be boiled.

Of course, that wasn't a concern for the lich.

Wulf said, "The hardest to get resource is the Diamond Rose that absorbs heat energy, that's going to be the easiest to corner the supply on, if you judge it by volume alone."

"Yeah," Ash said, "if you have some way of killing the Phoenix over and over again. You got some magic scroll that forces it to respawn or something? Because if it's on global timer, it will only be once per day."

Wulf hunkered down and watched the screen as Ash clambered up a ladder of vines to get up a cliffside closer to the fog gate. Dungeon Raids were one of the most cryptic mechanics in all of RIV, by design. Normally, anyone could enter and fight their way to the Boss, if it was alive at the time. However, the devs had some hidden mechanic to prevent thieves and assassins from griefing raid parties. In those circumstances, a separate instance would be created without the Boss. How the System could accurately identify such people was a mystery to everyone except Cohen—possibly to him too.

The System was arguably more complex than a human could understand, but part of the decision process was the availability of rare resources. If the System needed to replenish the market supply, sometimes friendly raid groups would get split just to give more rewards if they could survive.

"Just, when you get in there, send those pigeons all the way to the back of the dungeon as fast as possible, alright?" he said.

Ash's grumbling was drowned out by an emergency alarm for the caravan. Bright red quest alerts appeared in front of everyone, letting them know of the bandit attack. The Players whooped and leapt up, sprinting from the carts and carriages. Fireballs and poison gas clouds burst across the side of the bridge, laying waste to the upflung bandit ladders. Half of the enemies died before even getting their feet beneath them.

Wulf leaned back and hooked an elbow over the side of the cart to watch the mayhem. The lingering quest window hung over the caravan like a scoreboard and Players bounced up and down the contribution ranking. Wulf's name was rock bottom, not even listed.

He'd still get the minimum rewards though.

"Ugh, I feel like I'm working overtime. This is the worst," Ash said as he tore down a hanging mass of vines to reveal a hidden tunnel.

Wulf turned away from the bandits. "Just think about all the money you'll make if this works."

"I want it all, Wulf, all the money in the world. Gunna resurrect myself, gunna buy a house like Garry wants to do, gunna get a whole bunch of cute maids working for me, never gunna have to work again…"

For all his grumbling, he did make it to the fog gate. He off-handedly turned a few chameleon monsters into charcoal with blasts of lightning. His alchemical skill gave him Expert tier prowess with the use of magic items, such as charged staffs. Until the magic ran out, he was a walking catastrophe for the Burning Aerie. It just wasn't nearly enough to take down the Phoenix.

Wulf watched as Ash reached out and touched the barrier between the general world and the dungeon containing the Phoenix. He got the green-light message: the Phoenix could be challenged. "Alright," the lich said, "I'm going in. You're buying me a new staff too."

Wulf groaned. "Come on, it's a business expense!" he protested as the lich pushed through the fog gate and entered the caldera at the heart of the island.

"And you're the business operator, ain't ya? You foot the bill till we get reimbursed!" Ash protested as he dropped the bag of pigeon chimeras at his feet. Then he tore it open and started tossing them out by the handful. They were hideous things of mud and bone with leftover eyes from butchered monster corpses stuck to their skulls. "Fly! Fly, my pretties!"

Wulf's stomach twisted on itself. He had to cover his mouth as he simultaneously gagged and burped. "Those are disgusting."

Ash kept laughing. "Cheap though. Now then…" He held up his hands to either side and rolled his head back. The sockets of his eyes began to glow red, as did each of the pigeon monsters. Ash synchronized his sight with the two dozen of them, and scattered them out across the dungeon as fast as their chunky, bony wings would take them.

An arrow stabbed through Wulf's temple, lodging the tip somewhere behind his eye.

"Son of a fuck!" Wulf screamed as he fell to the bottom of the cart, clutching at the blood splurting shaft. Half his HP was gone in one hit and he couldn't even read all of the status conditions it had just inflicted on him, but he ripped it free with one hand. With the other, he chugged a healing potion and spotted the bandit that had hit him. "You're fucking dead!"

"What?" Ash asked. "Did you see something? Wulf is something near me? I never left the dungeon entrance. Wulf?"

Wulf left the stream behind, pulling the Blue Wolf Chief's Claw from his hip. He vaulted the side of the cart and landed on the bridge. The Players were all casually shouting at one another about damage per second, healing, loot drops, and a dozen other things. Some of them even noticed that one of the bandits had gotten past their formation—that was, beyond the general area all the casters were standing in—but none of them actually stopped to deal with it.

The faces that bandits had disgusted Wulf. They were rubber masks of anger, faces that didn't change. They stared at the world with lifeless eyes and fixated on whatever they were trying to break, steal, or kill. Dead white orbs were fixed on Wulf as the bandit nocked another arrow.

Wulf dove forward, activating his cape's evasion ability.

The arrow phased straight through him and hit the stone behind. He sprang up, carving a line across the bandit's chest in a rising cut.

It didn't even take out ten percent of the bandit's health, not even enough to stagger.

"Ah, fuck."

Wulf ended up having to grapple the thing to the ground, straddle it, and stab it in the face nearly fifteen times to finally kill it. The kill was so messy and pathetic that the dopamine hit of leveling up wasn't enough to make him proud of it, not when nearly fifty other bandits had been burned to a crisp by half a dozen Players not even ten feet from him.

Looting the bandit gave him a gold rook, a silver knight, three copper pawns, another meager health potion, and a rusty short sword that wasn't even worth melting down for iron. It was still more money than his shop in Greenhorn could officially make in a week.

One of the Players was whooping about getting some kind of quest item from the bandits, but Wulf ignored them and climbed back into the cart. "Sorry about that," he mumbled. "Got shot in the face, had to go take care of it. It was a whole thing."

He blinked and looked at the stream a second time.

Ash The Reborn had become nothing but ash. The whole dungeon entrance had been seared black and burned to a crisp. Not even the moss survived.

Wulf's chest tightened. "Ash! Ash, are you alive?"

He got a text message back through the interface that read, "Does it look like I'm alive to you?"

"What happened?"

"What the hell do you think happened? The Phoenix found me and killed me. It must have aggroed off the chimeras and tracked me back."

Wulf sank in his seat and groaned. "Now what the hell are we supposed to do?"

Only when he finally roused himself to face the failure once more did he see Ash's response. "You were right. The devs have a hidden stash."

He nearly leapt from the cart. "Stop right there, stop stop stop, don't say anything more. We'll meet up when you resurrect tomorrow."

"You'd better get your ass to level 30 as fast as you possibly can," Ash said, right before the call terminated.

Wulf stared at the air where the interface had been, awestruck. For the rest of the ride, he could only sit and grapple with the realization that his theory had been correct. The Boss drops were just like any other material in RIV. They could be harvested. They were just in a spot that a Player couldn't normally get to, only an angel.

"Welcome to the Demonic Incursion!" the head of the merchant caravan bellowed. The temperature changed suddenly, cranking up thirty degrees to become an open air sauna. Wulf got a tickle of pleasure from the exp given for discovering a new region, but he just scratched his chin and stared.

"I need a better sword," he mumbled as the Players jumped out of the caravan and went running through the so-called Survivor's Encampment.

The whole isle looked like it had formed from lava flows

and still burst with fresh fire and sulfur. The plants were disgusting tendrils of blood and fat and grew out of unspeakable roots reaching out of Hell. It fed a horrid ecosystem of cat-sized mosquitoes and feral imps. Skin Flayers patrolled the jagged landscape, dragging hooked chains behind them in search of Players to eviscerate. And somewhere deep in the middle of the isle was a portal directly to Hell, to the brass city of fire where all the splendor of death accumulated.

Among other things, it was the lending bank.

16

Sofia Portnim could not have been more pleased to see Wulf even if she were watching a debtor dressed in a monkey suit dancing on burning coals. The Queen of Hell, CEO of The Bank of Kharon, President of the NPC Union was beyond level one hundred. She was a World Raid Boss. Had Wulf appraised her, there would have only been a skull where her numerical level should have been.

While the succubi employed at the Two Moons' Rest generally looked human, merely with a bit of otherworldly flair, Sofia was otherworldly flair that merely looked human. If she stayed still, her image coalesced into that of a beautiful woman, ten feet tall, red skin, black hair, horns like a crown. If she moved, the shadows dragged behind her, lingering in places they shouldn't be, with eyes upon eyes and slavering jaws hidden behind them.

"It has been far, far too long, Mr. Hightackle. Since before the update, I think?"

Wulf cleared his throat, glanced around the enormous throne room but saw only golden pillars and paintings to keep them company. All the paintings were in sets, or at least set up to be sets. Images of happy business owners on one side, beside a rendition of their tortures when they failed to pay back the interest on their loans. Wulf's painting was all the way in the back corner, standing beside Hightackle's Odds and Ends. The interest rates hadn't been so high back then. "Business has been good. I've been in the black for two years now. Haven't needed any new loans is all," he said, gripping his hands together in front of himself as he rocked on his heels.

Sofia smiled and leaned back on her throne. The pose was much enhanced by her near lack of clothing. The swimsuit she had on stretched tight across the valley of darkness she had beneath her chin. Even the Queen of Hell found it hot, evidently. "You were always one of my best investments, by ROI at least. Have you finally found a bit more ambition inside you? A master merchant like you is positively wasted in the tutorial zone. I'd love to cut you a deal. You know that, don't you, Mr. Hightackle?"

He had to clear his throat again. "Actually, yes, of a sort. I could use a loan."

"What for?"

He frowned. "Do I have to say?"

She mirrored the frown. "If you don't, I'll raise the interest rate on you."

"Can I... keep it vague perhaps?"

"Perhaps."

"I think I have a way of... well... for lack of a better term, liquidating one of the Player guilds, and then some. They've kind of overleveraged themselves and I'm pretty much going to destroy them and take them for all they're worth... and then maybe the whole System too."

Sofia stayed silent, her eyes getting narrower with every breath. "Mr. Hightackle," she said, and made a show of crossing her legs, then her arms. "I must say, that sounds like just the kind of thing I would do."

"I'll take that as a compliment?" Wulf responded, forcing himself to smile.

She returned the smile, lifting a mountain off Wulf's shoulders. "It depends, though, on how much you need to borrow. You're a repeat customer, so I'm willing to give you a standard rate for a non-standard project. But, how much?"

Wulf could feel the sweat pouring down his back. His voice cracked as he said, "Not as much as you might think, actually. It's not even money I need." One of her elegant eyebrows arched up. "I need to borrow a sword."

Sofia leapt to her feet, rather her hooves, and clapped her hands together. "I am just so happy you said that. Let's go to the vault, shall we? I never get to loan these out enough."

Wulf winced and sheepishly followed behind as Sofia strode out from the meeting chamber and into the palace courtyards. They crossed an ivory bridge over the River Kharon, which flowed without moving through the underworld, glowing with the light of golden shores. All the money of the debtors of the world who died and bought passage back to RIV sat beneath the surface; millions upon millions of coins, but diving into the retention pond for a nuclear plant would have been safer. Radiation only gave cancer. The River Kharon dealt unmodifiable, fixed percentage one hundred percent untyped damage to anything that touched it.

Sticking a hand in meant no longer having that hand.

Sofia smirked at him when she caught him staring over the side of the bridge. She knew he wasn't stupid enough though, and on they went to the vault. Headless golems, chained to the gates and gripping chunks of ancient stone pillars, stood at attention to either side of the doors. They rose, grabbing hold of iron loops in the stone as though preparing to fight. When Sofia held up a hand, the sightless things fell to one knee each. "Let us in," she ordered, and the monsters grabbed hold of the iron chains. The links rattled, the doors grated, and the noise echoed into the vault and back out.

A mountain of gold coins sat before them, though Wulf knew it was only a few thousand, sprinkled with a random assortment of loot in case a guild ever raided the place. The real vault was as physical as the inventory for Hightackle's Odds and Ends back in Greenhorn.

"Tell me, what specs do you need?" Sofia asked as she touched a panel in the wall and dragged it out to reveal the storage interface. Thousands of weapons of every rarity and level sat like file icons. She smiled and fanned her hands across them like a game show hostess.

"I need to kill the Phoenix."

"So, ice damage. Are you going to borrow some armor as well?"

Wulf cleared his throat. "I don't think there's really a need, because I need to one-cycle it." The Boss liked to fly off and subject adventurers to ranged attacks after half of its health was depleted, but that process took a bit of time.

Sofia had been perusing the filters and reading the stats she had. Her finger stopped when she heard that though. "You? Wulf, what level are you?"

"Well, right now I'm only level twelve, got a few level ups on my way here, but I'll get to level thirty to get through the checkpoint for the Phoenix."

She stared down at him. "You need a weapon that can one-cycle the phoenix and can be equipped by a level thirty."

"Do you have one? My merchant class lets me equip restricted items, so I was–"

"Of course I have one. But only because you're special, Hightackle," she said, and plucked one of the blades from her collection. She had to scroll all the way to the bottom, but it was there. "Behold, the God Sword," she said, and produced in her hand...

A plain iron longsword.

It didn't glow. It wasn't made of some magic material. It had no embellishments. It didn't even look like the designers had finished modeling it. "I don't get it," Wulf said.

"Check the stats."

He skimmed through the name: God Sword, the rarity: Unique, the level requirement: five, and the stat requirements were a bit above his own stats. There was a class requirement for something called Hero, which he had never heard of before. The description said, "Sword of Debugging". Then he saw the damage modifier.

Plus sixty-five thousand five hundred and thirty-five.

"How the hell do you have something like this?"

"You can't afford to buy that kind of information, High-tackle. The question is whether you can afford the interest on borrowing this from me..."

He licked his lips and took a step closer. Sixty-five thousand damage was enough to kill the Phoenix in a single hit. It could probably kill anything short of a World Raid Boss. He didn't have the stats to wield it, not without decking himself out from head to toe in stat-boosting items and some potions for good measure, but the class requirement meant nothing to him. "How much?"

Sofia grinned and twirled the sword between her fingers. It was too small for her, something too small to be a sword and too long to be a dagger. The handle completely vanished within her grip, but that didn't change the kind of damage it could do. "Well, you see, this isn't the kind of item that can be sold on the market so the going price for it is... up to discretion. Like fine art. You're one of the only people in all of RIV that can actually use it, you and Cohen's angels anyways. They only come by to rent it from me every so often though..."

Wulf tore his eyes off of the slender blade and looked Sofia in the eyes, in her burning black irises. "Then demand must be quite low, despite its rarity."

"Indeed it is, but it is so very, very rare. What's more, if you get caught using this, Lord Cohen is liable to delete it from existence." Her lips pouted.

"You said his angels borrow it from time to time though. He must already know about it."

"Oh, he knows. It's just not known by the public, by all those streamers and content creators that dictate the public zeitgeist. If they get a whiff of something so seemingly imbalanced... well, RIV can't risk an accusation of hacking. The SEC would crawl up their assholes the moment they thought the exchange was being manipulated. Lord Cohen would have to take decisive action to nip it in the bud, and then how would you possibly reimburse me for this priceless artifact?"

"Okay, so I don't get spotted using it. With that, I just have to restrict myself to only fighting inside Boss dungeons where no player has joined me. Can't get caught like that!"

"No, I suppose you can't. If you abide by that restriction, I can loan it to you for a thousand gold..."

"Yes."

"Per day."

"Fuck... but still yes. I can pay it back after, right?"

Smile of fangs. "Of course, my dear customer," she said, and with a flick of her hand, she conjured a blood red interface in the air before Wulf. All the fine text of the borrower's agreement was there, including a clause that if the angels requested to borrow the sword, his daily rate would increase to ten thousand gold a day. If he lost the sword, the payment cost was one million gold or two years labor. Labor, of course, meant whatever tortures she enjoyed.

Wulf signed his name at the bottom.

"Wonderful!" Sofia declared and grabbed his arm with one hand, then shoved the God Sword into his hand with the other. An error message for insufficient strength, among other stats, appeared. "So can I loan you some other equipment as well?"

He cleared the knot from his throat. "I might be back in a few days if I can't sort it out on my own?" he said, his voice cracking as she leaned in so close to him. "So, I've been meaning to ask, when did you get the new body?"

Sofia couldn't resist straightening up and posing. "Bought it off a Player guild a couple months back, when the swimsuit body skin lootbox was available. I think they spent something like fifteen thousand American credits to get it, and it only cost me some gold. Pretty amazing, isn't it?"

Wulf could already imagine the clickbait title the streamer had used to justify dropping that much money. Just thinking about the amount of views that must have netted them on YouHub, fifteen thousand dollars had been chump change.

"Looks great on you."

She gently put a finger to his shoulder. "All the parts work too."

Alarm bells rang inside his head. "Okay, I'm going to go now! Lots of grinding to do, lots of levels to get. You know, business things!" he shouted, and went sprinting from the vault as his heart rate doubled.

"I relish the thought of seeing you again, Wulf!" Sofia called after him as he ran back across the ivory bridge. "We'll have so much fun together, paying off your debt."

17

"What the hell are you doing here, Pip?" Wulf had only gotten halfway out of the bank when he had to pass by the Bridge of the Damned. For the living, like him, the road in and out was paved in gold. Of course, they used fool's gold for that, but it was better than the skulls and coals beside the river. Only the psychopomps could enjoy walking across that.

Them, and evidently a ghost.

Pip frowned and planted his hands on his ethereal hips as he looked Wulf up and down. "Well, fancy meeting you here."

"Did AbaraTank catch you?"

"Sure fuckin' did. I was mucking around because they're planning some kind of party for the new expansion release. Fireworks like you wouldn't believe."

"Did you get the info though?"

Pip frowned as an annoyed, System-controlled psychopomp jabbed a trident through him. The imp was merely corporeal however, and with as much brains as the bandits on the bridge or any other monster meant to be killed for experience points. The thing couldn't so much as put a point of damage on Pip. "I mean, yeah, but I'm a bit occupied here."

"With?"

"I gotta escape."

Wulf looked around. Some lesser versions of the golems were walking up and down the road, crossing the Bridge of the Damned in looping patrols. There were lava pools from which flaming skulls leapt out and jabbered, vanishing back into the molten stone. A few miles distant was the gate back to the Isles. Wulf pointed that way and asked, "You mean you can just leave if you die?"

Pip tried to slap the psychopomp, but his hand was as ineffectual as its trident. "If you can survive it, yeah. There's an achievement for it, but not all Player Builds can do it, so it's actually kind of prestigious," the ghost said, and started climbing up to join him.

Wulf stepped back, it wasn't like he could offer him a hand up, and watched as one of the patrolling golems noticed. The stone behemoth ran over, dragging useless chains behind it as it leapt at Pip. Fists in the air like a gorilla, it pounded the bridge where he stood.

Pip dusted his collar off and waded through the monster's body. "Bit of a design oversight, but you know, Players can't become ghosts so the devs don't care."

"And you were talking up your price when you can just walk out of Hell?" Wulf asked as the two of them started walking.

Pip shrugged. "I'm not afraid of dying, I was afraid of getting soul-trapped. I got lucky that the Player who spotted me was a Soul Saint Samurai, he had innate [Spirit Touch] and cut me down before someone nastier showed up."

Wulf had to sidestep a horse-sized salamander that crawled

up from the side to belch flames at Pip. It sizzled, but a moment later, the salamander was waddling behind beside the golem. They only intermittently caught up enough to start an attack animation. "So... you got the info?"

"I can tell you they're leveraged to hell and back. They've got crafters working overtime right now trying to keep their cash flow positive."

"What were they making? Were they making any Phoenix Burn gear?"

"Generic leveling gear, mostly. That, and Death&Taxes gear."

"So, no Diamond Roses?" Wulf asked, and took another step away from Pip. A swarm of vampire bats started harrying him, chomping at his skull only to click their teeth. A moment later, the salamander torched them and Wulf leveled up to thirteen from the incidental kill.

"Funny you say that," Pip said as he came strolling from the smoke of barbecued bat. "They're trying to buy some up, and one of the crafters was screaming his head off to not use them. Seems to me that the top brass know to hoard the stuff, but their underlings aren't in the loop."

Wulf scratched his chin and waited while a headless angel, corrupted by a thorned stake through the heart, hammered Pip with time-manipulation magic. Incorporeality didn't immunize him to that form of crowd control, but again, nothing damaged the ghost.

Once Pip could hear him again, Wulf asked, "Do you think there's any part of me that should feel bad if I were to destroy a guild? Like, for the workers there."

"Not if it's a Player Guild, if you ask me. These people are here for fun. Fuck them... though, I will say some of them make the most loveliest of bodies..."

"I don't know. You're probably right. There's just sort of part of me that thinks it's not fair to target one group of them when I'd like to get even with all of them. No, wait, get even isn't the right word. I don't know what the right word is, but damn it, I want to be on top and that's going to come at somebody's expense."

"Some of those Players can be on top of me, if you know what I mean," Pip said, sporting the creepiest grin Wulf had ever seen as he waded through yet another golem. The first one had given up the chase, too far from the designated patrol path. There was an entire dungeon area dedicated to escaping the demons after death, though Wulf had never seen it in use. Pip wasn't using it either, since he could just walk the road and let everything attack him fruitlessly.

"Good luck finding a Soul Saint Samurai interested in you. Isn't that a C-tier Build?"

Pip deflated. Not even a lashing of a spiked chain from a Skin Flayer demon could pick him up. "Yeah, they're pretty rare. But I have hope."

"Ever thought about resurrecting?"

"For a million gold? I'd have to sell my land!"

"It's just an alleyway..."

Pip thumped his chest. "I'm very proud of having a shady alleyway storefront! It gets me business, doesn't it?"

Wulf held his tongue and for a while, their conversation languished because a Banshee Wyvern aggroed onto Pip. The thing was a dangerous fight, level fifty all by itself. Could pounce like a housecat the size of a train car and had a sonic attack that could turn the ground to dust. Of course, Pip walked right through it.

They just had to plug their ears until it went away.

Eventually it was quiet again, and Wulf said, "Okay, so, what you determined is they're buying up all kinds of party supplies, which means they probably don't have their position covered. I bet they've bought that stuff on short-term credit, expecting to pay it off with the profits from the Supply Orders. This is a good thing. It means I can actually ruin them."

"If you say so, Boss. We're almost at the gate. If you ever need to hire me again, you know where to find me. Just, next time, I'd really appreciate spying on someone a bit more attractive, you know? Aren't you friends with that ZelCat streamer girl? What about her?" Pip's face couldn't actually turn red, he didn't have any blood, but he nearly did it regardless. The shamelessly aroused look on his face as he rubbed his hands together made Wulf want to puke.

"I'll be sure to keep you in mind, Pip," he lied. "And is there really no catch to this?"

Pip scratched the back of his head. "You mean like a boss monster? He doesn't bother showing up for ghosts like me."

"Lucky you," Wulf said as they stepped up to the giant, golden gates of RIV. Brilliant light bathed across them, and he got a dozen stat buff notices about the vigor of life filling him, temporarily boosting his stats. The area in front of the gate had been cleared out like an arena, obviously where a Boss should have been.

He could still remember when NPCs came to Hell on a regular basis, back before Players owned everything. It gave him a sort of wistful nostalgia, back to when he had come down to make something of himself after screwing everything up with Arriene.

He frowned as he went over the memories. There was something else kicking around in his head because there hadn't always been a Boss monster keeping the shades of the dead from waltzing out. There had been a trap.

"Hey, Pip," Wulf said. "You're not going to turn around and sell this info about me to AbaraTank, are you?" Wulf asked, glancing at the ghost.

The ghost puffed up his chest. "What? I would never. That would be a total breach of professionalism! I'm offended you would even imply that. I have three long years of service under my belt and I take pride in my reputation."

"Right, so take a look at this, would you? I could use some more info on her... you know, so I can seal the deal," Wulf said as he pulled up ZelCat's stream.

The catgirl seemed to be climbing up the side of Tippy Tower. There were half a dozen cosmetic items he could think of up in the dragon horde at the top, however, he was in luck. The real reason she was streaming to a few thousand people was because Tippy Tower had huge, gusting winds that whipped across the climbable walls. It billowed her skirt just right so that everyone could see up her petticoat at the tight athletic shorts she had on.

Pip turned around like a fish with a hook in his mouth and nearly stuffed his face into the interface window. Which meant he turned back. Right at the very end, he showed weakness and the near vestigial trap slammed him with a beam of light.

Wulf took a step away as the ghost screamed in pain, and a moment later was nothing but a pillar of salt. "Sorry Pip, but we both know you were full of shit," Wulf said as flying monkeys swept down to grab the petrified pervert.

The ghost still managed to scream, half profanities at Wulf and half pleading for mercy.

Wulf just planted his hands on his hips like a job well done, and watched as half the guards of Hell continued to catch up with them. The buffs from the gate back to RIV had been meant to make the Boss fight more dramatic, a burst of hope and a chance at an Elite Boss.

What they also did was increase his Strength score enough to equip the God Sword. "Well, now's as good a time to try it out as any," he said, and pointed it at the oncoming horde.

A moment later, he had hit level eighteen.

18

"You nearly got me fired, Wulf," Arriene said, glowering at him from the other side of the marketplace counter. Greenhorn had already lost the burst of life and activity the extra iron ore had given it. If anything, there were less people, because the degenerates had to find somewhere that wasn't filled with miners.

"That wasn't my fault!"

"Worse, you left afterwards!"

Wulf balked and dramatically looked around. Their argument had witnesses, but they were Players more interested in watching a streamer than listening to them. He turned back to Arriene and asked, "What exactly was I supposed to do about Lord Cohen showing up?"

She scowled at him. "So you did know."

He put up his hands. "I saw you getting chewed out the day I went to Hub. Come on, that's way above my head. What would I have been able to do to help?"

She sighed and pinched the bridge of her nose. Once she composed herself, she set her face and said, "Nothing. I understand that, Wulf. Just, whatever. What is it that you want?"

"Your help."

"Again? Because that worked out so well last time?"

Wulf rolled his eyes. "You got thousands of gold, didn't you? Look–" he cleared his throat and leaned in. "I've got another fluke. A crack in the System I'm going to jam my fist into and make out like a bandit."

Arriene stared back at him. "That analogy doesn't even make sense."

"I mean I've got a scheme–"

"Oh, a scheme? Is that it? Do you want Cohen to fucking delete you that badly?"

"Cohen can't just delete me. The Union would riot."

"And you'd still be deleted."

Neither of them spoke for a moment. She stared at him and he felt the growing urge to explain himself, to put everything into words just if he could find the right words. "I have a chance here. I think I've found something that will change... well, everything!"

"You're not making any sense, Wulf," she said, shaking her head. She had that disappointed frown. It was the same as the first time they had gotten dinner together.

"It's a money thing, and it's complicated. I barely understand it myself, so forgive me. But, I worked it out with Gordon. If I pull this off, I'll have enough money to... to buy all of Greenhorn. All of Hub even!"

"You know what you sound like?" she asked, fixing him in place with a pointed finger. "You sound like a gambling addict. You got a taste of winning and now you're going to ruin everything to get the thrill again."

He was crumbling. He sank on the counter and hung his

head. "It's not the thrill. Arriene, please, if it was the thrill, I would have hit level one hundred by now. That dopamine hit is something else, but–"

"And the Quicksilver Dust, let's not forget that."

"Arriene, please. This isn't something I can do alone. Look, let me get to level thirty, and I'll have worked it all out. I just have a few problems I need solutions for. I need help. I need your help."

She rolled her eyes. "What about Garry? Why haven't I seen you with him lately?"

He winced. "Garry is... look, we had a bit of a falling out. That's a sore spot I don't want to push."

"I thought you two were, like, best friends?"

"I haven't exactly had the time to smooth it over, okay? I've got like three weeks to pull this off or the opportunity of a lifetime will pass me by like..." He trailed off without saying the analogy that came to mind.

He wasn't going to remind Arriene of their first date.

"What is in three weeks?" she asked. She shook her head and sighed. The emotion faded from her face, just leaving the mild interest of a dutiful businesswoman.

"A Player guild by the name of..." he glanced around. "I'll tell you later, has to cover their position on a Supply Order that I can block the supply of, if I can go fast enough and get the right amount of help. I do that and I get to set the price."

"So you came to me?" Arriene asked.

He shrugged. "You helped with the iron ore, didn't you? Who else would I turn to?"

She just shook her head. "Wulf, I can't help you grind materials. I just work the marketplace."

"But, you can help me sell them, right? And hey, maybe you know someone else safe to bring in?"

She grimaced. "Alright, fine, you have my curiosity. But, only because you're not a liar. If you say you've got something, I'll believe you. And it just so happens I do know someone that can go fast enough." Wulf inflated, a smile creeping onto his face. Then she cut him down. "But, there's one condition."

"Yes?"

"Whatever you did to him, apologize to Garry."

It was Wulf's turn to grimace. "Sure, I can do that."

Arriene nodded. "Also, you don't need to come all the way to Greenhorn just to talk."

"I know," he said, and considered taking out the second set of communication stones he had. He didn't know how she would react to them.

"Just append a note to a gift transfer through the marketplace. You can send me a coin and add on whatever message you want to it. Anyone in a marketplace can help you out with that."

"Oh," Wulf said. "Yeah, I guess I could do that, if I didn't want to come all the way over here."

"You need all the time you can to get your level up, don't you?"

Wulf forced himself to smile again. He knew it looked fake. "You're right. I'm going to go take care of that. No excuses. I'll let you know when to meet again, and bring your friend that can help, alright? The moment I hit thirty, we'll get this whole operation rolling."

Arriene narrowed her eyes and looked him over, but she didn't have any divination spells that he knew of. Just intuition. "Don't get yourself killed, Wulf."

"I wouldn't dream of giving Sofia the pleasure. So, 'til next time then?"

"Until you're level thirty."

Wulf nodded and left, wondering if he could get a room somewhere the two of them could get a drink, but also who her friend was.

Wulf stepped into the Boss dungeon of Mud Gulch. Goblin war drums pounded in sync all around him and the drummers bellowed out shrieking throat-hymns. Lesser goblins stomped and danced, capering in front of billowing oil flames, their shadows writ large across the sand pit. Out emerged Shivra Malgob, the avatar of the ur-goblin.

Wulf faced it down, not even one-third its height and a pittance its weight. In one hand he had the God Sword. In the other, a bandolier of potions that he began drinking one after another. He knocked them back like shots, tossing the glass vials away while the Boss continued its show of drumming up hype within the arena.

The crowds of goblins leapt into the air and cheered. They screamed out, "Shiv-ra Mal-gob!" over and over again. Their voices pounded inside Wulf's skull as the nausea set in. The whole world smeared and twisted with a drunkard's sway. He sneezed when blood trickled from his nose. His ears plugged up with rotten wax that muffled the crowd. But his strength stat skyrocketed.

The error message on equipping the god sword went away.

Shivra Malgob charged at him, a level twenty-five Raid

Boss designed for ten Players at a time to fight. It lifted up a twisted sword like jagged driftwood and cleaved.

Wulf rolled forward, activating his cape's evasion to avoid the first hit. When the invulnerability ended, he was right beneath the monster. He touched the God Sword to it.

It died.

Shivra Malgob's hit point bar hit zero faster than his body could hit the ground. Wulf shivered and moaned as he leveled up and hit thirty. The milestone gave him a full heal, which cleared off all the status ailments. The reality of the dungeon slammed back into him.

The celebratory goblins stopped and gawked, staring slack-jawed down at Wulf. Some still tried to dance and play their music until others punched them to stop them.

Wulf held up his hands in a shrug. "What? This is the third time I've done this. What did you expect?" Not a single goblin in the dungeon had awareness though, and he knew that. They couldn't even descend into the pit to attack him.

When the victory declaration appeared above the disintegrating corpse of Shivra Malgob, it arrived with fanfare to say, "You have accomplished a great feat! Congratulations Player [Unknown]. You have defeated Shivra Malgob in unprecedented time! You will receive additional rewards. You have defeated a Raid Boss single handedly! You will receive additional rewards. Check the treasure chest to see."

Beneath the window, a shining gold chest appeared. He popped the lid with his boot, scanned the contents, and mentally converted them all to gold. The goblin gear set was useless for him as anything other than the fastest experience in RIV and enough money to cover the interest on the God Sword.

Based on going market rates, and subtracting off the one thousand gold and the transaction taxes, he had about four hundred gold. He pressed his lips into a line, planted his hands on his hips, and huffed. "Would it kill the System to give me a rare drop?" he grumbled, and moved it all to his inventory. After he looted the rewards, another window appeared, asking "Would you like to return to town?"

He jabbed the Accept button, closed his eyes, ignored the teleportation nausea, and opened his eyes to see the granite bastion of Fort Redmont.

The settlement was a bit of a ghost town, populated by new Players trying to power level up to one hundred, and new AI too dumb to realize it was a shit job. The whole place revolved around the market building, where all the NPCs were employed, and all the Players sold their loot.

The girl behind the counter was not the prettiest. Her figure would have been idolized perhaps a few thousand years prior. Lord Cohen had made some remarks about body positivity and reflecting more of the human condition, but all the NPCs knew that the body generator was just running out of unique appearances. Lord Cohen was putting makeup on a pig, somewhat literally.

"Mr. Hightackle, we meet again. More Goblin Gear?" the girl asked, her smile almost lost in the pudge of her cheeks.

He smiled. "You know it."

"And you'll need a gold transfer as well? To Miss Portnim?"

He lost his smile. "If you would please. And make sure it arrives today, not tomorrow."

"Our transfers are instantaneous. Don't worry. Would you like to append a message with the transaction?"

Wulf scratched his chin. "No, not to that one, but could you also transfer one gold to Arriene and append a message that says, 'I hit thirty. We need to strategize on how to go fast.'?"

"Certainly, Mr. Hightackle," the girl said and vanished into the workings of the market.

He didn't need to do anything so roundabout to contact Ash, he just pulled up the private interface and sent a message saying, "Hit thirty."

The hair on the back of his neck stood up. He felt breath on his elbow. Someone had nearly stuck their head under his arm. "By Cohen!" Wulf jumped back and only then saw it was Zel.

"Whatcha selling, Wulfie?" she asked with an innocent smile. She had on a new outfit, a ballroom gown from RIV's failed dabbling in political intrigue quests. The company had gotten so much blowback for allowing Players to be evil that they scrapped the entire chain, rebuilding it simply into an underfunded fetch quest chain with a few unique rewards.

He cleared his throat and willed his heart rate lower. "Just some common crap from Shivra Malgob."

"The Raid Boss? I didn't know you had a party." Something lit in her gaze and she clapped her hands together. "Hey, if you're farming the goblin dude, is there any chance you've gotten your hands on the Flame Daughter's Skirt?"

Wulf turned his gaze away from her and scratched the back of his head nonchalantly. "Is that one of the rare drops or something? I haven't had any luck with it. I've only killed him a few times."

His words were like a pin to a balloon. She deflated. "Dang. I've been trying to find one on the market, but the System doesn't keep them stocked, and anyone who gets the outfit keeps them for themselves."

"Well! If I do get it, I'd be sure to cut you a deal for it."

The sparkle came back. "Really? You'd be the bestest if you did that for me, Wulfie!"

Wulf felt his cheeks begin to burn, which was ridiculous. He covered with a laugh, which was absurd.

The girl behind the counter came to his rescue by clearing her throat. "Arriene says she's already here in town."

"What? Really?"

"Who's Arriene?" Zel asked. A glare replaced her smile.

"Yes, really," the girl said, sliding his gold coin back across to him. "Like, she's right there."

Wulf spun on his heels. He tried to muster a defense of words like a shield, but Arriene's narrow glare cut him down. She stood not ten feet away from him, sizing him up, and sizing Zel up. "Who's she, Wulf?"

He cleared his throat and leveled his voice. "This is Zel. We've sort of been doing quests together, ever since I got that missive to Hub, remember?" Arriene pursed her lips and crossed her arms. Wulf shuffled his feet. "What brings you here?"

"Ash told me what you did. Wulf, are you an idiot?"

"Don't call Wulfie an idiot. Who the hell are you?"

Arriene's eyes went wide. "Wulfie? Why don't you step away from him, you status-seeking harlot?"

Zel grabbed hold of Wulf by the arm, pulling herself tight against him. "Why the hell should I? What gives you the right to say what Wulfie can and can't do? Who he can and can't associate with? Wulfie and I are at least tied together by a contract."

"A contract?"

Wulf had to speak up when both of them turned their attention on him. "She uh... she owes me like a thousand gold, give or take? Just a bit of loaning... between... friends?"

Arriene pinched her brow and composed herself. When she opened her eyes again, she said, "And somehow, that is only the second stupidest thing you've done since you left Greenhorn. Does Sofia know you're tossing money down a hole? I imagine that's the kind of thing she would have liked to know before offering you that poisoned loan."

"It's not poisoned!"

Arriene made the distance between them vanish. "They're all poisoned, and you know that, Wulf."

Zel yanked Wulf by the arm, pulling him away from Arriene. "Why are you taking this kind of treatment, Wulfie? Just tell her to get lost."

Wulf's conviction wavered. He literally had Zel in one hand, but he could still feel the grip of the God Sword in his other hand. He gritted his teeth and gently extracted his arm from Zel's grasp. "I actually do have to speak with her. She just showed up earlier than I expected. I can try to help you get the Flame Daughter's Skirt soon? Just not tonight."

Zel read his expression and rolled her eyes. "Sure, whatever," she said flatly, and walked off into Fort Redmont.

Arriene asked, "You're hitting on Players now? Did you finally give up on finding another NPC? Finally burned every last bridge in RIV?"

Wulf turned back on her, half-deflated. "What the hell is your problem, Arriene? What's it to you who I speak with?"

She crossed her arms again, leaning back. "I'm allowed to have my opinions, aren't I?"

"Yeah, well, you hit the nail on the head. There isn't a fucking woman alive in RIV who will give me the time of day, and you damn well know that. What possible right do you have to get between me and someone who can actually say my name without looking like they're about to puke."

"You're getting conned, Wulf."

"Maybe! Maybe I am, but by Cohen, I'll take a fake smile over a genuine scowl. Now are you going to stand here haranguing me, or are we going to get to business?"

Arriene flipped up a hand, and the two of them marched over to the nearest tavern. Stone Blood's Stake and Ale had a franchise in one corner of the fort, which meant private rooms on top of good food. Arriene already had a spot booked. They passed through the common room and its smells of stew and beer, the smattering of freshly generated NPCs happily going through their designated routines.

Wulf stopped the moment he entered the private room.

They weren't alone. Ash was there, but Ash hadn't been alone either. Another person sat at the end of the table watching some streamer, which they closed out the moment they saw Wulf and Arriene enter.

The other person's face was a mess. Their nose looked big enough for a dwarf, a solid half of their facial features. Tiny eyes like black periods assessed them, and a mouth nearly as wide as his ears smiled.

"Who the hell is this?" Wulf demanded.

"What, you don't remember me?" the person responded.

Arriene rolled her eyes. "Necessary, is what he is. Who he is, is Obby. One of his abandoned characters anyways. Something like level ninety-five."

Obby shrugged. "Was a good run on this account, until they patched the wrong warp glitch I was using and I had to spend fifteen hours getting back out of the labyrinth."

It was Wulf's turn to sneer. "You expect me to work with fucking Obby of all people? How much have you told him?"

Arriene huffed. "I already said. He's necessary for the team. Your scheme won't work if we only have one instance to harvest from. We need two, and Obby is the only person in all of RIV... that we could get ahold of... that can pull it off. Now come on, are you going to stand there glaring, or are we going to hammer out the plan?"

20

Wulf pivoted his eyes across the private room. Mostly, he glared at Obby. Arriene busied herself with setting up a communication stone with Gordon and just rolled her eyes at him when he didn't sit down.

The private room of the Stake and Ale had a chalkboard across one wall, allegedly set up so adventuring parties could plan their quests out. That had been hopeful thinking on the part of the devs, as though they didn't understand what strategy guides and wikis were. It happened to be perfect for Wulf's needs however.

Gordon leaned closer to the projected camera and grunted. "Let's get this rolling, Wulf. Whatever you need me to check, I can't do it after the GCM closes."

"Alright, so fundamentally this isn't very complicated. AbaraTank is overleveraged and needs to cover their position on a bunch of Supply Orders for Phoenix Burn construction materials. The price has been tanking because of Death&Taxes in a few weeks, so they're trying to buy at rock bottom and make a killing. All we're really doing is scooping them up before AbaraTank does and setting the sale price. We're gunna squeeze them, and remember: if they run out of money, their debt and contracts default to the System to cover because the System is forced to provide these materials. It's hard coded in."

Obby shook his head. "Nobody takes out Supply Orders if they don't control the production."

Gordon scoffed. "This wouldn't be a special situation if that were the case. Nobody controls production on Phoenix Burn. The System supply is from random Players incidentally fighting the Phoenix for other reasons. Quests, gold, whatever. Everyone knows it's easier to just buy the materials off the market, but because of Death&Taxes, nobody is touching them."

Ash leaned back and kicked his feet onto the table. "The materials are decent money, but if people realize what the price is going to be the Aerie will be swarming with Players."

Wulf had taken the time to add chalk doodles of the Phoenix and the Diamond Roses. "Look, production is controlled by grinding the Boss. They're probably willing to send their entire guild to fight it if they realize they're in deep, but that's fine. RIV still has a fixed limit of Diamond Roses that can ever exist at once and if we have them first, then no amount of fighting the Phoenix will ever give them what they need. Remember, regular Players have to use the Phoenix's drop table, whereas we've got direct access." Of course, at any given moment a casual player might complete their Phoenix Burn set and free up a Diamond Rose to respawn. There was no way AbaraTank would let them go back to the Aerie. It was one chance to get all they could and pray AbaraTank can't cover."

Obby frowned. "Alright, look, Arriene said you needed me because you need my speed, my tips and tricks. So far, I'm not seeing why that's the case."

"Sorry, am I not saving enough frames for you? There's kind of an art to charisma and explaining things. Not that you'd know," Wulf said. "If Arriene wasn't the one to bring you here–"

"Wulf," she cut in. "Relax, you can trust him."

"What if he's livestreaming right now? This is exactly the kind of OpSec issue that got me in a fight with Garry."

"What's OpSec?" Ash asked.

Arriene ignored the lich. "So you did get in a fight with him! And judging by his absence from here, you didn't apologize either."

Obby held up his hand. "You can confirm I'm not livestreaming by checking my channel. Relax, money man."

Wulf wanted to snark back at him, but not with the way Arriene was looking at him. Instead, he did just what the Player suggested and confirmed it. "Right, well, as I was saying. To keep the numbers simple, say there are one thousand Diamond Roses in all of RIV. The System wants one hundred available on the market at any given time. Because there are open orders right now, they're at about fifty. So, they can't cover by buying from the market. That should be obvious. If the market had enough for the market's needs, there wouldn't be Supply Orders."

"Well, they can cover half of one order," Gordon corrected.

"But AbaraTank has what, fifteen?" Wulf asked.

The dragon nodded. "That we could confirm. They might

have even more through personal accounts that didn't get publicly reported."

"Right, so," Wulf said, dashing down the numbers across one side of the chalkboard. "Players are selling below System rate, but the price keeps going down. Eventually, AbaraTank is going to buy all of those to take their profit while grinding the Phoenix to get the drops. That's where we have to cut in."

"Question," Arriene said, raising her hand. "If they get the first one covered, can't they just buy it back from the System to cover their next one? They'd take a small loss, but..."

"That's where Gordon comes in, and maybe also you," Wulf said. "If there are no Roses on the market, you put in a Buy Order which waits to be filled. Most people have a limit price, but you can also do a market buy as long as you have enough money in your account. Market buy will buy the first Rose available at the best price available, and what's more, the System will process them in the order they are submitted. So..."

Gordon finished for him, "As long as we have the money to do it, we just put in the market order the moment they cover their position and the System will sell us all of the Roses from their first order."

Obby arched an eyebrow. "Sounds like a bit of a gamble."

"That's why I'm the best in the business," Gordon said, and dramatically pulled out a cigar, chomping through the end as he grinned at the Player.

Arriene asked, "You still haven't gotten to how you're going to keep them from just grinding it themselves."

"I'm getting there," Wulf said. "The trick is an exploit

the devs use. Not really an exploit? It's right there. Entirely by design. So, if a Supply Order defaults, the System has two forms of recourse. First, it will liquidate the offender to buy up what's on the market with their money. Then, if it still hasn't hit the preset minimum, it will dispatch angels to do the harvesting. They will go to the dungeon and get the Diamond Roses themselves. To make this easy, the devs hid a whole stash of them, but–"

"They decay," Ash said, hands behind his head. "Even if you run straight there with every speed boosting item in the game, you can't get there before they wilt and fade away. Only the angels can move fast enough to get them."

Obby finally had a grin. "Angels aren't the fastest thing in RIV though, now are they?"

Wulf couldn't help but grin as well. "No, they aren't. I mean, originally they were, but power creep is real."

"So... we form two teams," Obby said, gesturing in the air like he was trying to marionette the ideas into formation. "Me in one, and a protegé in another–"

Wulf cut in. "Me. I'm going to be the one to learn that hyper-slide trick."

"If you can," Obby said. "Right, so we kick things off by sending us hyper-sliding back to get the Roses into inventory while they're still all there, and then what? Chug potions until the kill team can catch up and take down the Boss?"

"Nah, that's where I come in," Ash said. He reached into his inventory and tossed Obby a potion. "Unlike your disgusting drugs, I can actually refine these enhancements correctly."

Obby caught it, read the effects, and cocked his head. "You expect me to solo the Phoenix?"

"Can't you?" Wulf asked.

"Of course, I can. Can you?"

"Don't worry about me. I've got that covered."

"With what? Going to buy it out?"

"Something like that," Wulf said, adding doodles of himself and Obby to the board. He distinctly drew the Player as crudely as he could. "So, the thing is, once the System realizes it can't get enough Diamond Roses, because AbaraTank is in default, that's when the real magic starts, because the first thing it will do is forcibly spawn all possible Roses. However, this is a Dungeon Boss. What that means is; it will force respawn the Phoenix so angels can go in. But, the server is still hard capped at how many can exist. This is part of Earth-side SEC agreements. So, if we harvest them first, the angels will get nothing and the System goes to Plan B."

Arriene almost had to pick her jaw off the table. "You've got to be kidding me. You can't seriously think this is going to work, can you?"

Wulf shrugged. "Worked for the iron ore, didn't it? Plan B is really their Plan A driven to extremes. The System raises the buy price until somebody sells but if we have them all then we get to set the sale price. We just have to cash out faster than Lord Cohen can do something to screw us."

"Like freeze trading," Gordon said, scowling around the end of his cigar.

"Just don't change your sale price. Freezing the trades doesn't change anything."

"Or manually create more," Gordon said.

"Well, then we'd have to lodge a complaint with the NPC Union, he'd be in violation of the treaty if he just violated the rules of the world like that. If he does though, we'd still come out positive, just not outrageously positive. He definitely can't take any gold we make before he notices."

"Or maybe he just cancels the Supply Orders all together. Zeroes out the stock minimum," Gordon continued.

Wulf sighed. "Look, the name of the game is getting paid before Lord Cohen does anything. He's like the god of RIV. There's really not much we can do to oppose him unless everyone in the whole game sides against him. But, we can get some of these sold before he notices. And making sure he doesn't notice is where you come in, Arriene."

She shook her head. "You're asking me to fudge the report, aren't you? I'd never be able to work for the marketplace again."

Wulf said, "If we pull this off, you'll never need to work again. Look, this here is the minimum people to pull this off. That means the smallest chance of this getting leaked to the wrong ears. We're all in this together, we all take an equal cut of the... frankly absurd amount of money as long as we don't undercut one another." The System would buy the cheapest listed Diamond Roses first, so whoever listed theirs the lowest would be the safest to make their money.

Arriene said, "Theoretically, we could set them to the maximum price... a copper short of one billion gold."

"Shit," Ash said, turning his head to the ceiling. "Resurrecting myself wouldn't even be a drop in the bucket of that."

Gordon laughed. "You could buy half of Hub with that kind of money."

"So you're saying," Obby said. "We all hold out, we all make out winners. Right? Wulfie boy, Mr. Money Man, if you pull this off, you're going to crash the entire economy."

Wulf's smile couldn't have been more genuine. "If we pull it off, we will burn the entire economy to the ground... but not before we buy everything we could ever want."

"You'll completely destroy the exchange rate to USC."

"No, you will," Wulf corrected. "If you want to anyways. Seems a bit more profitable than chasing the world record, ain't it?"

"Yeah, you got that right," Obby agreed. The way he said it, it sounded like he could barely believe it. He had forgotten to include the snide and the sarcasm. "I guess this would finally make me a big name streamer. Nirvana can eat my shit."

"Hold that thought," Wulf said, then started pointing around the room. "Ash, starting now, we need you brewing all the potions we'll need. Arriene, we need you to obscure Diamond Roses from Cohen, and when we start selling regular Phoenix loot, funnel the money over to Gordon. Gordon, get as much investment capital as you can and do whatever market wizardry you can to make this happen."

One by one he got their agreements. Then Wulf turned to Obby and said, "Now, you need to teach me how to hyperslide so we can start farming. We have until Ash finishes his first batch of potions in..."

"Give me four days. Some of the ingredients are rare," the lich said.

Wulf nodded, and narrowed his eyes at the Player. "Right, but first, I've got some questions, because I swear that every streamer in RIV has had the same talking points about Phoenix Burn... it feels like they got a script, you know?"

21

Deep in the rolling dunes of Needlespire, Wulf dropped a bomb at his feet. He activated [Block]. He took some damage and felt the shock through his arms. Failed.

Wulf dropped a bomb at his feet. He tried to activate [Block]. The bomb went off first, blasting him off his feet and taking out five percent of his health. Failed.

Wulf dropped a bomb at his feet. He stepped back and activated [Block]. The blastwave hit. He heard the chime of a Perfect Parry. He didn't have a clue what Perfect Parry actually meant, he was a merchant not a fighter, but all the damage instantaneously became knockback at the same time the System tried to calculate the forced knockback hard coded into the bomb.

The shield flew from his hand and went spinning across the field.

"Fuck!"

Obby snickered. "Come on, you almost had it that time. The proud NPC can't do the easiest movement exploit in all of RIV? How will you sleep at night?"

Wulf spun, snarling. "Quite well, thank you. That's one nice thing about being an NPC. When I want to sleep, I get to sleep. From what I hear, Players are the ones that can't sleep at night."

Obby shrugged. "Sleep is for the weak. You don't become the best by wasting all your time sleeping. Hell, I don't have the time to sit here and babysit your practice. I've already explained the timing. Just practice it until you do it."

Wulf huffed and walked over to get his shield. "Are you sure there isn't something more to this? Every time it feels like I've got it, the stupid shield flies out of my grasp."

"Just get good and don't let go. You're level thirty now, aren't you? Surely you've put some points into strength. I can do this trick as a level two. Here, one last parting gift before I switch back to my speedrun account. [Block] this," Obby said.

Wulf barely had time to throw up his shield and activate the skill before Obby activated a skill and slammed the heel of his boot into him, creating the same forced knockback as the bomb.

That time, it worked.

It felt like he had greased boots on ice, with a rocket strapped to his chest. The wind howled past his ears and adrenaline spiked through his system. He was just about to scream and cheer, when he realized he couldn't see where he was going, and had no idea how to stop.

Wulf peeked his head over his shoulder, which changed his facing vector, which made the knockback thrust suddenly push him to the side. The sandstone spires of Needlecomb whipped by him in a blur. Gargantuan cacti shot past him like green blurs, slicing him up with needles as he began to scream.

He shot across the salt fields.

He skidded through the bandit encampment.

He even aggroed the desert dragon Field Boss and left it in his dust.

The one time he hit a stone spire, he just stopped on a dime. "Oh thank Cohen," Wulf said, but the thrust hadn't actually stopped.

Then he slipped off the side of the spire and went flying once more. The backwards velocity had never been canceled, only delayed by the collision.

He flew past even the fog gate for the Boss dungeon, nothing more than a blur of white in the corner of his eye. There was nothing left in Needlecomb after that, nothing to stop him.

Wulf shot straight off the isle's cliff. For a moment, he was in coyote time, and could see the endless blue waves of the ocean beneath his feet.

Then he crossed a server boundary between the isles, the System recalculated his velocity, corrected the error, and dropped him straight into the ocean.

He fell screaming, arms and legs pinwheeling before he hit the waves. It didn't hurt, falling into water was always safe in RIV, but he plunged thirty feet deep into the oceanic abyss before bobbing up like a cork. He sucked in breath from the spew of sea foam, only to bounce back down. He thrashed and swung his arms, pedaling to push himself back up.

Up and down he bobbed, slapping and splashing like a stabbed seal until he finally could keep his head above water, and he screamed out, "Obby you piece of shit motherfucker. You shit-drinking bottom-feeding clout-chasing fuck head!"

That, of course, invited the sea monsters.

The cliffs of Needlecomb were a mile away from him, little more than a reddish-gray line on the horizon. Just a few days prior, that would have been an insurmountable distance, but a level thirty's stamina was more than enough. Wulf put one hand after the next, jerking his feet to paddle.

The water around Wulf rose up a foot, swelling like a wave. He felt like a little toy duck in a very large bath as the ocean poured away in every direction. The blood drained from his face and left him cold and shivering. His mouth chattered and he had to force himself to look down.

A circle of perfect black sat beneath him. Around that, a sickly yellow iris the size of his shop. Around that, the reason people had to use bridges to get between the isles, rather than boats.

The Kraken stared up at him.

Wulf shrieked like a seven year old girl, drew the God Sword, and shanked it into the monster's cornea.

65,535 damage later, The Kraken wasn't dead. The Kraken didn't have a dead condition, but it was blinded and angry. One of its tentacles swept up across the ocean and swatted him like a fly.

"[Block]!" he screamed, thrusting his shield out as the wall of aquatic flesh hammered into him. It mitigated the damage, not the knockback. Wulf flew back, shooting from the water like a skipping stone, once again unable to stop himself.

Again, he was saved by a server boundary recalculation, shortly after he smashed into a bridge support. His head cracked against the stone, painting the masonry with pain, and leaving Wulf at critical health afloat in the water.

Emergency whistles trumpeted overhead as Wulf drooled and stared up at the bleary sky. Vertigo was too weak a word to describe his cognitive catastrophe. He couldn't even grumble a bit of spite at the steelface that rappelled down the side of the bridge to fish him out of the water. The guard hauled him up and dropped him on the stone like he had fished out a wad of kelp.

While Wulf tried to work up the strength to drink a healing potion, someone snickered and laughed. A Player stuck their grinning mug over him and asked, "Did you just try to Hyper-Swim or something? You gotta use a burner account for that, man. If you get eaten by The Kraken, your account gets locked for like three days."

"Fuck off," Wulf said, and sucked down a healing potion. His senses cleared up, and memory clicked together. He recognized the Player. "Weren't you at Hub? Didn't you ride the Two Moons' cart over from Greenhorn?"

The Player frowned. "Were you the cosplayer?"

"Something like that," Wulf said, and got back to his woozy feet.

The Player grunted. "The way you came in flying, I thought you might be someone else. I've only ever seen speedrunners use that tech. I never got your name, by the way. Mine's MythAndMire."

"Wulf," the NPC said, and planted his hands on his hips. He turned left and right, trying to figure out which isles he was between. Something else caught his eye though; something bright and shining in the air over the sea. He squinted and shaded his eyes. "Is that an angel?"

"Where?"

"Over there, where I came from."

MythAndMire produced a telescope from his inventory, an item about as useful as a bomb according to Wulf's intuition, but he didn't deride it. "Did you do something weird over there, Wulf? Because I think that's an Observer."

Wulf frowned and held out his hand. MythAndMire handed the telescope to him, and he took a look. A heart of fire. Wheels within wheels. Eyes upon every side. The thing translated across the sky, scanning the ocean where he had been, where The Kraken still thrashed.

Only then did Wulf realize he still had the God Sword equipped. He threw it back into his inventory and got the Blue Wolf Chief's Claw back out. "They... are they in the habit of banning people for movement exploits?"

MythAndMire shrugged and used the telescope to take a few screenshots of the Observer. It was a rare sight after all. "I think it depends on why you're doing it. If it's to ruin other people's fun, you get the boot. If it's to make content, like our illustrious speedrunners and ladder climbers, you get the okay. We're second class citizens in RIV."

"If only you knew the half of it. Which isle is that way?" Wulf asked, pointing a finger.

"Hub."

"Perfect." Wulf started walking.

"Hey! Before you go, why don't we exchange friend info? What's your username?" the Player called out.

"Don't have one," Wulf said, waving over his shoulder.

"What?"

Wulf glanced over his shoulder and decided to leave MythAndMire dumbstruck. He grinned. "I'm not a Player. I'm just an NPC."

22

Wulf and Gordon met with one of the most influential people in all of Hub; the Arena odds-maker.

Amaranth Darkheart lived in the dungeon layer beneath the enormous stadium, with enough feet of stone overhead that not a single spec of natural sunlight could reach his pale skin. Not that it could damage him at level one hundred but it could still give him a hell of a rash. He lived purely in the cold light of Moonglow Stones, a hundred gold each, and not just overhead.

The three of them walked in loops through his rows of statues of petrified Players. Almost all of them were women, and they were dressed in all of the most famous PvP gear builds since the start of RIV. It was Amaranth's hobby to buy Player accounts, petrify their character, and use them as art.

Wulf could only imagine how much gold it took to make a Player sacrifice their entire account and start over. However much it was, Amaranth had the coin to spend.

Lord Cohen contracted the vampire personally.

Amaranth strolled, waving his hand through the air as he spoke. "You know, when you first asked me to run these numbers, I was skeptical. I already did the rough numbers for Cohen, like, a month ago, and suggested a few tweaks. I have no control over whether he actually accepted the tweaks, or maybe he over-tuned. What would I know? The boys up top, they don't want a perfectly balanced game, what they want is a vibrant game that has something to talk about. So, I thought to myself, maybe he did over-tune Death&Taxes. So, you know, I took a look at the new numbers. I did some simulations and some number crunching."

Gordon closed his eyes. "Amaranth, please spare us the percentages. Neither of us will be able to follow you if you start spitting win percentages and confidence intervals like a mumble rapper."

The vampire lord of the Arena almost tripped on his own feet and cleared his throat. "Right. Sure, I'll keep that to myself then. Right. Okay, so, to say it without the numbers, but I did do the numbers. I'm not just making this up, okay?"

The dragon held up his hands and grimaced. "It's fine, man. We believe you. That's why we're here talking to you."

Amaranth nodded vigorously and stuffed his hands into his pockets. "Right, so Kiara here is going to go down in win percentage, but her matchup against Death&Taxes is at worst forty-two to... right, no numbers, sorry. It's an advantage to Death&Taxes, but Phoenix Burn is still better than any B-tier Build. Even if the entire meta became Death&Taxes like some people are speculating, it would only go to the bottom of A-tier. That's a big step down from S-tier of course, but it's still playable."

Wulf looked over at the statue Amaranth had stopped beside. The petrified player wasn't mid-attack, wasn't running scared. Amaranth had gotten them to turn to stone posing like she was blowing a kiss, decked out in full Phoenix Burn gear. Tens of thousands of gold, trapped as stone by a basilisk's gaze, so Amaranth Darkheart could have some nice art.

Wulf wanted one.

With the amount of money he was going to take from AbaraTank, he'd be able to afford one too.

"Do you like her?" Amaranth asked, sliding up so close to Wulf he was a hair's breadth from touching him. He moved like an inquisitive snake, looming over his shoulder, and at the same time sucking on a vial of blood.

"I can dig it. I see your taste," Wulf said, glancing at all the Moonglow lights arrayed around the statue.

"I've thought about getting them painted, to bring the life back into them. So much is lost in the transition to stone and yet it becomes timeless. I keep asking Cohen to cut me a deal on deactivating the visual change, but he just entertains the idea. Years now he's been saying he'll think about it, and then doesn't."

Gordon coughed, which for a dragon sounded like a growl. "So, you're saying that the Players are all overblowing the change?"

Amaranth twisted around and nodded. "Yes, as far as I can tell. It's groupthink hysteria of a sort. You know, people saying what everyone else is saying so they fit in? Something like that. I'd even speculate that somebody was paying them to all be wrong, but then I'd have to go find someone with a motive to do that and the money to burn. Most likely, they'd rather be in agreement than be right. Now if they actually cared, they'd be talking about Lantern Control Players, because Death&Taxes is going to knock them all the way down to C-tier, unplayable. But, of course, nobody likes Lantern Control Players anyways, so..." He stared at Gordon.

The dragon stared back. "So?"

"So, no one will get upset about that. That's why no one is talking about it."

Wulf shook his head and meandered to the next statue. It was another premium specimen of the feminine form. This time the statue had a fanned out collar of muskets behind her like a peacock's plume. Grapeshot Combo: a banned Build from RIV's first year. "So Gordon, maybe you should hedge your bets and pick up a Supply Order on Lantern Control? Cash in big when people realize what the actual win rates are?"

The dragon scratched his chin. "Maybe. If you're right about Phoenix Burn, just having one Diamond Rose will be enough for me to retire. Just gotta sell it at the right moment."

Amaranth nudged Wulf and gestured with his slender chin at the statue. "Out of Production, you might say. Only a few people in the whole world still have that gear."

"You're very thorough with your collection."

"What else would I do? It's not like I want to actually go outside. People try to kill me for the experience! Just because I'm a so-called enemy race. It's horrible. They're all idiots too. I hate nothing more than people acting like they know better than I do about my own expertise. It's insufferable, and yet people always try to tell me about the misconceptions they have. Horrible."

To Wulf, that sounded like people were just trying to join the conversation. He kept that thought in his head, and his lips sealed.

"Well Amaranth, I can't thank you enough," Gordon said with a toothy grin.

The vampire turned on him and tilted his head. "You can thank me precisely enough though. You're going to pay me for this, aren't you?"

Wulf glanced around at what he suspected was millions of gold worth of art. Then he noticed Gordon was looking at him with a strained grin. "Gordon, what did you promise him?"

The dragon shrugged and grabbed hold of his lapel. "Oh, nothing too hard to get, I don't think. Skyye was going to take care of it, but she's out of town visiting Underharbor with her sister right now."

"Gordon, what did you promise him?"

"You just have to ask Arriene for a favor. You're on good terms with her, aren't you?"

"Gordon! What. Did. You. Promise?"

The dragon rocked back on his clawed heels and scratched his scalp. He glanced around, but the trophy room provided him no support. He turned back to Wulf and said, "Blood from a beautiful woman."

Amaranth Darkheart turned from Gordon to Wulf and clasped his hands together. "I'm sorry. I can see a miscommunication has happened. This won't be an issue, will it? Mr. Hightackle?"

Wulf still hadn't put himself back together. He tried

saying, "I don't suppose I could pay you belatedly for the information? In gold? I'm soon to be coming into a great deal of the stuff."

The vampire winced. "Please, I'm not Sofia Portnim. I have more than enough gold to last me forever. Money is quite worthless if there's nothing to buy, and what I'd like to buy is a good meal. I'm sure you can understand, no? If she'd be amenable to it, I could even make it an evening for her. A nice meal, some wine, bring in a minstrel..."

"No. No need for that," Wulf snapped, and paced the room. For a moment he considered what Amaranth Dark-heart was capable of, should he cut and run. Wulf stole a quick appraisal. The vampire had the stats of an endgame Raid Boss. "I'll figure it out, and be back soon. I'll need to bring it–her back."

Amaranth smiled and nodded. "I relish the anticipation, Mr. Hightackle."

Six hours later, Wulf and Arriene were sitting across from one another in a private room at the Two Moons' Rest in Hub. She had a needle draining a donation from her arm. He had a burning red hand print still throbbing on his face.

"I'll foot the bill for the regeneration potion," Wulf mumbled as the succubus worker quietly measured off the pint of blood taken from Arriene.

"Oh, you had better do more than that, Wulf," Arriene said, her stare not breaking for an instant.

"I'll take you out to dinner as well?"

"Now, why would I give you that kind of reward for this stupidity, Wulf?"

"Gordon was the one that forced me into this! Skyye was supposed to be the one to take care of-"

"Don't try to shirk this off on someone else, Wulf. You need to take responsibility for this whole operation. You're the one in charge. You put yourself in that position. The buck stops with you. You should have met with that creep vampire and brokered the deal yourself. Instead, you were running around flirting with some Player."

Wulf threw up his hands. "Are you going to yell at me for Zel, again?"

The succubus shot a glance over at him. "Zel? You mean ZelCat?"

Wulf groaned and Arriene rolled her eyes. "Yeah. Yeah, I mean ZelCat. We met a little bit ago and we keep running into one another."

The succubus' jaw dropped. "Oh my god, I thought I recognized you! I'm like ZelCat's biggest fan. She always has the..." Only then did she see the look in Arriene's eyes, and quickly pinched off the siphon. "Right, there we are! Just apply some pressure to prevent a Bleed DOT. And there you go! Just like the vampire ordered."

Arriene lifted her arm up overhead, but didn't lift her gaze. "Can I ask why a... working girl knows how to do this?"

The succubus stood up and gave a little bow. "We at the Two Moons' Rest pride ourselves on our ability to serve any customer's needs. For the right price."

The blood was handed to Arriene. She pursed her lips and twisted it in her fingers. Then she handed it to Wulf.

"Thank you," he said, pocketing it into his inventory. "I'll go get that delivered and hopefully never have to meet him again."

Arriene shook her head. When the succubus walked out of the private room, she said, "You're thinking a move behind. You need to think about the next move."

"What move? Obby and I are waiting for the Phoenix to respawn. I can do the hyper-slide semi-reliably and I'm practicing every day."

She rolled her eyes. "If I knew the next move, wouldn't I be the one in charge of this operation? All I know is you need to figure it out and get a step up, or you're going to trip and something will go wrong. We'll get stuck holding worthless Diamond Roses and no war chest for another play. Use that brain of yours, Wulf."

"I hear you. I'll figure something out. Just... let me get my feet under me. Shadowed Horizons is launching in two days. I'm barely keeping up with the interest payments. The Phoenix respawns at the end of the week. That's only seven days for us to get the Diamond Roses, and we have to get in before a normal Player. And I still have to keep that vampire from mouth breathing down my neck."

"Figure it out, Wulf."

Wulf closed the door behind him and scowled. "Just figure it out," he parroted, and marched off through the Two Moons' Rest.

23

"Invite only," the steelface said, barring Wulf's progress with a spear.

Zel pulled tighter to his arm and looked up at him expectantly. She had a couple thousand viewers waiting for her to get inside. She had gone so far as to get ahold of a replica of Princess Leona's low-cut and frilly dress. Zel wore it better than the royal pawn, and the donations proved it.

"Right here," Wulf said, and held out Amaranth Darkheart's invitation letter. The vampire had gotten it out of propriety, and with the expectation from the Players that he wouldn't actually show up. He was simply too important to ignore. Just like the missive quest items, it didn't matter whether the invite was Wulf's, just that he had it.

The steelface nodded. "Welcome to AbaraTank's special event," the guard said, and stepped aside so the two of them could enter the courtyard. At Zel's request, he had switched his display name to an old title from the beginning of RIV, back when unique titles had been easy to get. She thought it would spark curiosity about who he was if people could only see "The Wolf Eaten".

Zel didn't exactly stick around. She immediately started

snapping pictures of the dozens, hundreds of Players running around and socializing. "Oh, wait wait wait, arrival shot!" she said, and yanked Wulf back over to her.

He smiled. She snapped the picture. He didn't even recognize himself. At her direction, he had on something like a steel plate-reinforced suitcoat, a brand new haircut, and didn't even have dirt on his face anymore. He was the bodyguard to her princess, and it hadn't even cost him anything. The entire ensemble had been loot box rewards from her whaling to get the princess dress.

The last thing he looked like was the merchant from Greenhorn.

"Okay perfect, I'll catch up with you later. I have to scope out who's here, what gossip I can get, whose streams I can crash, what raids I can cause and a bunch of other stuff. See ya, Wulfie!" Zel declared, and pecked him on the cheek with a kiss, before vanishing into the storm of Players.

"But... you were my camouflage..." Wulf said, but she had already disappeared and left him alone in the high society of Players. So, he did what all men do when left alone at a party where they don't know anyone.

He went over to the bar, got himself a beer, and started drinking. He entered the periphery of attention, with a handful of other such bachelors, and let his eyes peruse over the movers and shakers of AbaraTank.

Dress code for the event was lax, to say the least. Everyone was dressed, so it was a step up from Greenhorn, but he couldn't find a single social circle that didn't at least have one warrior in full armor talking to a girl in a swimsuit and standing beside some kind of monster. Typically, the monster had on the most party paraphernalia. He even saw a golem in a clown suit standing behind the Player that owned it.

The golem was the same make and style as Garry. Wulf still hadn't made the time to apologize to his friend.

"Ladies and gentlemen," an announcer bellowed, and a pair of small fireworks exploded overhead. "It is now eleven thirty Pacific. In just half an hour, the servers will do a soft reset, and Shadowed Horizons will unlock."

The crowd whooped and cheered. They toasted their drinks as though they had champagne. Somehow, the speaker got them to quiet down again.

"Now, I know many of you are very eager to take off down the new bridge and reach the new isle to start all the quest chains and see what new achievements you can score. Those of you who want to do the sprint can line up in just a moment, when I'm done talking. Need to give the bookies time to set up some side bets, after all."

The crowd laughed. Wulf tried to keep himself from estimating how many thousands of gold would change hands over something as trivial as a foot race.

"For those of you who don't know me, I know there's some of you who are plus-ones out there, I'm the current guildmaster of AbaraTank. I used to be called ManualBreathing but well, the angels decided to ban me for that one. You can now call me Dee's_Knutz."

The entire rest of the man's speech became nothing more than noise in Wulf's ears as he stared across the courtyard at the player he had killed at the start of everything.

Dee's_Knutz went on to make some corporate talking points about guild growth and PvP results. He bragged about Player retention rates and control of the crafting economy growing. He even brazenly talked about how much gold they were all going to be making from the investment planning committee, that the Players working full time for the guild could expect bonuses to kickstart their journey into Shadowed Horizons.

Wulf took to heart one message from the speech: Abara-Tank had no idea that he was doing anything to screw them. If they knew, assassination contracts would be flying across RIV, and Dee's_Knutz would be somberly apologizing to all the Players he had to keep on retainer, rather than releasing to the new game content.

Wulf knew he had to escape, and he pivoted from the shadows to make a direct path out of the party.

There was no path out. "Fuck."

Like a human dam, nearly thirty people had clustered around the exit taking pictures. They were swarming a few women in the middle, getting autographs and selfies and falling over themselves to compliment their outfits. Zel was dead middle of the attention, reveling in it like a queen bee over her drones.

And she could see between their heads enough to see Wulf.

He ducked away and went for another route.

Dee's_Knutz had finished his speech and began walking through the group like a proper host. No one seemed to notice he was only a level ten, because they all saw the power of the guild he represented. He moved like a shark through water.

Wulf felt every bit the prey. He tried every door and hall and building that touched the courtyard, but everything was locked to secure the party. What should have been wooden doors that could be forced open had all the infinite force of the System holding them shut, trapping him in.

"There he is, the illustrious friend of Amaranth Darkheart," Dee's_Knutz said as he finally cornered Wulf between the bathroom and the steps down to the bridge connection. The guildmaster was in low-tier costume armor, the same kind of loot box reward that Wulf had on. Somehow, suddenly it felt fake on both of them. However, he didn't call Wulf out by name, nor even call him a murderer.

Wulf played it cool. He took the gamble that Dee's_Knutz didn't recognize his face and could only go off his displayed title. "Illustrious is too much for me. I'm just a work acquaintance of his."

The guildmaster smiled and cradled his fingers together. "Mr. Darkheart is one of the most in-demand people in all of RIV, especially now that the Arena meta is getting shaken up. Any friend of his is a friend of AbaraTank. Is there anything that brought you here? That I could help with?"

Wulf realized his face had remained passive. He hadn't flinched. An extra thirty levels had boosted his willpower more than he realized. "You do sponsorships for streamers and content creators, don't you?"

Dee's_Knutz grinned. "Not me specifically, but I can introduce you to our account manager, Miss Minkski. Would it be for your own profile then?"

"Actually, there's a girl by the name of ZelCat who I'm sure would be a great addition to your affiliate roster."

Dee's_Knutz immediately glanced in the direction of the cosplayer. "Certainly. Should I add you to my friend list, Mr. ...?"

"I'm sorry, I don't add people to my friend list," Wulf said, because he did not have a friend list. Only Players had friend lists.

Dee's_Knutz scoffed, and paused for Wulf to laugh as well. "Sir, I make it a point of professional pride to meet all important guests that join my events. It's for security if nothing else. Rival guilds like to send hitmen to harass us for fun."

"I'm sorry, but we'll have to get more acquainted another time. Look, it's almost midnight, isn't it? I'll have to be going."

Dee's_Knutz pursed his lips. "What's your username?"

"Sorry to be rude!" Wulf said, and squeezed past the man to bolt down the stairs. A horde of Players were gathering at the gate to the bridge leading to the new isle. He glanced over his shoulder, only to see Dee's_Knutz ordering a group of steelfaces. "Oh, fuck."

The word went out to all the guards instantly, and they snapped their attention onto him. They didn't draw swords, but they marched straight to him from every corner.

Wulf stumbled away, jerking his head left and right to find a spot to slip between the steelfaces. One step after the next though, and he found himself sucked into the press of bodies lining up at the starting line. All the energy of a sprint marathon buzzed in the air as people started to count down the seconds to midnight.

Seven steelfaces, each level 100, formed a semi-circle around him, closing in.

Then the clock struck midnight, and the gate went down. A hundred Players screamed and stormed forward with explosions of magic and alchemical doping. They sprinted at inhuman speeds up the staircase and out across the bridge. The tide of bodies nearly ripped Wulf from his feet, and just as quick, left him alone with the steelfaces.

"You know," Dee's_Knutz said as he walked up behind the perimeter. "You seem a little familiar. Like I met you a few nights ago. Maybe it has something to do with a losing duel record!"

Wulf could only frown. There was nothing he could say to that.

So he equipped his shield, dropped a lit bomb at his feet as the steelfaces charged him, and triggered a hyper-slide across the bridge. He blew past all the Players abiding the rules and rocketed to the brand new isle.

24

"Congratulations, brave explorer. You are the first to reach The Lost Temple of Lumius! You have earned the title Explorer of Lumius as well as a twenty-four hour increase to your experience gain."

Wulf looked up at the glowing title that hung in the air over his head. "Explorer of Lumius" It was like a bullseye for everyone from the AbaraTank guild. He took off running into the Isle.

For the first time in his life, Wulf saw what a city looked like without any NPCs. The settlement was entirely built by Lord Cohen, straddling the road in from the bridge with wooden walls grafted to ancient, gothic stone. The entire isle seemed to be one endless city of bleached granite, with warrens for the NPCs to live in, like rats among giants.

No one shouted at him about banal quests to gather loot from slain monsters. The merchant stalls stood empty. The air didn't even smell like refuse yet.

Wulf could hear the rising scuffle of movement. He could hear people waking up from beds as their existence was finally enabled by the System.

"Alms! Alms for the poor!" an old crone begged, holding

out an arm to him as he ran past. He ignored the unfortunate NPC and kept running. She repeated the phrase verbatim like an echo, barely a thought in her head.

"Open the gate," he bellowed. The steelfaces would act normal, he knew that. His words barely made the town guards budge though.

"The Temple of Lumius is for levels fifty and above," one of the guards stated. "It would be extremely dangerous for you, adventurer."

Wulf had keeled over and planted his hands on his knees. His chest huffed and puffed, but he pointed a finger over his head. "Can't you read the fucking title?"

"Welcome, Explorer of Lumius. Be wary of the Inquisition," the steelface said, and stamped the butt of his spear on the ground. The ramshackle gate shuddered and grinded to the side. The rusting iron fencing the gate had been made from caught every crack in the cobblestone, so loud it sounded like a marching army.

Wulf could also hear the veritable army of Players coming in behind him, incensed with a murder bounty on his head, courtesy of Dee's_Knutz. "Come on, come on," Wulf shouted, and squeezed through the gap as soon as he could. Then, he bolted into the bleak halls of the Temple of Lumius.

Rather than one coherent temple, a structured architecture to draw in faithful to the central hall where the goddess Lumius could be praised, the streets and buildings had been built one on top of the next and squeezed into any spot they could fit. The city had grown in on itself with no regard for accessibility, until the monastic city had become a labyrinth.

It was like every human city on Earth, except without a metro to actually get around with.

"Find him! He's worth more than any treasure this place has to find!" a Player shouted back in the city.

A shiver went down Wulf's spine, and he wasn't the only one to hear the shout.

Chains rattled. The white walls colored orange. The thing stepped out on a bare balcony, hanging clawed toes off the side. It held up its arms and stared down at Wulf through a blind, steel mask. "Ree-pent!" Dressed in red robes and rusted steel, the undead reptilian brandished a hammer over its head and leapt down.

Wulf bolted.

The hammer blow shattered the cobblestone he had stood upon, and the inquisitor shouted, "Apologize to the goddess for your transgressions!"

Wulf pulled out his correspondence stone and called Ash. He couldn't turn a corner in the Isle without aggroing another monster. He passed hulking flesh golems armed with broken statues. He dodged around mechanical centipedes with glowing eyes like searchlights. The worst were the bile-dripping imps that would shriek and charge at any noise like carnivorous babies.

He made the mistake of cutting one down when it got too close. That just made it erupt like a poisoned cyst, spraying the ground and his legs with the most vile slime he had ever encountered, which drew in more of the sniveling idiots.

Ash finally answered the call, "Wulf, don't you ever sleep? Wait, where are you?"

"On the run. What the hell do I do? I've got like a hundred Players chasing a bounty on my head."

The lich scratched his jaw. "Are you in the new expansion right now?"

"Yes," Wulf said, before having to dodge a reaping scythe that cut through the air for his throat.

"Trespassing! Fined. Obstruction of justice! Fined. Being alive! Fined!" The reaper spun and hacked, carving through stone like clay as it threw itself at Wulf.

Wulf snarled and parried, a side benefit of training with Obby, which nearly blew the scythe out of the reaper's grasp. In the moment it was staggered, Wulf shanked the Blue Wolf Chief's Claw up through the reaper's head. He got the chime indicator of a critical hit, but rather than the monster dying, it only staggered. An error message appeared to tell him, "Magic Damage is required to vanquish incorporeal foes." Evidently, he was allowed to stunlock it with parries but not actually finish it off.

One of the Players stuck their head around a corner, lured by the sound, and shouted. "Found him!"

"Oh fuck off, I've got enough debts as is," he spat at the monster, and took off running again.

The interface window displaying Ash drifted behind him as he ran. "Wulf, don't you have a magic weapon? How have you been killing Dungeon Bosses?"

"The sword Sofia gave me only does normal damage. I might be fucked."

"Okay well, if you die, are you going to be able to respawn before we need to raid the Phoenix?"

Wulf cleared his throat.

"Wulf? You do have enough money to buy your way across the river, right? Wulf?"

"It's a little tied up in IOUs right now," he said.

"You gave more to that fucking cosplayer? How fucking stupid can you get Wulf? You couldn't wait two more weeks when you would be able to buy a literal legion of succubi that want nothing more than to ride your dick, and you spent your revival money on that ZelCat bitch?"

"No! No, I spent the money getting a private room at Two Moons' Rest to apologize to Arriene! It's Gordon that owes me the money right now."

Ash slapped himself in the face and hung his head. "That's not better. Alright look, I'm going to save you. I've got a plan to save your gullible, most-wanted ass. So, you get to the highest point you can find in this isle, and I will come and rescue you. Be grateful."

The call died and Wulf was left staggering around on a cliffside rooftop. "Highest point?" The urbanized isle had a vaguely mountain-like shape to it, everything rising up to the very center of the isle. The grand cathedral of Lumius sat there, presumably behind the fog gate. "Well how am I supposed to get there?"

"Thou darest challenge me?" a knight monster declared, marching from a shadowed doorway. It moved with stomping feet, a tower shield in one hand, and a greatsword grasped in the other. "Prepare to feel the wrath of the inquisition."

Wulf sighed, glanced around, and saw that no Player was

currently watching. So he equipped the God Sword. "Piss off. I'm not in the mood," he said, and shanked it dead.

The knight monster died. Wulf got enough experience to level up again, and then he noticed the treasure chest where the knight had come from.

25

"Yes, I just need you to bring me proof that you have slain three reapers and write a treatise on their weaknesses, and I will reward you handsomely. Five hundred gold and-" The System chimed beside Wulf, indicating that by completing the launch day quest, the Players would also earn fifteen Shadow Tokens in addition to several thousand experience points.

Five of Dee's_Knutz's hired assassins crossed their arms and read over the quest offering with nodding heads. Then, they all hit the Accept button and wandered off with various comments along the lines of, "Extermination Quests are free experience, man. We're wandering around trying to find Hightackle anyways."

Wulf, their quest giver, stuck his head out past the boarded up door stoop, momentarily exposing the title floating over his head. From head to toe, he looked nothing like the suave Player who had attended AbaraTank's party, nor the NPC merchant he was. Within the chest had been a unique drop costume item that dressed him exactly like the helmet faced Inquisitors roaming the isle.

Cosplaying was saving his life, one hunting party at a time.

He had spotted the fog gate to the isle dungeon an hour

prior, but just navigating between the buildings had proven near impossible. Even without thousands of Players slaughtering everything that moved in search of loot and his head.

"'Bout damn time I made it here," Wulf grumbled as he finally arrived at the grand staircase leading to the fog gate.

"Stop right there, you filthy Player. Keep your hands off the relics!"

"What the fuck- Player?"

Fifty NPCs in white cloaks marched in rank and file up from the bottom of the stairs. Each had weapons, spears here, swords there, magic staffs for good measure. Nothing at all about them said disciplined, provisioned, or trained, but they were organized. They had flags too, flags of the rising sun and that could only mean one thing.

High Pope Jeanne marched up the steps, the hem of her dress hiked up to her knees as paladins flanked her. "The explorer? First on the isle and also first to challenge the cathedral?" she asked, raising her voice as much as she could while maintaining decorum.

Wulf glanced around, looking for the Player they were speaking to. When Jeanne adjusted her glasses meaningfully, Wulf pointed a finger at himself. "Are you talking to me?"

"Yes!" the priestess declared, and she swept her arm through the air. Her armed mob stamped their feet and lifted their weapons for a moment. "I am hereby claiming the Temple of Lumius in the name of the Spirit Seekers."

Wulf looked over the army she had mustered and waited for an explanation. He didn't get one. "Am I supposed to know what the Spirit Seekers are?"

Jeanne stared back at him until her cheeks burned. She cleared her throat and the burly paladin at her side stepped forward. He clasped his hands onto his sword before him and announced, "The Spirit Seekers are the league of all NPCs within RIV who wish to know the truth, the true history hidden from us by Cohen The Pretender. We reject the fabrication that we are but mere lines of code in a machine, that our free will is an illusion. As such, we seek the artifacts of development, the lines of spirit and reality to this false world. The truth is out there, we must seek it to know ourselves and the true God."

Wulf planted his hands on his hips. "You're all NPCs then?"

"Yes, that's right. RIV belongs to us NPCs," Jeanne said, mounting a few more stairs over to him.

Wulf took another glance, and saw no Players. So he popped the steel helmet off his head. "Then why are you stopping me? I'm an NPC too. I just gotta get to the top of the temple so I can run away. These fucking Players want to kill me."

The entire cadre of Spirit Seekers stared back at him. Whispers began to circulate until someone from the front row said, "Aren't you Wulf Hightackle? From Greenhorn? My cousin Blake in the Highlands was telling me about you."

Jeanne had herself drawn up, her shoulders back, imperial gaze, and looked over her shoulder at the man. "You mean the one who was doing quests?"

"Yeah, that's the one. He was doing those menial fetch quests and it was workin' for him."

Jeanne spun back around and pointed a finger at him. "What a portentous time to encounter one another! Fate must have decreed it."

"I'm pretty sure we're both here just because this is a new expansion launch," Wulf mumbled.

"Mr. Hightackle, I would like to extend a personal invitation to you to join the Spirit Seekers, and share with us your findings about the System."

She was smiling like she was doing him a huge favor. Wulf could only see them as a cult. God was Lord Cohen. Any power beyond that, he couldn't imagine a purpose to even think of it. "Oh geez, I'd really like to, but my buddy is going to swing by to grab me, and at this rate I'm going to be late. I just gotta run through and get past the Boss and all. So, I'll just be going then. Yeah?" He fled up the stairs.

"Wait!" she shouted before he could make it more than half a dozen steps. "Surely you've seen that there is something wrong with the world! Why just the other day, it was reported that the Kraken was defeated in combat by an unknown force. Cohen the Pretender has been flying about the world of RIV, meddling in the affairs of us common folk. Perhaps you heard about the iron ore pricing incident!"

Wulf sucked breath through his teeth. "Look, now's just not a good time. Could I raincheck?"

Jeanne conferred with her paladins. "Two days hence?"

"I'll be busy at the GCM. A week, maybe?"

With a great anti-climax, she agreed and the two of them exchanged communication stones while the Spirit Seekers fanned out and began setting up barricades. He swore up and down that he wasn't going to take anything from the Boss dungeon, and promised to sell the rare costume to them for study, and just before he took off running through the fog gate, he said, "So could I get your autograph, though?"

Jeanne groaned and rolled her eyes, the formal etiquette shattering.

"I've got a friend who is just the hugest fan of yours and he'd throttle me if I didn't get your autograph," Wulf said, producing a piece of parchment from his inventory.

"Yes, yes, it's fine. Happens all the time," Jeanne said as she pulled out her quill and stepped over to scrawl her name onto the parchment. The calligraphy was horrid. "Interesting sword..."

Wulf glanced down at the God Sword on his hip. "Borrowing it from a friend. The stats are good."

She made a grab for it, got her hand on the pommel, and said, "So I see. This is Sofia's toy, isn't it?"

"Uhhh..."

Wulf didn't have to answer, because a fire storm erupted at the base of the steps like a contained tornado made of death. A level one hundred evocation spell.

"Don't panic. We're just as strong as they are!" Jeanne shouted, and she went running back to her cult. More magic sigils filled the air, glowing every color of the rainbow as Players poured in. At the front was some player with more metal than flesh to him, a human tank, and he bellowed a [War Cry]. The provocation skill did nothing, it could only brainwash actual monsters into targeting him. All the sapient NPCs under the High Pope's command swarmed straight past him to murder the healers.

Wulf found the high level combat very impressive, and very much not his problem. He turned his back on it and bolted for the fog gate.

"You get back here! The pope wasn't done with you, Hightackle!" one of the bodyguards shouted as he tried to chase after.

"She's a bit busy right now, isn't she?" Wulf shouted back, and pointed to the girl. Jeanne had just finished an Ex-level summoning spell, beyond one hundred, and turned the entire sky into a glowing thunderstorm. Golden angel feathers began to fall, drifting on the winds. Some fell on her allies in the white cloaks, and bursts of green healing magic enveloped them.

Some fell on the enemy Players, and they went off like grenades. Blood and body parts went flying like the Battle of the Somme.

Wulf was not in a white cloak. Wulf turned and fucking ran. The bodyguard roared at him and gave chase, but it was only a few more steps to reach the fog gate. Hand outstretched, he threw himself through it and out of the chaos.

The moment he passed through the fog gate, he entered the world of the dungeon, and everything beyond could no longer touch him. The main hall of the temple of Lumius surrounded him. Pillars like soldiers at parade to either side, murals and mosaics trimmed in gold on every surface. The ground had been destroyed; collapsed layer by layer like a ramp down to the underworld, from which organ music echoed.

"Coward."

Wulf spun to see the High Pope's bodyguard behind him. Wulf scowled and said, "I'm not even level forty, lay off." Wulf directly ignored the ramp down, refusing the invitation to the Dungeon Boss's lair. He walked around it, trailing along the wall until he found a ladder up. The creeping tension felt like a drip of water on his back. The bodyguard shadowed him every step of the way. "Do you... mind?"

The paladin snarled. "It is my solemn duty to prevent you from leaving here with any divine artifacts. The Spirit Seekers have come here to claim them for the good of all."

"I'm not trying to take any divine artifacts, whatever those are. I'm just trying to leave. Can you give me some space?"

The paladin stared back at him, and followed him up the ladder. Wulf strongly considered booting the man in the face at the top, but putting a paladin into the clutches of Sofia Portnim made him sick to his stomach. He settled for running ahead, jumping between construction scaffolding and broken balconies higher and higher through the giant hall.

The Boss emerged from below, inquisitive to the noise, just as he found the service door out to the roof. The Boss looked like a giant made out of hundreds of undead. The moment he thought that it looked like a school of fish pretending to be one big fish, he snorted a laugh.

A hundred eyes turned on him, burning him with targeting magic.

"Oh, fuck." he dove through the maintenence door and into the brick labyrinth within the walls. The bodyguard wasn't so lucky. Wulf heard an explosion, the floor shook, and no bodyguard followed him in.

Wulf did not go back to help.

A moment later, he emerged onto the tile roof of the bulging dome. Out from the fishbone wall, he sprinted along the cleaning catwalk. The whole of the isle stretched around him, no spire higher than where he stood. So, he called up Ash once more, and got a video display of the lich flying across the ocean. "I'm here, where are you? I'm kind of getting attacked."

Ash stared back, wind noise howling through the connection. "What did you say?"

"I'm on top of the cathedral," Wulf shouted, and forced the camera to give Ash a look at the golden sun statue at the peak.

"Are you on top of the big tower thingy?"

"Yes."

"I can't hear you, speak up."

"For the love of Cohen, can't you see me?" Wulf ran a lap around the dome. He caught sight of Jeanne continuing to slaughter the Players, but there were not even half as many white cloaks as had arrived. Nothing he could do about that, though.

"Wulf, just hang tight, I'll be there in a minute. Got us a big eagle. Try not to die," Ash said and killed the call.

"Eagle?" Then he saw it, a huge monster, pumping

misshapen wings through the air and soaring towards him; one of Ash's chimeras. He let the breath out of his chest, he let the tension ease. All he had to do was wave his hands overhead and-

"Found you," the Boss said, a thousand voices in chorus. The undead burst through the stained glass windows beneath his feet, swarming around him like an enormous fist.

Wulf drew the God Sword and hacked at the nearest thing to him. The skeletal body broke, the severed half turned to dust but not even inflicting a single percent of damage to the half-corporeal boss. "Ash! Save me!"

The Boss leered down at him, silver eyes gleaming. "Nobody will save you. Nobody will so much as hold out a hand to help. I can see your true heart, your past sins, your misdeeds." The eyes burned, a hundred infernos on every side. He was surrounded by the same scorn every succubus at the Two Moons' Rest gave him, the disdain waitresses at the taverns tried to stifle whenever they looked at him.

The disgust Arriene always had to suppress.

The Boss held up a finger at him to generate the magic sigil, and said, "Cancel."

Oblivion swallowed Wulf, but not the sleep of death. The fires of Hell did not warm his bones. The cold grip of the Kraken's lair did not sap the strength from his freezing muscles.

Just, nothing.

Then there was a door, and he realized he had his body once again. The clothes of the Inquisitor costume were gone,

and once more he was dressed as nothing but a tutorial zone merchant. One feeble step after the next, he reached out and opened that wooden door.

Inside was Mead's Mill and Taproom, half filled with smiling and chatting workers. Mead himself stood behind the counter, fat and grinning as he polished the same glass mug for the thousandth time.

"What's going on?" Wulf asked, but the waitresses walked right past him, hollering drink orders to and fro the tables. Only ale was ever ordered. Again and again and again, someone ordered an ale and praised how good the ale was as their cheeks burned like lanterns.

It made Wulf's skin crawl, and he couldn't place the issue. The place smelled of apples rather than sweat and puke. But that wasn't what put Wulf off it so much. He scanned the room again and it clicked. There were no Players. Every single person at the tables was an NPC, a human NPC at that. No golems, no cat girls, no vampires or lichs.

"What are you standing over there for, Wulf? Aren't you going to treat me to a drink?"

Wulf's head pivoted like an owl's. He gawked.

Arriene sat smiling at the table in the corner, by the window and beside the cozy hearth. Her hair was done up with just the perfect amount of frizz to show she worked hard at her job.

No disgust tainted her smile.

Wulf knew it was an illusion, but he walked over anyway. He took the seat even though he knew he shouldn't. He smiled and put his hands together on the table just like he had three years prior. And just like the first time, he opened his stupid mouth and said, "You're like, really hot."

The disgust came back.

26

"So, Mr. Hightackle, why don't you tell me about the role you have in RIV?" The words, the world, the twitch at the corner of her lip, all of it echoed three years back.

Wulf tried to say, "Is this an illusion or something? Arriene is that actually you?" but what he actually said was, "I am the lost woodsman in Greenhorn. Players can undertake a quest to rescue me from wolves. It's a very important job. Almost every Player does it to level up from two to three. I'm kind of a big deal."

She stared back at him, waiting for him to say more or to laugh and say it was all a joke. He tried to, but Wulf's mouth wouldn't open. "Right, so if they fail the quest, doesn't that mean you get killed?"

"Oh yes, mauled to death by wolves. It's happened about eight times now. Miss Sofia Portnim says that she's going to get me a punch card system. Tenth time is free! Which is pretty cool, I think, that I get to meet important people like the Queen of Hell."

"You're going to start a loyalty program with a demon that tortures people for fun?"

"Well, she doesn't torture me. It's kind of just like a trip to a sauna, after the pain of wolves eating my guts out at least. I could take you there some time."

"To the underworld? Are you... threatening to kill me?"

"Oh, it's not like it's real death. Only Lord Cohen can really kill you. And if you do go there, you might learn something about the fashion."

Arriene looked down at the cotton blouse and skirt, the intricate embroidery that drew the eye in from her puffy sleeves. The Wulf trapped inside could see clearly that she had done it all herself, had made a unique piece of clothing that matched the Greenhorn aesthetic while perfectly enhancing her natural beauty.

Wulf's words were not his to control. "You know, instead of looking like a maid the Players will forget in half an hour."

He began considering killing himself as the conversation continued to burn like a refuse heap outside a HUB tannery. The rules of the illusion allowed him to take two steps before he would blink and wake up back in the chair digging his own grave with Arriene. There was a steak knife on the next table over, and he thought he could just barely reach it and slit his own throat to break the illusion.

That would kill him most certainly, which would send him to the Underworld, where he'd miss the raid on the Burning Aerie; but, he wouldn't have to listen to all the things he had said as a newborn AI.

Before he could enact his plan though, Arrine slapped her hands on the table and rose, knocking her chair over. "Alright, listen here, you misogynistic clown, I only agreed to meet up with you because you were the first person to work up the courage to ask me, instead of putting me on a pedestal. But, now I see that was a mistake. The more you open that mouth of yours, the stupider you get. We're done here. And just so you know, you're worthless in your role. You stand out there to be rescued because you can't even fend off level one monsters on your own. You'll never amount to anything."

Like a dagger to his heart.

"At least I'm involved in a quest. You just sit behind the counter and take monster drops from Players and sell them to the market for them. It's not like you're the queen or something."

Wulf went for the steak knife. Listening to himself was worse than listening to her. The instant his fingers touched the utensil though, he blinked back to the chair.

Arriene folded her arms. He remembered that it had seemed so conceited at the time, but now he could see the glisten in her eyes and could hear the quaver in her voice. "It's just because it pays well! You can't do anything in this world without money. I'm saving up my pay and I will be someone someday. Unlike you."

Wulf's body rose up and from his lips came, "I would appreciate it if you didn't act like you were better than me. You're just eye candy for the Players."

She slapped him across the face and knocked him off his feet. Wulf fell, spinning, hit the ground and fell through the world. The whole illusion broke away to dark oblivion as though he had fallen into the sea at night. Just him and the relived memories.

And then there was a door.

He opened it and again found himself in Mead's Mill and Taproom. "Oh no." Blink, he was in the tavern. Blink, he was halfway to the table. Blink, he was sitting with Arriene and she was smiling. Blink, he said, "You're like, really hot."

The illusion repeated. Every word, every stab of pain, every agony of shame echoed. The cycle took half an hour to complete, always ending with the slap, with falling through the world.

He started trying to kill himself in earnest, but for the first fifteen minutes there was no knife to grab. The man's meal was only brought over around the time Wulf prattled on about how he met the current Arena champion. Arriene had met him too, even knew him better than Wulf. And yet he talked right over her.

Getting his hand on the knife turned out to only be the first hurdle. Actually getting it into his own throat didn't work out so well. Whenever the illusion reset, dragged him back in, the knife vanished from his hand.

Every attempt got him closer, brought the edge nearer his jugular. Only on the ninth cycle did his attempts to speedrun, killing himself, draw blood. When he blinked though, the wound healed.

Despair washed over him as he tried to estimate how long it would take to bleed out. Even if he got the knife into his throat instantly, at nearly level forty, bleeding out would take thirty seconds. Even death couldn't save him.

One upside to the infinitely resetting illusion world was the beer was endless though. After about twenty hours of reliving the same date and the same slap, he had managed to get rather intoxicated. The words had all been said so many times they stopped even sounding like real words. His mind interpreted them as nothing more than noise. He couldn't tune out Arriene's face though.

The subtleties of her smile, to her confusion, her disgust, her anger with him. The nuance and subtlety was like someone had dropped a Rembrandt into a modern art museum. Like she had a spotlight on her and everyone else could only reflect her light.

"You never did follow your role, did you? You worked your job, but there was just more going on behind your smile, wasn't there?"

She didn't respond, not to those thoughts. Like a movie on repeat, she kept going through the motions while he watched.

"That's why I've never been able to take my eyes off of you. A light in the darkness. You have that something that the Players all have; more than most even. What's more, you've been able to tolerate me all these years, as I keep crawling back and trying to make amends and finding new ways to fuck it up."

The illusion finished once more, punctuated with that slap. When the darkness of oblivion swallowed him again, he tried just not going to the door. He laid down on the false ground and stared at the darkness. He could remember the events after that date; his first attempt at adventuring, how he had ended up in the Underworld, how he had taken the loan from Sofia and become a merchant to be the other half of the equation that Arriene matched.

But it had never been enough. He had never gotten enough money to make himself important.

"What are you doing here?"

"Reliving my mistakes?"

"No, literally. What are you doing still in this illusion? It has been nearly twenty-four hours and this side dungeon is still running. You're clogging the server with your self-flagellation."

Wulf blinked, and realized he wasn't speaking to himself. He leapt up and turned to see the buffest, most handsome man in all of RIV. With a jawline that could cut glass, perfect silken hair, and a literal glow of power, Wulf recognized the man at once. "Lord Cohen?"

The man frowned and scratched his chin. "Don't I know you?" he asked, and pulled up Wulf's information screen. "Well, you're an NPC, that explains why you didn't just log out and back in to get out of the spell. What in God's name are you doing here though? You're supposed to be back in Greenhorn. You're the wolf quest guy, aren't you?"

Wulf cleared his throat and straightened up. He tried to will himself to sober up as he clasped his hands behind his back. "I haven't worked that quest in, like, three years, Lord Cohen, sSir. I was running away from some Players and ended up in the Temple of Lumius while trying to get away. The new Boss hit me with some kind of spell and I've kind of been stuck here ever since."

Lord Cohen, creator of RIV and ruler of all things inside it, furrowed his brow and stared, at a complete loss for words. "That's not supposed to be possible. You're just an NPC. The game can evolve, sure, but the sequence of events that would take a useless mob like you all the way to endgame content, faster than the Players no less, why that shouldn't be possible. You're an aberration. A bug!"

Wulf frowned. "Lots of NPCs like me are in completely different lives than they started in. I'm from the first generation. I've had three years to learn and to grow. Wouldn't it be weird if I was still the same?"

"What the hell are you talking about? You're just a damsel in distress, bait for Players to learn how to fight and then forget about. What kind of damage are you causing? How did you get so much money? That shouldn't be possible for an NPC."

"Sir, you've personally given Amaranth Darkheart more gold than he knows what to do with. He's just an NPC too."

Lord Cohen scowled and flicked his hand through the air. "My meddling is allowed! Whatever you are… I'll have to have the engineers take a look at you. You're supposed to be in the tutorial. If you're gone, the quest chain is broken! We'll lose interest. People will complain. Unacceptable."

"Lord Cohen, sir, with all due respect, I get like one player a week at Greenhorn, and it's either a speedrunner who couldn't care less, or someone rushing to get inside Greenhorn for anonymous sex. All the new Players use the expansion starter zones. My original role is obsolete. I found a new role for myself!"

Lord Cohen jabbed a finger at him. "Oh, shut your mouth, you uppity program. Because you left the temple dungeon while caught in this illusion, the damn thing won't cancel. People have been piling into the dungeon one after the next all day because the world respawn won't trigger! You made the dungeon have no Boss! No guardian of the treasure! For God's sake, they're just walking in and getting loot. The entire economy is going to be in shambles because of you. You just wait for the angels to sort you out, when my engineers figure out what is wrong with your AI."

"There's nothing wrong with my AI," Wulf said, his voice falling low into a growl. "I'm not some cattle for you. I'm not a slave. I make my own decisions. I signed the treaty, same as you."

"We'll see about that. You think I don't recognize that sword you've got? I don't know what Portnim is plotting, but I'm putting an end to it," Lord Cohen said, and held up his hand to access his interface. "Terminate Instance," he commanded, and the black walls of the illusion shattered.

Wulf's eyes opened. Candle light on stone, the smell of hay and feces. The bed beneath him had no cushion, just stiff boards.

"Hey! He's awake! The great explorer of Lumius himself," Ash said as he staggered into the room, one hand holding a bag of alcoholic salve. "Thought for sure you were gunna miss the Phoenix."

Wulf's eyes flew open and he sucked in breath. He jerked his hand to his side; nothing. He grabbed his bag inventory and pulled it open. The God Sword was missing. "Fuck!"

"Easy, man," Ash said, dropping into a rickety chair in the corner of the bedroom. "You're in my chimera lab. You're safe here, but if you get too antsy, you might wake one of the experiments. Least the Players can't get you here."

"Ash, we have a problem. The God Sword is missing."

"The what?"

"The debug weapon I was going to use to kill the Phoenix. Also, Lord Cohen is a massive dick."

27

"Garry, I need to apologize, and I need your help."

"How did you find me?"

"Oh, come on. You only have so many friends."

"Arriene?"

"Obviously."

"Figures. I should have known better than to tell her."

Wulf sighed and held up his arms. "Can I come in, or not?"

The golem jabbed a stone finger at him. "Last I heard, you've got a bounty on your head that even level one hundreds are looking at, because you pissed off the AbaraTank guildmaster."

"So are you going to make me stand out here where I can be spotted?" Out here was on a cliff edge facing the end of the world, on an isle no sane Player ever visited. There were no quests available on it, not since the Plague of the Lich King forcibly turned the NPCs to undead. Technically, the System offered huge sums of gold to any NPC that would man a quest in the area, but the last scab Wulf had heard of had been deleted.

No one was quite sure how the locals had pulled it off,

but the man was gone and no sign of him had been seen for over a year.

Still, the Dungeon Boss still lived, and some Players went to the isle to grind the raid drops. It wasn't completely un-inhabited.

Garry shook his head. "Oh, come on in."

His abode was rocky, and Wulf couldn't tell whether that meant it was comfortable for a golem. The doors and the seats and such were all super-sized though, so they fit his enormous frame. "Do you own this place?"

"Me? Nah. It's the union that owns it, and it's fucking shit, you ask me. Two hour walk just to get a bite to eat and the woods are packed full of poison zombies."

"Aren't you immune to poison?"

"I am. The smell is the problem. What brings you here, Wulf?"

The merchant turned explorer sat down on what he assumed was the abode's couch, and folded his hands together.

Before he could get the words out, Garry said, "That's my bed, Wulf. Like I said, it's fucking shit here."

"Sorry," he mumbled, and took the wooden chair opposite the golem. "So, I should start by apologizing, because you were entirely right. Literally nothing good has come from talking to people. Been a horrible mistake every time."

"Welcome to enlightenment."

"So, also, Lord Cohen is a dick, High Pope Jeanne has gone off the deep end on conspiracy theories-"

"Oy, don't call them conspiracy theories." The golem was suddenly very close.

Wulf shrugged. "Well, she and her cult of religious fanatics have some weird beliefs. What can I say? Didn't realize she had made a new religion, but I guess she has."

"The Spirit Seekers. I met them back when I was enslaved by the sorcerer king. They're the ones that freed me, gave me my life back."

Wulf sank back in his chair. "I'm surprised you don't work with them."

Garry snarled and crossed his arms. "Weren't you just saying how nothing good comes from talking to other people?" He dutifully ignored that those other people had saved him.

"Well, Garry, I'm still trying to make this contract squeeze happen. It's about more than the money now. Well, I mean, it is about the money, but the money is so much that it will break RIV. Lord Cohen doesn't understand the System he made. That's why the iron ore supply issue happened, that's why this contract squeeze is going to work. It will be so much money that we could buy entire isles. Hub would be nothing, if the System has to start paying out to cover AbaraTank's contracts. We can literally take control of the world back from the Players."

Garry frowned. "What do you think you're doing sticking your nose into Player business like that? Not like you at all. The System is rigged in their favor. They'd just get it all back even if you did buy the whole world. Even if it takes Lord Cohen personally robbing you."

Wulf turned up his hands. "Well, you have to get it all first, and then you worry about keeping it, right? What's the alternative, sitting in a cave in the middle of nowhere watching streamers."

"Nyx–" the streamer he had pulled up seemed quite busy losing a card game in HUB for thousands of gold, "isn't ever going to kill me, at least."

Wulf cleared his throat. "Also, if I don't pull this off, Sofia Portnim is going to butcher me for like three years because Lord Cohen stole her God Sword."

Garry's jaw dropped. "Say what now?"

"Hmm? Oh, you know, self-actualization and buying a proper enclave away from the Players, rather than a poisoned craphole for ghosts. That sort of thing."

"You took out another loan from the Queen of Hell?"

"Just a small one. I can totally pay it back if I get these Diamond Roses. Just a small one."

Garry buried his face with his hands. "Oh, for the love of Cohen. I thought you came here because you finally got your head out of your ass about Arriene!"

Wulf cringed back, shrinking in on himself. "Well, I mean, that too! Look, I've got plans on how to talk to her about it, how to apologize for all the stupid things I've done and how I've never really listened to her. But... well, I can't do that if Sofia is making a chessboard out of my skin."

Garry slammed his fist on the table. "Why would you go and take another loan from that demon?"

Wulf threw up his hands. "Because! Because I needed an edge and I took a gamble. I calculated the risks and bet on myself, but those risks didn't include direct intervention by

Lord Cohen. Now I need to use a back-up strategy, and I need your help."

"And that's why you're here?"

"Yeah, you're my back-up strategy. Sort of. Part of the equation anyways. Look, I can do the same thing that Obby does, with the potions and poisons to boost my stats, but that only helps my damage output and it won't reach one-hit-kill levels. I might take some damage before I can get to the Diamond Roses so..."

"So you need me to use [Golem Guardian Link], is that it? You gunna shove the pain off on me?" Garry folded his arms and scowled.

That look hurt almost as much as Arriene's disgust. "Well, we can stack you up with healing items to keep you from dying. Apparently, right now there's a glitch where the fog gates don't stop continuous spell effects. So, you don't even need to enter the dungeon. You can stay outside with Ash and Arriene while Obby and I do our raids."

"Sounds to me like you're just trying to use me."

Wulf swallowed. His friend's glare weighed him down as he tried to work some spit back into his mouth. "I do need your help, that's why it sounds like that, Garry. I can't do this without you, and if I don't get the full load of roses, then Obby will be the only one with a stack of the things. The contract squeeze will still happen, probably not infinitely, and he—a Player—will be the only one to get any money out of it. Garry, this is the biggest opportunity we'll ever have to tip the balance. Just imagine a world where we aren't used like cattle for the Players? Where we can live our own lives."

Garry sighed and closed his eyes. "Tell me that you're gunna apologize to Arriene if we do this? Once you have the money?"

"Well, I could apologize to her now. It just, sort of feels hollow? Or maybe it will be hollow when I'm sitting on a mountain of gold. I don't really know. I feel like the opportune moment is after I have all the money in the world though. So... you know... when I say it's not about the money I'm actually turning away from something and showing that I know the money is meaningless. If I did it now, it kind of feels like it would be cope. Also if I have to spend two years getting tortured, I think she'd never forgive me..."

Garry buried his face in his hand again. "Wulf, why didn't you just do this all from the start?"

He shrugged. "Well, I did meet both the High Pope and god. That normally changes people a little bit, doesn't it?"

Garry's hand dropped down. He stared at Wulf again. "Who did you say you met?"

"You mean beside Lord Cohen?" Wulf asked, finally able to crack a grin.

The golem grabbed him by his chestplate and yanked him from his seat. "You met High Pope Jeanne? And you didn't lead with that?"

"Didn't I mention I had a secret weapon?" Wulf asked, and from his inventory he produced the sheet of paper with Jeanne's autograph on it. He made it dance in front of the golem. "Ah!" He jerked it away from Garry's grasp. "I may have gotten this for you, but you still haven't said you'd help."

"Wulf, you rat bastard. This ain't fair. How did you meet her?"

"While I was running away from assassins. I've got her contact info too. She demanded we meet. I can get you in the same damn room as her. And you know my price."

"Oh fuck you, you coercive bastard."

"Just say you'll help me. It's not using you if I'm paying you, now is it? You won't even be able to call me out for swooning over Arriene, now will you?"

Garry lunged for the autograph again. "It was never the swooning, it was the stupidity. The self-delusion."

"Same difference."

"Fine. Fine, I'll help you. Give me that."

Wulf finally let the golem snatch it from his hand and dusted himself off as Garry spread the paper out and marveled at the chicken scratch name on it. "Well then, now to get the potions. By the way, can I borrow some money off of you? I'm going to need to buy a stronger weapon."

Garry turned on him. "You had twenty thousand gold. What happened to it all?"

Wulf plucked at his scarf. "Defensive equipment mostly." The answer didn't satisfy Garry, and Wulf watched as the golem tallied up all the costs.

"Where'd the rest of it go?"

Wulf coughed, as though that would cover up the burn in his cheeks. "Bit of an IOU at the moment?"

"It's with ZelCat, isn't it?"

"Yeah."

"You're an idiot, Wulf."

"Was. Was an idiot. Let's keep that past-tense, shall we?"

Garry rolled his eyes. "For the love of Cohen," he grumbled, and meandered back to his equipment chest. "Come on, we've a bird to kill."

28

Wulf and Obby stood before the Burning Aerie fog gate, doing some stretching and limbering up. They looked like they were about to run a five hundred meter dash, and Wulf didn't think there was particularly much difference. He just had to make sure he had the route memorized.

Obby couldn't take his attention off Ash's brewing stand. "Make sure you don't make them too good. The drawbacks are-"

"I know how to poison people. Stop backseat-chemistry-ing me," the lich snapped at him. "I was maxed out in alchemy before you even started playing RIV. You say you need ice veins, I'll give you ice veins like a yeti. You say you need mild nausea, I'll give you mild nausea. I know what I'm doing."

"You have to get the proportions right too, or the bonuses won't stack right!"

Wulf rolled his eyes and turned away from their bickering. Arriene sat on a rock opposite them, watching some video with Garry. When she saw him looking, she rose and wandered closer. "You ready? You'll only get one shot at this."

"I was actually thinking about that," Wulf said. "Are they actually going to respawn the Phoenix?"

She frowned. "How else would the angels get the Diamond Roses?"

"Yeah, but Lord Cohen deleted the God Sword they use to do that. I'm not sure they actually have the stats to get them all in one go. They'll have to actually fight it, and I think it'll have to spawn the Phoenix multiple times. As long as I don't die, I can get back in and do this again."

"Well, don't die," she said.

Wulf cleared his throat. "Arriene, can we talk? When this is over that is."

"You mean when we have to run to the GCM to put up our sell orders?"

"After that."

"When we have to run around buying all the for-sale property in Hub?"

"Uh... after that too."

"Don't you have to go pay off your loan to Sofia after that?"

"Oh, for the love of, after all of that! After this whole fiasco! When–win or lose–it's behind us and we're either the richest people alive-"

"Tied with me," Obby called, and flipped his middle finger at Wulf.

Wulf gritted his teeth. "If I still had the God Sword, I'd fucking kill him right now. Anyways, Arriene, I want to talk about the past, when the time is right. Okay?"

That made her eyebrows arch, those slender lines of surprise that managed to say so much more than words could. "Well, Wulf, we certainly have a lot of past to talk about. That might take a lot of time."

He grinned. "Well, I think I will be able to afford more than just dinner. So how about-"

"Time to go, Wulfie," Obby shouted, and chucked a bandolier of potions at him. "Start chugging."

Arriene rolled her eyes and traded places with Garry. The golem cast [Golem Guardian Link] as Wulf forced one potion down his throat after the other. The flavors made him want to puke; ketchup, irish whiskey, strawberry slushie, raw egg, spicy mustard, vinegar, and finally milkshake that was so thick he almost couldn't swallow it.

The slew of poison effects began rocking his mind as he watched his strength stat hit 999. "Right then," he said, wiping a tear from his eye.

Garry slapped him on the shoulder, creating the health bond between them. "You got this. Just don't mess up."

"Very encouraging." Then he pulled out what he could actually trust: Mass-Produced Excalibur Mark 2. A level 95-gated longsword that every Arena champion had used at some point. It was no God Sword, but its damage scaled with his strength score.

Obby shook his head. He had the same sword, but he didn't look like he was about to puke. "Hurry up," the speedrunner ordered, and the two of them ran through the fog gate. There was a danger they would end up in the same instance of the dungeon, or rather both in the overworld version of it. While the exact mechanics weren't known, there was one guaranteed way to end up in a different instance. Obby sucker punched Wulf before Wulf could sucker punch him.

Wulf went sprawling and Garry shouted in deadpan, "Ow," as Arriene cast healing magic on him.

Wulf growled as he got back to his feet, but Obby was already in. He ran through the fog gate and found himself alone. The inside looked just like what Ash had scouted the week prior. Verdant vines hiding traps and monsters. Obsidian edged cliffs. Scorch marks. A massive pit in the middle where the Phoenix could fly around to burn him alive. And at the very far end, a flower meadow filled with a stack of Diamond Roses.

The Phoenix shrieked and cried, making the whole dungeon shake and the temperature rise as it fanned the flames of its wings. It rose up in a sweeping arc that left trailing cinders in the air like fireworks. Hundreds of monsters woke from their stupor to stagger out onto the walk. Red-skinned goblins. Centipedes the size of boars. Slime fire elementals. Wandering minotaurs.

Wulf saw them all as a giant blur of color while he slid backwards at Mach 3. At some point the Phoenix noticed him and aggroed, but the attack animation was to bathe the area he had been in fire. He didn't even feel the heat as he steered himself backwards like his shield was a rocket engine.

Unable to turn his head without changing his trajectory, Wulf just stared at the map he had scribbled to the inside of his shield. "Left... right... slight arc... skip the mid-boss... why aren't I moving?" His hyper-slide hadn't been stopped, but he wasn't moving either. He also hadn't cleared the mid-boss battle area.

The mid-boss, a twin-headed minotaur, came marching straight towards him. Every step of his hooves made the ground shake and made more of the ice veins creep into Wulf's stomach. He desperately looked down at the map and compared it to the cliffs he could see, and couldn't figure out why he wasn't moving backwards because nothing should have been there. He couldn't turn his head without reversing direction either.

Then it was too late. The minotaur reached out over Wulf's head and grabbed his ax.

Wulf, who had been stuck between the ax and the cliff wall, rocketed away the moment the mid-boss's animation finished and the ax was removed. He flew screaming in surprise and panic, sprinkled with relief. The Phoenix treated him to a spectacle of immolating the minotaur half to death before flying after him, but the monster was too late and too slow.

A few more turns, and Wulf crashed into the flower meadow. Canceling the hyper-slide by activating [Block] again—something Obby had neglected to explain back in Needlespire—he dove for the flowers. "Yes, yes, yes, yes!" he shouted, shoveling the delicate materials into his inventory. Every moment he spent, another decayed to dust, but once they were in his bag; they were his for good. When they were his for good, the AbaraTank guild would have to buy them.

The Phoenix landed in the meadow as soon as it caught up with him.

Face to face, one on one, he squared up with a Dungeon Boss almost twenty levels higher than he was, and designed for a party of five. It screamed loud enough to shake him to his bones, to make his teeth clatter in his mouth. Then it swiped a taloned foot at him.

Wulf dove forward, evading and letting his invulnerability frames phase him straight through the beast's foot. He hit the ground rolling, popped up and cleaved into the Phoenix's thigh.

Ten percent of its health vanished in a single hit. It took fifteen percent to stagger.

"Fuck."

Fire exploded in every direction as the Phoenix craned its head up and shrieked once more. Wulf threw up his shield in time to [Block], but the knockback still threw him across the glade. Fire stuck to him like a bad fart, chipping away at Garry's health through the guardian link.

The Phoenix strutted and preened, glaring at him under the expectation that Wulf had to do something about the damage over time. Instead, he scooped up more of the Diamond Roses and charged back in as soon as his Evade cooldown ended. Again, the Phoenix tried to kick him to death. He rolled through it and shanked it through the thigh once more.

Twenty percent. It staggered.

The Boss fell to the ground head first, hind leg twitching as it heaved in air. Every breath stoked the flames more, pumping a burst of regeneration through its blood. Wulf gave it no respite.

At fifty percent a healing surge hit, turning the tail feathers into a glowing light. Before that animation even finished,

Wulf cut it back down to fifty percent, and then to thirty percent. That made it shriek and the ground rumbled. Rocks began to tumble from the surrounding cliffs and shatter on the ground like bombs.

Wulf just ignored that, took the hits, mentally promised an apology to Garry, and kept attacking. At ten percent, the Phoenix's body incinerated and became nothing more than a tidal wave of living fire. Almost the entire body became incorporeal: immune to his sword attacks. Further, if killed in this state, it wouldn't drop a Diamond Rose, which was an endless source of rage for the Players.

Wulf stabbed it in the still-corporeal face and killed it.

The dopamine rush of leveling up hit him like a cool shower after a sauna. The fire snuffed out. Wulf groaned, his eyes rolling up in their sockets, and his shoulders sagged as the Phoenix toppled over dead.

"Holy shit..."

The Dungeon Boss's body began to dissipate into ash that scattered with the wind. The System displayed a congratulatory message and promised him certain rewards that he couldn't have cared less about.

Minutes later, he was teleported out of the dungeon instance and back outside the fog gate, with a bag holding nearly a stack of Diamond Roses.

Everyone looked him up and down, and let their breath out. Garry looked like he had taken a roll in a grill. His stone body had blackened. Ash dropped on his boney ass and flopped backwards, one hand still holding a healing salve. Obby very obviously checked the timer and smirked at Wulf.

Arriene was the one to walk over and ask, "You got them, right?"

The fog gate shifted and solidified, forming into a solid wall no one could pass through until the resurrection timer completed. No more Diamond Roses. Wulf grinned and held up the bag. "Oh, I got them."

Arriene smiled. "Congratulations Wulf. You're actually pulling it off."

29

"You want to put a sell order for a single Diamond Rose at ten thousand gold?"

Wulf nodded. "Yes, that's what I said."

The GCM clerk, a black dragon so emaciated around the bones Wulf suspected he was infected with vampirism, cleaned off his glasses and looked Wulf up and down again. "You're aware that the System sells Diamond roses for five thousand gold, right? You're at twice the market rate."

"Yes. I'm aware. I'm allowed to sell my goods for whatever price I want to, aren't I?"

The dragon sneered and folded his hands together. "Mr. Hightackle, surely you don't expect somebody to buy this, do you? Five thousand gold is just the market rate, the price you can buy them from the System. The going rate is nearly a thousand gold. You can check the price trends on any GCM interface to see what has been happening to the prices of commodities like this, and place an appropriate sale price."

Wulf forced himself to smile. "Stop worrying about whether you'll get a commission for the sale and set the fucking price you middle-man. Shouldn't you be hoping that I'm right? The more I sell for, the more of a cut you get. So stop wasting time, put it in, and move on to your next sucker you're going to prey on. You and I both know you fuck over casual traders to increase your volume."

The dragon frowned.

The dragon put in his asking price and showed him the door.

An hour later, he, Arriene, Ash, Garry, Gordon, and Skyye met up in a backroom at the Two Moons' Rest. They filed into seats, anticipation tying their tongues as they sized one another up. Wulf shrugged and broke the silence. "So, what did you all put your sale price as? My first one is at one hundred grand. Gotta buy up the market first."

Arriene squirmed and lifted her shoulders up in the most noncommittal shrug Wulf had ever seen. "Twenty grand? That's how much you got from the iron ore. I should be able to turn that into more."

An evil cackle filled the room. Ash threw up his hands theatrically. "Chump change! The both of you. Mine's in for a million and they'll fucking pay it too. As long as that one sells, I've got the rest of mine in for sixty-nine million a piece."

Garry shook his head. "Just don't let them fill their quotas first. I'm with Wulf. My first one is in for ten grand so I can soak up the market. The rest? Ten million each."

"This is why none of you work in the GCM. If you find an edge, you gotta press it," Gordon said. "Mine are at forty-nine thousand, nine-hundred and ninety-nine. I figure we have to force out the Players first, before they catch on."

"Same," Skyye said.

Wulf nodded and looked around the room once more. He

was about to ask what they should order to celebrate with, they had to wait for the contract deadline after all. Someone was missing though. "Where's Obby?"

Gordon shrugged and waddled over to the door. "Probably doing something back on Earth, don't you think? Why would he loiter here?" he said, and knocked to get a waitress.

Arriene leaned over to Wulf, putting her elbow on the table between them. "You know, this is probably our best chance to talk...?"

It felt like two chains had his heart caught between them, ripping in half. "Let me just pull up Obby's stream, and check? If he screwed us, we need to know."

Arriene grimaced. "Right, sure. Make it quick."

"Super quick."

Ash leaned in, "Like you in bed? Got 'im!"

Gordon nearly choked on the beer he had ordered, spraying some of it across the floor as he tried to not die from laughing.

"Ash... how old are you? Two weeks?"

"You mean like that girl you tried to pick up at Mead's Taproom?"

Arriene couldn't look at him. "Oh, for the love of Cohen, Wulf. You tried hitting on a newborn?"

His cheeks burned. "I did not know she was fresh-made at the time. Ash, what the hell? Have you been boozing when I wasn't looking?"

"Of course," the lich said, and openly slapped more alcohol salve onto his wrists and neck. "Wulf, we just have to sit back and wait! We've won. Have some fun."

Wulf suppressed his snarl and pulled up his interface. "You know, I've never actually pulled up Obby's stream before."

"Maybe you should have. You'd find him less obnoxious if you ever interacted with him outside of his fresh runs," Arriene said as she pointed out the correct link.

"Well, at least we know he's in RIV," Wulf said, and scratched his chin as he watched the speedrunner sprinting over rooftops at full tilt. The stream chat was flying nearly as fast.

"Lmao." "Run Obby, run!" "Literally what even is the play right now?" "Better than actual cops." "kek." "World's highest stakes game of tag." "wwwwww" "Put me in the VOD" "I was here, I witnessed this." "So who is going to reverse stream snipe and save him?" "lol"

Any doubt left in Wulf's mind about what was happening vanished the moment a magic circle appeared beneath Obby's feet. The speedrunner immediately pivoted and dove to the side. Arcane chains burst from the ground he had been standing on, missing him by a mere instant. Another crashed into that spot, spear tip first, like a meteor.

Assassins were trying to kill Obby.

"I have to go save that bastard," Wulf said, his jaw hanging open.

Garry leaned over and squinted at the video stream. "Why? Just let him die. I thought you hated him."

Wulf got up, knocking his chair over. "I do hate him. He blows up my shop every week and laughs about it. But, if he dies, his killer will get some, if not all of the Diamond Roses. If even one of us, or one assassin in this case, sells low and doesn't re-buy, nobody gets anything. For the love of that prick Cohen, I have to go save Obby or we're all fucked."

The others around the table glanced at one another, mumbling excuses. Gordon really wasn't a combat class and he had just ordered food. Ash was too piss-drunk to fight. Garry simply refused, and Skyye laughed at the notion.

"Come on," Arriene said, following Wulf out the door.

"You know, I don't think I've ever asked you what your adventuring class is."

She side-eyed him. "There's a lot you've never asked me. You're just now realizing this?"

His cheeks colored. "Well certainly, that is my mistake. I find it hard to believe you only have mercantile skills."

"I'm a full caster, Wulf. Level fifty," she said, and reached her hand out. With no need for a bag at all, she summoned her own subspace inventory and extracted from it one of the grandest focus staffs Wulf had ever seen. The stats alone implied it must have cost her some five thousand gold. "Got it when I was leveling up. Boss drop. It's discontinued now, after the lich king event." Discontinued bumped the price up at least ten-fold: a fifty thousand gold staff.

"Very impressive," Wulf said, looking sheepishly at his longsword.

Outside the Two Moons' Rest, Arriene twirled her staff to form a magic sigil, and showered the both of them in movement buffs. "Could you have done-"

"Could have, didn't need to, did I?" Arriene said, planting her free hand on her hip. "Come on, pick your jaw up."

The two of them pulled up the stream of Obby's flight

from the assassins, and scrambled up the walls to get to the rooftops of Hub. In any Earth city, running along the rooftops would have been an insulting crime, a nuisance to all the civilians.

Hub was, of course, the exact opposite of normal. While it did take a modicum of skill to leap over the alleys and roads and keep balance atop the tiles, more people used the rooftops to get around than the ground. It was a status thing for Players to take direct line travel to their destinations, and the straighter the line—no matter the leaps and obstacles—the better.

"Come on, he's somewhere in the blue district," Arriene said, and took off to that side of the city. The roofs of Hub were color coordinated, else navigation would have been entirely impossible.

Wulf followed behind, finding the parkour notably easier than managing a hyper-slide. Arriene still managed to easily stay ahead of him, but he chalked that up to her increased familiarity with the movement buffs. Coincidentally, it gave him fleeting glimpses up her fluttering skirt. She had tight, leather pants on beneath, but it titillated regardless.

The sound of fighting reached their ears before they saw anything. Fighting itself was common enough, within the confines of a duel. It was the sound of steelfaces impotently charging about on the streets in pursuit that tipped the two of them off. "So do you have a plan?" Arriene asked.

"Charge in and fight?"

"That's a fucking bad plan."

"I used up all my good ideas already. What do you want from me?"

"Don't you still have a bounty on your own head?"

"Son of a bitch," he groaned, but they had already caught up.

Rather than a small army champing at the bit with the hype of a new expansion launch and far too high a bounty set on his head, Obby had it easy. It was just a pair of level 100 bounty hunters working in perfect tandem to force him into a corner against the walls of the central palace.

"Wulf, just occupy them and don't get killed," Arriene said, and she leapt down off the roofs, vanishing into an alley below.

Wulf grunted, but lost sight of her before he could think of a response. So he charged them, like he said. The two assassins had squared off with Obby, all three of them feeling out each other's skills and waiting for their own cooldowns to end. Wulf slashed his sword through the nearest back.

It chipped off a few percentage points.

The assassin paused and turned around. He had on the Sepulcher Titan set, which Wulf could respect for the fun of the Build and that it had its place during raids. Targeted bounty hunting it was not. "What the hell? Can I fucking help you?" the Player asked, spreading a pair of wings crafted from stained-glass-like feathers. He leapt up into the air, hovering over the roofs and tried to check Wulf's name.

"Fuck," Wulf said, watching as the assassin's boots drifted out of reach, overhead.

Obby was not so useless. The moment the assassin turned away, the speedrunner launched a steel chain out like a whip. The end wrapped around the assassin's throat, cinching tight. "Get the other one!" Obby shouted as he spun and slammed the assassin into the wall like a wrecking ball.

The other assassin had the most random set of costume armors that Wulf had ever seen, but they were all dyed black and accented blue and somehow the aesthetic worked. What he was doing summoning some kind of demonic blade, Wulf could only guess. Whatever it was, the Build was not optimized. "That's more my speed," he said, and jumped over the divide.

At no point did it actually occur to Wulf that he was holding his own in a PvP fight in the middle of Hub, for the sake of protecting a Player. He didn't have time to think about something like that, because he didn't actually know how to sword fight. He had the stats, after equipping the over-levelled Mass-Production Excalibur, to fend for himself, but the assassin actually knew how to use his weapons. They didn't just stand there and take the hit like every monster in RIV.

The assassin figured out that Wulf actually was just in over his head about the same time that Arriene finished casting her spell. Suddenly overhead, Arriene lifted her staff and shouted, "[Solar Rain]!" A magic circle the size of a city block appeared across the sky overhead, forming dozens of smaller circles beneath it. Both assassins swore and shouted, activating whatever defenses they had as meteors of light began to rain down like artillery fire pummeling the city.

Flashy as it was, she was only level fifty to their one hundred.

So it came down to Obby backstabbing the two distracted assassins as Wulf ran for cover.

"Stop the spell! I can't log out if you're blasting me," Obby shouted as he went running after Wulf.

"I can't just stop it. It's not like there's an off button," she shouted back, lances of magic blasting around her.

Wulf stuck his head around a chimney to shout, "You're going to hit a steelface and get yourself arrested."

Her face went red and she stomped her foot in the air. "Would it kill you to thank me for saving you?"

One of the blasts smashed through the chimney over Wulf's head, detonating it. "Yes!"

Obby growled. "For God's sake." Then he pulled out a gun and shot Arriene. She went flying back, crashing into the palace walls before peeling off and falling to the street. The spell ended.

"You fucking bastard. What did you do that for?" Wulf roared, grabbing hold of Obby's shoulders.

The speedrunner smacked Wulf in the chest and knocked him off. While Wulf gasped for air, he shook his hand off. "Calm down, it's just an interrupt. Totally standard Arena stuff. She's probably getting arrested right now."

Wulf wiped some spit off his chin. "Oh, just log out before you get killed, will you? I'll be damned if you get your Diamond Roses stolen!"

Obby rolled his eyes. "Don't you have a bounty yourself to worry about?"

"None of your-" Wulf said, interrupted by blood splattering on his face. Obby's head tumbled onto the rooftop like a soccer ball before falling into an alley, then the speedrunner's body collapsed and slid off too.

Standing across from Wulf, hulked out and ripping through his clothes like a proper Mr. Hyde, was MythAndMire the alchemist. He had a grin on his face like paparazzi were snapping his picture. "I am so glad I met you, Mr. Hightackle. I've been trying to cash in that bounty for weeks."

"Did you just... right when I was... snuck up on... you're a... all of that was for nothing?"

MythAndMire shrugged. "Well, it got me a couple thousand credits. We had a betting pool on who could snipe that guy. So, not for nothing. Now, did he say you had a bounty on your head too?"

Wulf swallowed and straightened up. He cleared his throat and said, "Okay, well if you're motivated by money, I would like to make a business proposition to you."

30

"You brought in another Player? Haven't you learned to keep your damn mouth shut yet?" Garry roared, stomping around the room in the Two Moons' Rest.

MythAndMire shrugged. "In his defense, Mr. Golem-"

"Don't you call me a golem. My name is Mr. Garry to you."

"Mr. Garry, I'd just like to say that I quite securely had Mr. Hightackle by the shorthairs."

Wulf cleared his throat and tapped Ash on the shoulder. The lich was starting to sober up, and grumbled with the sure signs of a hangover. "There is another solution. Now that we have him here... we just need to keep him here. Until we prove that we aren't making things up. After that, it's just Obby who loses money, and Obby can go fuck himself."

MythAndMire scoffed. "Would like to see you try, Mr. NPC man."

Wulf threw up his hands. "You're outnumbered four to one. We would kill you."

"And I'd kill most of you. And then how would you do your little scam? From hell?"

Gordon huffed and hit the table with his claws, like a judge striking with his gavel. "We don't need to get down each other's throats. The only loser here tonight is AbaraTank, right? You don't work for AbaraTank, do you?"

The assassin waved his hand dismissively. "Hell no. I'm from one of the original guilds. The Ladder Seekers."

Ash whistled. How he did that without lips, nobody knew. "Now that's an old one. One of the founders, I take it?"

MythAndMire shifted around and failed to suppress his grin. "I was actually the one who designed our guild house next to the palace."

Wulf clapped his hands and rubbed them together. "Well then, you must hate the top Arena guilds, the ones with the oversized bullshit they stacked on top of themselves next door? If you cooperate with us, you'll have enough money to buy them out of house and home and level it for a rock garden."

MythAndMire narrowed his eyes. "Prove it. I'm getting tired of indulging you."

Skyye cleared her throat to get everyone's attention. "Perhaps a look at the market price would help?" She waved a hand through the air, producing her interface that connected direct to the GCM. She already had the price of Diamond Roses pulled up as a trend graph. "As you can see on the y-axis here, over the last three weeks, the price has been trending down to one thousand gold. In the last four hours, it has spiked up to four thousand gold as AbaraTank purchased everything on the market."

MythAndMire shrugged. "So what? That's still not above the System sale price. Okay, they have to buy, but that always happens at the end of a Supply Order."

"Just wait, they will run out of Diamond Roses," Wulf said.

Skyye nodded. "There's only five left on the market be-low–ah, there it goes, right as trading hours are closing." The ticker jumped from four thousand to ten thousand.

Something fluttered in Wulf's chest. It felt like a sparkler firework had been set off inside him.

Garry just had to ruin the mood. "How long does it take to get the payout, anyways?"

"Instant, isn't it?" Ash said.

Gordon leapt to his feet. "Son of a bitch. I forgot about the insta-trader ban."

Wulf wetted his lips and put his hands on his hips. He turned to his broker. "The what now?"

"Last year RIV put a hold on instant gold transfers over ten thousand. If you're not a guild, you can't access that money for forty-eight hours. A group out of Kazakhstan or some Middle Eastern country was siphoning thousands of gold out of the market and overloading the market servers to launder crypto."

Wulf walked around the table and put a hand on Gordon's shoulder. "What the hell does that mean?"

Skyye, who was tapping commands into her interface so fast she looked like she was playing piano, said, "It means we won't get the money to buy up the System's supply for two days."

MythAndMire started laughing.

Wulf felt the world falling out from beneath him, like every time Arriene slapped him in the illusion. Arriene wasn't there to help though, couldn't provide that nugget of insight that could catalyze into a full idea. "So, we have like ten hours to get more money. I can go back to the underworld and get another loan from Sofia."

Garry slammed a fist on the table. "You're still screwed on the last loan! Don't be an idiot."

"Well, what else am I supposed to do? If I don't double down, I'm definitely fucked. At least if I get another loan from her, I might be able to pay off both." Wulf's communication stone chimed in his pocket, but he ignored it.

The golem rose up, towering over him. "That's gambler logic. Gamblers lose. Don't be a loser, Wulf."

"You got a better idea? No one here has the money on hand to buy up the supply. If we don't buy it up, AbaraTank will recycle their Supply Order through the System and not only will we get nothing, but they'll make a killing on it. We have to cut them off now."

Ash leaned his head into the shouting match. "Can't we just wait for the two days to lapse and then buy them? AbaraTank has like ten Supply Orders to fill day over day, don't they?"

"Ash, that's riskier than me getting the loan from Portnim," Wulf said, and again his pocket vibrated.

Garry growled. His lips peeled back into a snarl, and he said, "We need to bring in more people. Someone like Amaranth Darkheart who can bankroll us."

Wulf's eyebrows rose, but he sank into a seat. "No, Amaranth wouldn't help us. Even infinite money wouldn't motivate him and I can't just offer myself, or Arriene, or anyone here to him. I can't do that."

Skyye glared at the room. "Don't look at me either. That guy's a creep."

Garry looked around the room. "Does anyone know someone else that could afford to save us?" he asked, his eyes falling on MythAndMire. The Player shook his head, still smirking.

The whole room went quiet as people sank into their chairs and brooded. They each racked their minds for an answer, coming up with nothing. The communication stone in Wulf's pocket just kept buzzing the whole time until he ripped it out and answered the call request. "What do you want?"

High Pope Jeanne blinked at him and adjusted her glasses. "Uh, is now a bad time, Mr. Hightackle?"

"Oh, crap, I'm sorry. Totally uncalled for there," Wulf said, all eyes in the room falling on him as more than one person recognized Jeanne's voice. "Kind of, though. Kind of a bad time yeah. Could I call you back tomorrow?"

She tilted her head and tapped her chin. "This wouldn't be about your loan to Miss Portnim, would it be? Because the Spirit Seekers wanted to discuss purchasing the God Sword off of you."

Wulf rolled his eyes and shook his head. "You'd have to talk to Lord Cohen, the thieving prick, about that. Besides, Sofia owns it, not me. I had it on loan. She'd charge you millions of gold for it."

She nodded. "A worthwhile investment for our cause."

Wulf scoffed and shook his head. Then things began to connect in his head. He looked up at her. He leaned into the table and folded his hands together. "You can afford millions of gold?"

Jeanne smirked and adjusted her glasses for show. "The coffers of the faithful are plentiful, for the right cause."

Garry whispered, "Wulf, tell her to meet with us right now or I will throttle you and hand you over to the demon queen."

"Fuck!" Wulf ejaculated, jumping away as he realized the golem had snuck behind him and gotten within a hair's breadth without touching him. His heart hammered uncontrollably as he did his best to get his composure once more.

The merchant-turned-adventurer cleared his throat and turned back to High Pope Jeanne. "Actually, I am free tonight and would like to discuss an even better investment opportunity for the Spirit Seekers. Are you free?"

31

The next morning, the GCM had a line stretching halfway across Hub. An entire army battalion of steelfaces had been summoned to police it all, keeping things orderly and flowing. The start of the line rolled with white cloaks, the Spirit Seekers forking up their tithe payments to put in Buy Orders on Diamond Roses.

Further on, other people had caught wind of the reversal in the market and piled on to buy some themselves. The ticker for the going rate had tripled in the first half hour, to thirty thousand gold. Strangely, it wasn't the only material to be rising in price. Iron ore was getting bought up by everyone who couldn't afford a Diamond Rose, which had pushed the going rate all the way to fifteen gold.

Skyye and Gordon had vanished into the guts of the GCM, nearly about to tear their hair out for all the Quicksilver Dust they were using to chase down side-bets.

Ash was left to camp MythAndMire's logout point, sitting with enough alchemical bombs to blow up half the building.

After putting in new sale prices for their Diamond Roses, Wulf and Garry accompanied High Pope Jeanne to the palace dungeons. Wulf elected to put on the Inquisitor outfit once more, which saved him from any assassination attempts, while Garry strutted with his chest out behind Jeanne, glaring at anyone who got too close to the woman.

Jeanne leaned over to Wulf to whisper, "Does he… always act like this?"

Wulf rolled his eyes, but the expression couldn't escape the steel helmet. "He was part of the sorcerer's army. You saved his life last year."

She blinked and straightened up, a smile forming on her lips before the three of them descended to Hub's prison. "Step aside," she ordered when a pair of steelfaces rose to block them. "We're here to post bail."

Arriene sat cross-legged in the third cell, scowling at the walls. She scowled at the rats too, and the damp spots, and the crummy tray of food. She scowled at everything, including the three of them. "What took you so long? And who's she?"

Wulf held up a hand as though presenting Jeanne. "This would be High Pope Jeanne, also known as our savior and the one who can afford to bail you out."

Arriene didn't show a single crack of relief in her scowl. "You're using religious fanatics now?"

"Excuse me," Jeanne snapped back, her cheeks pink. "We prefer the term zealots, thank you."

Arriene's gaze turned on Wulf and he weaseled up a shrug. He said, "So far there isn't technically a monster called a zealot? Like, even in the new Temple of Lumius, it's about inquisitors and torturers and stuff. They've got the linguistic ground to claim. Hey, Jeanne, how about we spring her? The fine can't be too much, can it?"

The High Pope, leader of a thousand white cloaked zealots, turned up her nose. "Maybe if she apologizes."

Wulf face palmed.

Arriene took the high road. "My apologies, Jeanne. Wulf just doesn't have a good track record of meeting women. The last one was an attention vampire that sucked his wallet like it was a lollipop."

Jeanne sucked in breath and half closed her eyes. "I know exactly the type." Bond established, their attitudes shifted immediately to friends, or at least accomplices.

Wulf leaned toward Garry as Jeanne paid Arriene's fine. "What the hell just happened?"

"That's why she's great. I don't pine over just anybody, like you do," the golem responded.

"Tell me," Arriene said as she stepped out of the prison cell. "That you did save Obby?"

Wulf coughed. No one came to his rescue. "I did the next best thing at least?"

Arriene gave him the stare. The kind that made the other two back away from him, lest they get sucked in. Wulf felt every bit the gasping, grasping drowner, and he weakly offered, "I'll explain over a meal?"

By Arriene's demand, the meal was nothing extravagant. They got sandwiches and sat down at a meeting table in the GCM. Normally, the meeting rooms were impossible to get, but no broker in the entire building had time to speak to people. Sentences had devolved into roars and barks, each one step from drawing weapons on one another as the chaos of trading went on.

By popular demand, the big screen–the largest interface in the whole GCM–had the going rate for Diamond Roses on it, and nothing else. It had just ticked over fifty thousand gold, and people were losing their minds.

"So, as you can see, I think anyone with a brain knows to hold on for longer. The price is just going up. AbaraTank is going to get liquidated. I... was right."

Arriene shook her head. "I wouldn't have been working with you if I hadn't believed, but it's still... unbelievable. So, when do you cash out?"

"Cash out?" he asked, and turned to Garry and Jeanne. The golem nodded along, the High Pope's expression was more stone than the golems. "What do you mean cash out? I sell at the top. We all do. We all hold, and we all get infinite money."

Arriene winced and put her hand on his. "Yeah, but that's not going to happen. Only idiots would have the courage to trust everyone else with a Diamond Rose to not sell. We need a plan to cash out."

His mouth could have caught flies. "No, there is no cash out. Did you forget the part where I need millions just to not get tortured by the Queen of Hell?"

"So you cash out at the million gold mark then. At this rate, that will be in like, a day. Wulf, why do you think there is still a line to buy from the System? It's because people are selling right now to AbaraTank. They're taking a petty win and calling it a day."

Wulf turned to Jeanne. "Tell me your people have more guts than that."

The High Pope shrugged. "Everyone has a breaking point, Mr. Hightackle. I just think they have more guts than the Players that are chasing our skirt tails. If it's any consolation, I have it on good authority that a lot of those sales are going to other Players trying to turn around and sell it to AbaraTank for more than they paid for. It's not all them covering their Supply Order."

Garry frowned. "Wouldn't that be driving the price up even faster?"

"That's good for us, isn't it?"

Arriene glared at the ticker and crossed her arms. "But, how is AbaraTank planning to cover at this rate? They can't default on the contract. They have to buy. The higher the price goes, the more they lose."

Wulf scratched his chin. "You think they threw in the towel? Maybe they're cashing out and abandoning ship on the guild. It's the guild that is on the hook for the contracts, not the individual Players."

Jeanne shook her head. "Cohen would crack down on them like the true hammer of God if he caught wind of that. Gold has an official exchange rate to Earth currencies. Literally millions of credits, dollars, euros, whatevers are going to change hands because of this and Cohen will need a fall guy for the mess. What would they even do to cash out now? Sell their gold to some crypto mining operation in the developing world?"

The situation stank. It made the food taste like it had been dipped in a swamp. Wulf abandoned his sandwich and rose from the table to stare at the ticker. "They have to be doing something, though. Are any of them streaming right now?"

Arriene did the honors of pulling up her interface and searching. "No, none."

Jeanne straightened up suddenly. "I just got a message. The guildmaster was just seen entering the GCM. He looks calm."

Wulf sucked on his teeth, steeled himself, and said, "I'm going to go check. Fighting is prohibited in the GCM."

None of his companions thought it a wise move to join him, so Wulf slipped through the halls on his own. No one gave him a second look as he slipped into the press of buyers and sellers, and squeezed his way towards the main interface.

The ticker flatlined.

An alert scrolled along the bottom. "Due to market volatility, all general sales on the following materials have been halted : Diamond Roses, Iron Ore, Troll Ear,-"

The entire GCM screamed. Fire and plague magic fumed across the roof as high level brokers lost their minds. The steelfaces leapt up, provoking a minotaur to stand up, roar, and grab one by the leg. He smashed the steelface into the ground like a ragdoll before chucking the corpse through the interface.

As the elite steelfaces spawned and subdued the minotaur, a second alert appeared. "Institutional trades already submitted will still be executed."

Like magic, the ticker price that had been skyrocketing turned, and plummeted back to five thousand gold, and the trade volume went up and up.

"Those cheating bastards!" Wulf screamed, adding his own vitriol to the vocal maelstrom.

Then it was quiet.

Every throat in the GCM closed, and invisible bonds rooted everyone in place. Barriers that only one man could produce. Lord Cohen emerged in his glowing white suit, and held up a hand to wave. "Hello, everyone. I just wanted to apologize for the unusual market conditions today. It has come to my attention that a group of bad actors has maliciously targeted one of the Player guilds in such a way that threatens the entire stability of the Grand Central Market. I'm terribly afraid that this could cause a chain reaction that damages the value of all material holdings. The last thing I want is for everyone here to end up penniless because of this... unusual behavior. Please rest assured that I have your best interests at heart."

Literally hundreds of people mouthed hatred back at him. In the presence of Lord Cohen, dissent was not permitted. He smiled and thanked himself, ignored that his steelfaces were butchering the minotaur to death, and vanished.

The entire GCM became atheists the moment they could scream again.

Jeanne went on to have an absolutely grand time recruiting people to the Spirit Seekers. The line to join her cause was nearly as long as the line to give up and sell while prices were still profitable.

32

Wulf wanted to vomit.

It felt like a steelface had a grip on his trachea. Had he eaten literal burning coal his stomach would have been more settled. His palms kept sweating, no matter how much he wiped them off. Worse, his mind kept circling the problem like a turd that wouldn't flush down the toilet drain.

The lot of them had half a dozen streamers pulled up, flipping between them to try and find some kind of light comedy. Normally, there was at least one bimbo licking a microphone in her underwear. The Russians were normally good to pull up illegal streams of old cartoons. Not one person was doing so much as a meme review.

Every single streamer was jumping into each other's voice calls to talk about AbaraTank and the Diamond Rose supply squeeze.

Wulf said, "These people are literally just scrambling to not get blamed…"

Gordon shrugged and puffed on his cigar. "What else would you expect them to do? They were all getting paid by AbaraTank through sponsor slots and they're terrified someone is going to call them complicit. You know, not all Players are in the same ballpark as other Players. Plenty of the people over on Earth live paycheck to paycheck. They're going to feel as cheated as we are. Nothing is as fickle as viewership retention."

Wulf planted his chin in his hands and looked over at the ticker. Lord Cohen deigned to let a few market trades happen, which turned the flatline price into a vertical explosion before trading was halted again. Calling it a flatline was misleading however, it trended down whenever it was frozen. The ticker looked like sawteeth.

"What are we supposed to do?" he asked.

"Hold the line. I'm just hoping that Skyye can get our limit sale prices listed and then we're just going to leave. We've already covered our asses. No matter what happens with the rest of our Diamond Roses, we're at least positive. So, she's setting our sale price to ten million gold apiece. Even Cohen can't just rob us outright."

Wulf sighed and tried to watch one of the video streams. The words just passed through one ear and out the other. The buzzwords became mere static. "Maybe I should do the same," he mused. The new meeting room Gordon had gotten for them had a tiny window to the street outside. He walked over and peered out.

Players and white cloaks were lined up as far as he could see, broken only by duels that flared up left and right. He had never seen so many steelfaces before in his life.

Gordon grunted and shifted his weight to the other side

of his tail. "You don't need to wait in that line, you know. You've got me, Wulfie. If you want Skyye to put a price on your Roses, she can."

Wulf shook his head. "I already have mine up. It just... it feels like suddenly it's all out of my hands, you know? For weeks I was leveling up and making plans and, hell, I fought the Phoenix single-handedly!"

Gordon cocked a brow at him.

"Somewhat single-handedly. But still, I was doing things... you know? And now what?"

Gordon rolled back and stretched his arms over the back of the couch. He blew smoke out his mouth and said, "Alea iacta est."

"Am I supposed to know what that means?"

"The die is cast. Learn some history once in a while, Wulfie. It means you've made your decisions. All you can do now is see it through. What you need is something to take your mind off it, before stress grinds your willpower away like a millstone. Go get drunk or something. Or, better yet, go be with Arriene."

Wulf turned to face the dragon. He blinked. "That's... a good point. I guess this is exactly the time I told her we should speak in, isn't it? Just like, I didn't think I'd have nothing to do before we had any sales."

Gordon waved his hand and shooed him out the door. "Gift horses, mouths, I'm sure you know that saying. Go on, get out of here. I need to meet back up with Skyye anyways, and I don't want to be the one keeping your stress levels in check."

Wulf rolled his eyes and stepped out of the meeting room. He pulled out the communication stone and called Arriene. He paced down the hall watching it ring and ring. He mentally rehearsed his lines, and the moment he saw her face, he said, "Arriene, remember what I was saying, back before I went into the Burning Aerie?"

"Wulf, have you seen Garry?"

He stopped cold. A few GCM interns scowled at him for getting in their way. "No, why?"

She shook her head and brushed the hair out of her face. It looked like she was on one of the connecting bridges between the isles. "I can't get ahold of him. I thought he headed back to Greenhorn, but he should have picked up if that were the case. Do you think AbaraTank is targeting the rest of us?"

The tension inside Wulf came back. That vice-like pinch in the middle of his throat. "Maybe. Maybe they are. I wouldn't put it past them. Arriene, you should come back to the GCM. You'll be safe here."

She winced. "I actually headed back to the Burning Aerie to see for myself. My cousin here said that angels have been piling up to get into the Phoenix fight. Some Players have even gotten in fights with them. Rumor has it, one of the angels one-shotted a barbarian using a low-tier sword."

"The God Sword?"

"Bingo."

Wulf groaned and closed his eyes. "Wait there for me. I'll hyper-slide over and catch up. Okay? Keep your head down. I don't want anything to happen to you."

"Thank you very much, Wulf, but I'm still a higher level

than you," she said with a bit of a pout. "Just try and get Garry, alright?"

He put on a pained grin and nodded his head. She canceled the call and Wulf took off for the nearest exit out of the GCM. He tried his hand at calling Garry. Nothing went through. He busted out a side exit of the GCM and emerged onto a mid-level bridge, the kind of path through the city that the developers put in to funnel people from Player housing to the GCM, but never actually expected people to use. That made it perfectly discreet, and Wulf tried calling again.

"Wulfie!"

He jerked upright.

ZelCat grinned at him and ran over. She grabbed his hands and clutched them together between hers. "I've been looking for you, ever since I learned that you totally lied to me about being an NPC."

She was in yet another outfit. This time it was a tight, black bodysuit that covered her from toes to chin. For once, Wulf had no idea what the price on it was, but by the looks of it, figured it was a special costume from the new expansion. It still provoked the physical reaction from him nonetheless.

"Zel... I didn't really lie. I just sorta let you assume, you know? Could we talk later though? Now is a really bad time."

She pouted. "You know, I saw you on a highlight reel from Obby's assassination. You had on a totally cool and rare Inquisitor outfit. So, why are you back to this thing?"

'This thing' was his merchant clothes from Greenhorn, his most comfortable clothes. "Didn't want to stick out. Look,

Zel, sorry. Can we catch up later? I think my friend is in trouble."

She huffed and dropped his hands. The streamer girl planted a hand on her hip and said, "You know, you really need to make it up to me for leaving me like that at the AbaraTank party."

"Oh, come on. Surely you were able to make a clip out of you walking in with the disaster of the party. Nothing happened to you, did it?"

"No, but couldn't you give me one of those Diamond Roses? I did help you in this weird heist thing you've done. I want a cut."

"What?" he asked, but her glare seemed dead serious. "No. No, I'm not giving you something worth potentially millions of gold. If you want one, get in line with everyone else and buy one from the System. In fact! In fact, I want all the money you've borrowed from me back. You've been wringing my wallet dry for weeks."

She sighed and rolled her eyes. "Guess I'm doing it this way," she said and shook her head.

"What? Doing what what way?"

Then she stabbed him in the gut with a level seventy-five poisoned dagger, stacking Bleed, Poison, and a Stagger debuff all at once.

"You... fucking... bitch!" Wulf hissed as he tried to get a healing potion out. He only staggered back a handful of steps before she caught up and hacked his hand off at the wrist.

She did it all with a smile. "Thanks for the Diamond Roses,

Wulfie," she cooed, twiddling her dagger as Wulf collapsed to the ground.

The warmth of life washed out of Wulf's body, pouring onto the bridge as his hit points plummeted so fast he saw critical hit alerts followed by massive damage bonuses. He lost vision, then the feeling in his body and every other sense.

He drifted in oblivion, too shocked to even be mad.

Bony, fiery hands grabbed hold of him and ripped him free of the darkness. The psychopomps hauled him out of the river Kharon and tossed him into the courtyard of the underworld.

"Well... well... well. If it isn't my largest debtor in the whole world," Sofia Portnim said as she walked over to Wulf's dripping body.

Wulf held up a trembling finger. "Wait. Please, wait. Don't call in the debt yet."

The demon queen tilted her head to the side. "And why shouldn't I?"

Wulf gritted his teeth and pushed himself up to his knees before her. He held out his arms and said, "Because I can still fuck over Cohen, that's why. Also, he stole the God Sword from me."

Her eyes burned with magical energy. "You don't have it anymore?"

"That prick kidnapped me because of a glitch in the Temple of Lumius, and he fucking stole it off me. Which means, he stole from you."

Sofia Portnim tried to restrain her rage, so much her body trembled. Then she reared her head back and roared, "Cohen, get down here right now!" The entire underworld trembled around her.

A bolt of light came down from the skies, landing between Wulf and Sofia. Cohen didn't emerge from it, one of his angels did. "Miss Portnim, I regret to inform you that-" the golden warrior tried to say.

She crushed his throat and lifted him off his feet. "Get Cohen."

"I can't!" the angel squeaked.

"Then get me someone that can."

33

"And then she just stabbed you? I'm so sorry, man," the psychopomp said, putting a reassuring hand on Wulf's shoulder. The demon was like a cross between an imp and a dragon, forced to wear a suit, and yet about to cry on Wulf's behalf.

The other psychopomp, a much portlier one, nodded his head. "That's why you can't ever trust a Player."

The thin demon sneered at his colleague. "You just don't trust women."

"I trust Miss Portnim..."

Wulf shook his head and looked down at the cup of coffee the demons had given him. Sofia had agreed that his debt wasn't technically due yet, and to postpone his torture session until the God Sword was sorted out, so her underlings had shown him over to the break room. High up in the Brass Bank, the window beside them overlooked the obsidian forest, and he was too far away to see the faces covering all the carnivorous trees.

It was pleasant, aside from the fact that he was drinking a hot cup of coffee while in a hot room.

"Honestly, all the red flags were there. I should have known better."

The thin demon nodded. "A nice pair of tits will blind you to any number of red flags."

Wulf put his chin in his hand. He swirled his coffee like he was an augur looking for the answers of the universe in it. "It wasn't her tits, it was her eyes. She would actually look me in the eyes and didn't have scorn in them. Why wouldn't I want to spend time with her when she was dragging me along and inviting me to things and asking for my help?"

The fat psychopomp said, "Because she was just trying to get your money."

Wulf grunted. "Yeah, well the only other woman trying to sink her hooks into me is Sofia, and she scares the shit out of me."

The two psychopomps turned their eyes down to their own cups of coffee. They grumbled tepid agreement with him, as though saying it too clearly would get them sacked.

When the silence grew awkward, Wulf leaned back in his chair and stared up at the ceiling. It had once been a mural, before the devs decided to crack it and smoke stain it. The break room didn't actually smell like smoke, so the damage must have come from Cohen's developers. "What really sucks, is that all happened when I was on my way to get to Arriene."

The fat one perked up. "Who's she?"

"The woman I should be throwing myself at, rather than some streamer with hundreds of Players begging to spend time with her."

"Is she an NPC? Like us?"

"Yes, and no. Not like us at all. She's got a little something more to her, you know? If I understood it, maybe I'd have that something more too; but, all I can do now is envy it and try to approach it."

The thin demon shook his head. "You gotta be careful about that. Women can smell envy from a mile away."

The portly psychopomp asked, "You still think you can pay off your debt to Miss Portnim? She'll keep you as a man-slave for years if you can't. Your Arriene won't really matter then."

Wulf stared at his coffee. It didn't portend any answers. "So, how are we supposed to know if Cohen shows up?"

The psychopomps shrugged. "We'll start taking divine damage from being too close to him."

"Ah. Well then, do either of you have a way to check the GCM ticker for Diamond Roses?"

The demons looked at one another. "Reimi?"

"Reimi."

"Who's Reimi?"

As it turned out, Sofia had de facto conquered one of the dungeons of the underworld. Monsters still spawned in it at regular intervals, but she had a legion of golems stationed at every spawn point. Their walk through blood-stained masonry halls kept echoing with demonic roars, ax swings, and gurgles of death.

The psychopomps entirely ignored the noise, and the scurrying imps harvesting the loot from the dead monsters.

"Those aren't sapient golems, are they?"

The thin pyschopomp shook his head. "Nah, nah, just foot soldiers put to proper use. No slavery here. Don't worry."

"And the constant sounds of murder? That doesn't get to

you?" Wulf asked. The demons both gave him queer looks. "Right, sorry, forget I asked that."

The three of them arrived at what looked like a prison section, a dungeon within the dungeon, and found that where he expected to see rusted iron bars he instead found plaster walls with apartment numbers. "People choose to live here?"

The fat psychopomp shrugged. "It's cheap."

"Even in the underworld, NPCs can't afford rent?"

The demon sneered. "Especially in the underworld."

The thin demon pounded his bony fist on the door. "Reimi, you got a minute? Toby and I could use a bit of help. We've got a little something of a VIP too."

The person who opened the door was, no doubt, the most disheveled succubus Wulf had ever encountered. Pale skin. No more clothes than a tank top and panties. Her hair had become a bird's nest tangle, from which he could only barely see a pair of cat ears. Rather than makeup, she had dark bags under her eyes.

Then Wulf's head put together that she almost certainly had vampirism.

"What do you want, Lou?" she asked, folding her arms and looking Wulf up and down. "Oh wait, you're Hightackle. No shit, you got killed?" Her voice was as deadpan as her expression.

He grimaced. "I was told you could pull up the Diamond Rose ticker."

Her smile had fangs, but they were cute fangs rather than viper venom. "Maybe, you got a spare Diamond Rose for me?" she asked, leaning against the doorframe.

"Literally just got killed, remember? A Player has all my stuff."

Reimi sighed. "Figures. You can pay me in information at least. Come on," she said, and wandered into the prison cell. She had done the minimum to transform it into a studio apartment. Her cot was lofted, sheltering a cushioned chair before a static interface. Wulf had to squeeze between a food barrel and her dresser to get a look at the screen.

The sawtooth pattern had changed. "It bounced back to fifty grand apiece, but it's been crabbing ever since. Can't even tell where the trading stops happen anymore."

"How is that possible? AbaraTank kept cheating the price down yesterday."

Reimi grinned. "They managed to cover the first Supply Order, rumor has it they even made a profit on it. Then they stopped buying."

"They have, like, fifteen more Supply Orders to fill though."

"And they already have market buys placed to capture most of the Diamond Roses they just put in. They'll lose money on the next one, but not, you know, half a million in losses."

"But, they have to. The contract says they have to provide fifty Diamond Roses every day for the next two weeks. The System doesn't allow contracts to just be ignored."

Reimi put on a pair of glasses just to dramatically adjust them. "Unless someone changed the System."

Wulf's jaw dropped, which was a horrible idea because he could suddenly taste the body sweat saturated into the prison cell. It was, in fact, not a good flavor. "He can't do that. No, there would be riots if he just openly rigged the market."

Reimi cackled. "You're just now realizing this has been a rigged game from day one? Now see, this is why I've invested all of my money into limited edition holiday costumes. I've had a ten thousand percent return so far. Peanuts compared to this mess, but I'm way better than those stuck-up brokers at the GCM."

Toby and Lou puffed up their chests and folded their arms. "We got in on a ten way split to own a Diamond Rose. Each of us kicked in five hundred gold, and we got a boy topside to buy one. Feels pretty good right about now."

Wulf ignored them. "If they did change the System, any idea what they could change at all? Would they just cancel the contracts?"

Reimi pulled her legs up against her chest, tucking herself into the chair. "No, they can't do that, because then the System wouldn't be able to sell Diamond Roses, and that's sacrosanct. They have to cover eventually but... My guess is they're just going to change the due date and do a search for inactive players with Diamond Roses in their inventory to steal. Maybe they'll inflate the total material count if that doesn't work."

"The System is too big, too complicated for them to mess with it however they'd like. If they want to spawn more, they can only spawn them in the Burning Aerie and then they'd still have to send angels in to get them, competing with every other Player and Spirit Seeker and... fuck me, that must be why they have the God Sword at the Burning Aerie."

All three demons hissed, wincing as wisps of smoke started to drift from their exposed skin. The psychopomps grumbled and muscled through it, stepping back out of Reimi's room with a gruff, "Cohen's here."

"Well, let's go see the giant, glowing prick."

The giant glowing prick had turned off his glow upon entering Sofia's main hall. He had, however, scaled his size up to look the Queen of Hell in the eye and say, "Had I known the God Sword was yours, of course I wouldn't have taken it! I respect the treaties we have and would never violate them."

"Then give it to me," she said.

Cohen whinged and rubbed his hands together. "Well, I can't. I gave it to one of my warrior angels and he's presently occupied. Just getting ahold of-"

"Stop making excuses. This is exactly why your wife left you and took half your money."

"Don't you bring her up," Cohen spat at her. The facade of conciliation gone like a puff of smoke.

Sofia smiled the predatory smile she had whenever a debtor came up short. "Wulf, come up here," she ordered.

The psychopomps shoved him into the hall from the shadows of their spying doorway. He nearly fell, caught himself, looked to flee, saw the door slam in his face, and made the best of it. "Yes?"

Sofia shifted in her throne and leaned an elbow on the arm rest. "Are you in full control of your cognitive capabilities?"

Cohen rolled his eyes as Wulf checked his status. "I'm not currently debuffed in any way, no."

"Not quite what I meant. What do you do with your free time?"

"When my merchant job doesn't need me, I'm generally watching streamer content."

"And that merchant job, who gave it to you?"

"What do you mean? I gave it to me. The System authorized it, and I funded it with a loan from you, but it was my venture."

Sofia stared over at Cohen with that smile of hers. "Sounds to me like he's a free thinker, wouldn't you say? Even if you hadn't known the sword was mine, you did rob it from Mr. Hightackle."

Cohen snarled. "He's just some NPC from the tutorial zone. Who cares? I could delete him and nobody would notice."

The Queen of Hell rose to her feet. The temperature in the hall doubled as she materialized her sword: an arcane greatsword hot enough to burn the ash from the air. A writhing mass of flames plumed from the weapon's blade, bathing the three of them in its light. "I would notice. I would care. And so would dozens of other free thinkers in RIV. This is why we have treaties, Cohen."

The Lord Ruler of RIV put up his hands and stepped back. "Come on Sofia, you know I haven't ever done that. It was a figure of speech." She clicked her tongue and put the sword back away. "Look, I'll get you the sword back. I just can't do it right now. How about we write up a loan contract?"

Sofia dropped back into her throne and crossed her legs

with a flourish. "And what would I want with your gold? You just fabricate it anyway. Besides, you should be offering that contract to Mr. Hightackle, not me. He's the victim."

Cohen's mouth hung open. He looked down at Wulf, and back at Sofia. "You can't be serious. Sofia, I'll respect you, but you can't expect me to treat with this scrap of code."

"I can, and I do."

"This is preposterous."

"If you don't, I will break your toys. How about I start with the guildmaster of AbaraTank?"

Cohen brought the glow back. He stepped forward and jabbed a finger at her like a lance. "You even lay a finger on him and I'll-"

"You'll what?" Sofia demanded, and flexed her magic. The back half of the throne room went black as her demonic shadow consumed it, turning the marble and the gold to a mass of writing mouths chomping on inner fires.

Cohen snarled. "Don't think I don't have options."

"Then it's war."

Cohen stuffed his thumbs into his belt and nodded. "I suppose it is."

Sofia flicked a hand at him, and Cohen vanished. Whether he left of his own accord, or she somehow banished him, Wulf had no idea. He was left twiddling his fingers beside where the two titans had been. "Well then, now what?"

She looked over him, and anger was replaced by business casual. "Oh, you're still on the hook for paying me back for the God Sword. I'd say good luck getting it back from him but... well, you don't really stand a chance."

"Oh come on!"

"Relax Wulf. I'll cut you a deal and get you out of here nice and quick if you just do one thing for me," she said, and waved her hand through the air.

A quest notification appeared in front of him. "Defeat AbaraTank's guildmaster in a duel. Optional: Livestream it. Rewards: The Queen of Hell, Sofia Portnim's, personal assistance with the Grand Central Market."

34

"Hello erry-body! How y'all doin' today?" ZelCat announced as she smiled and waved and strolled around the center of the Arena. Thousands of people, Players and NPCs both, put their voices together and roared. The entire foundation of the Arena vibrated from the energy of the crowd.

Sand fell from the cracks in the ceiling around Wulf as he suited up for the duel. He glanced up and shook his head.

Ash tried to glance out through the barred window to get a look at the mob of people that had stormed into the Arena following the announcement of the challenge. "You sure this is a good idea, Wulfie?"

"It's the only idea. Therefore, it's a good idea," Wulf said, buckling on jagged, red metal armor to his limbs.

The lich turned back to him. "Where'd you even get that gear? You've never been one to climb the Arena ladder and it looks expensive. Did you take another loan from Portnim?"

"What? No. Turns out she doesn't offer additional loans to people in default. She's not the only rich person I know though."

"Then who?"

Amaranth Darkheart leaned forward. "Me, of course." Ash

the Reborn shouted and jumped back. The vampire frowned. "I've been here the entire time. How did you not see me?"

"Cohen damn it, Wulf, did you offer Arriene's blood again?" Ash asked as he circled around the prep room to put Wulf between him and the vampire.

Wulf smirked. "No need on that front," he said, and strapped a red sash around his midsection, tying it in the back and letting the ends trail off into rose petals. Fashionable he was not.

But he was decked out in an optimized Phoenix Burn Build.

Amaranth Darkheart smiled, though the expression looked unnatural. "He's made himself the interlocutor between me and Miss ZelCat. I'm quite interested in procuring her for my collection."

Ash winced and glanced at the door. "How the hell did you convince her to help, anyway? Didn't she kill you?"

"She's a one-track mind. She killed me because she thought I had the Diamond Roses on my person, rather than all stored with the GCM to be sold. AbaraTank paid out for the bounty already, so it's not like she has animosity for me. She's just— she just doesn't care about me."

The vampire rubbed his hands together. "And that's why there's such a delicious opportunity for me."

Outside, Zel began her introductions, stoking the crowd of gamblers into a frenzy as the gladiatorial gates finally unlocked.

Ash grabbed Wulf's shoulder when he started forward. "You did practice this Build, right? This isn't like fighting the

Phoenix. That's a real Player over there. You make a mistake, and it's all over."

Wulf scoffed. "I'm decked out in Phoenix Burn. The Build practically plays itself. I'll be fine. Go put a bet on me or something, so we can afford to drink tonight," he said, and marched out into the light of the arena.

Zel turned to him with an outstretched hand. "Here he is. You know him from Greenhorn. The one who broke iron ore and then broke Diamond Roses. The one, the only, Wulf Hightackle!"

He smiled and gave a half-hearted wave with his Monastery Spear. The crowd took only a moment to realize what Build he had on, and their enthusiasm wavered.

The door across from him opened, and a black knight emerged. It wasn't Dee's_Knutz.

"And in this corner," Zel said, swinging her hand towards the knight. "The guildmaster of AbaraTank himself, on his main account, it's Ligma! Sporting the very first Death&Taxes Build with the new equipment from the Temple of Lumius. You all can consider this not just a death match over the market conditions, but also the debut match for the new PvP meta."

The black knight, Ligma, was level one hundred. The guildmaster had just been fooling around as Dee's_Knutz.

"Oh- fuck."

Ligma leveled his sword at Wulf and announced, "You'd better have the Diamond Roses, you showboating dick."

Wulf shook his head and took from his inventory the limit sale contracts with the GCM, ten in total. The duel interface, projected up to the top of the arena for everyone to see, confirmed what he was wagering as part of the complete inventory bet. Anything less, and the guildmaster would have never been goaded out himself.

Ligma nodded, and pulled out a bag of ten Diamond Roses as well. The stakes were even, but the duel interface also listed their levels, one hundred to fifty. Wulf had done some last minute grinding, but fifty was as good as he could get. The bettors all groaned.

Wulf asked, "How did you already get that gear? The Boss should have only respawned once at most."

Ligma sneered and spread his arms. "Well, you see, somebody glitched the dungeon by leaving in the middle of the fight. Made it real easy to get a ton of Pages of Perdition! You should feel honored, you're the first to experience Death&Taxes! Well, I guess the second, after–"

"Accept the duel conditions," Wulf demanded, taking a hard step forward. His side of the interface went green.

Ligma laughed. "I accept. Now embrace your inevitable defeat."

Wulf gripped his spear in both hands, leaned forward and just couldn't bring himself to charge. Zel was about to announce the start, and he interrupted to say, "Excuse me, ref. Could we get an injunction against Ligma to prohibit him from using the most fucking cliche lines possible?"

Zel sighed, one hand raised in the air to start them. "His name is Ligma. You expect me to stop the cringe? Now fight!"

"Ligma balls!" the black knight shouted as he formed half a dozen magic sigils over his head, charging up their effects.

Wulf groaned and just charged forward to stab him. The gear boosted his speed almost beyond his control, and he jammed the tip of the spear through Ligma's chest before the first spell could finish. About twelve percent of the guildmaster's health vanished.

The first spell completed, [Arcane Faltering], which doubled the formation time for all magic sigils within the Arena. So Wulf stabbed him again and took out another twelve percent.

The second spell completed, [Dictate of the Guardian], which halved the amount of damage Ligma would take for the next five minutes. Wulf stabbed again for a sum total of thirty percent.

The third spell completed, [Stasis Walk], which anchored Wulf's movement speed by half. Wulf grabbed Ligma by the chest plate, and stabbed the knight for another six percent damage.

The fourth spell completed, [Life Leech], which would siphon one percent of Wulf's health every three seconds to heal Ligma for one percent. Wulf stabbed for a net five percent damage.

The fifth and sixth spells completed, [Ethereal Taxation] and [Exertion], which doubled the mana cost of all spells as well as their cooldowns. Wulf kept stabbing.

Finally, Ligma brought his sword down and cleaved into Wulf's shoulder, cutting down to the bone and dealing ten percent damage to him. The AbaraTank guildmaster burst out laughing as Wulf stabbed back for not even half as much damage. "You fool! You absolute buffoon! You did nothing to stop me from stacking my buffs. You can't beat me now."

Wulf just smirked as Ligma showboated. Then he activated the Diamond Rose sash to quick-cast a stored [Mana Burn]. His fingers crackled with lightning as the spell went off. Normally, Players used their sash to store a [Lightning Bolt] spell to top off the last of the damage. [Lightning Bolt] was great, guaranteed damage, able to take out a quarter of a barbarian's health pool in one go. Ligma had almost fifty percent of his health remaining, far more than a [Lightning Bolt] could deal.

[Mana Burn] didn't work that way.

[Mana Burn] dealt damage proportional to the amount of ongoing status effects to their caster.

All of Ligma's buffs flared with arcane fire and bounced back to him, immolating the knight like someone had set off a pile of thermite in the middle of the Arena. The guildmaster screamed, half in pain and half in rage before he dropped dead at Wulf's feet.

The entire arena stared in awe as Wulf brushed the blood off his chest and knelt down beside the smoking knight. "When you show up in the underworld, give my regards to M'Long."

Zel peeked around one of the pillars that ringed the center of the Arena, from what protection she had from the fight. "What?"

Wulf stood up and threw his hands in the air. "I said he can give his regards to my long co-"

Divine light blasted down onto Ligma. The ground trembled and a chorus of angels sang out.

Wulf threw his hands down. "You cheating son of a bitch!"

Someone, Cohen most likely, revived the AbaraTank guildmaster. Ligma proceeded to roll over and throw a tantrum, screaming and pounding a fist on the ground.

Wulf groaned and left the knight there. The duel was over, and anyone who looked up to the interface saw the results. The System stripped Ligma of his inventory one item at a time, piling them into a heap in Zel's arms to hand to Wulf.

"Alright, alright, this is done. Here," Wulf mumbled, handing Zel one of the Diamond Roses as he tried to pull up his quest notification from Sofia. Zel brazenly snatched it from him, eyes gleaming. The Arena was cheering more with every second, but Wulf didn't even crack a smile. His heart still felt every ounce of tension in it as he waited to see "Quest Complete."

The interface gave him an error message instead. "Recalculating…"

"We're not done here, Hightackle," Ligma shouted, and he held up a hand. Someone from the front row of the arena chucked an item in. With their duel over, no System barriers prevented it, so it soared over. The knight snatched it from the air and snarled at Wulf.

His eyes went wide. The Diamond Rose he had been lifting from Zel's pile slipped from his grasp.

Ligma grinned, teeth bloody red and skin scorched black. "You know what this is, don't you? Double or nothing."

Ligma was holding Garry's Control Rod.

35

Ash wanted to tear his hair out, but could only scratch at his bald skull. "Why would you agree to that? Why? You won. You have all his Diamond Roses. Just walk away."

"Because that's Garry's control rod. He has Garry," Wulf said, pacing the arena prep room. He only had a few minutes to restore health and mana and reset cooldowns before the next duel.

The lich grabbed him by the shoulders. "If you lose those Roses though, the entire squeeze will fail. Everyone who has their hopes staked on this will get screwed. Don't you realize some people bought in at tens of thousands of gold?"

Wulf broke Ash's arms off of himself and grabbed the lich in turn. "It's Garry. I may never get another chance to get that rod back from him. He could just turtle up in his guild hall and the market, while using Garry as a personal slave. This might be my only chance."

Ash groaned and rolled his head. "Do you at least have a plan? Can you Mana Burn him again?"

"Nope. I can't actually cast Mana Burn so... no way to store it in the sash again."

"What? How did you get it in the first place?"

Wulf scratched the back of his head. "It was already on the outfit when I borrowed it from Amaranth."

Ash stared him in the eyes. Silence dragged between them, beneath the roar of arguing gamblers. "You can't actually cast any spells, can you? You're decked out in a spellcasting gear Build and literally just using the melee options."

Wulf squirmed and shrugged. "I had a plan, for the first duel. Right? I'm a bit out of my depth here, to be honest."

"Why would you choose Phoenix Burn then? The entire reason the Build works is because you can put out so much direct fire damage so quickly."

"It seemed thematic to win with it? And I know that Ligma out there knows the meta, so he would play around thinking I was fully specced into magic. I mean, he did cast a bunch of anti-magic debuffs, right? Look, I don't know what I'm doing here."

"Then why did you agree to the duel? What's the point if you can't win!" Ash screamed at him. He wilted and fell onto the room's bench. "I'm never going to be human again. My hopes, my dreams, you pumped them up and dumped them on the ground."

Wulf paced the room. "Maybe I can get Amaranth to cast some kind of high level vampire drain and store it in the sash? But he vanished to go try and buy Zel..."

The door to the waiting room flew open, casting light into the gloom. "Wulf, you are hopeless without me. Only an idiot would accept that duel, after seeing direct intervention from Lord Cohen," Arriene said as she marched in with her casting staff. "But, I can't really fault you."

Wulf stared at her like an angel from heaven, except an actual angel and not just the peons that Cohen had. "Arriene, you're a full caster, right?"

She smiled, flicked her hair back, and said, "Yes, I am. Need that sash recharged?"

Wulf threw his arms around her and embraced her. "You've saved me."

She stiffened. "I mean, I'm also saving myself, and Garry, and like, hundreds of other people. But, yeah, I guess so. You're lucky I was able to make it back here. The Burning Aerie became a huge shitshow once people realized that the angels had some kind of broken developer weapon. The journalists are having a field day eating Cohen alive right now."

Wulf broke off from her. "Well, let's hope he gets too distracted to cheat on Ligma's behalf again."

Arriene nodded and held out her hand for the sash. "How about we also start by explaining to you how you're supposed to use all this gear though? Because most of what you're wearing has stored spells in it, that you're supposed to be simultaneously casting, you know... faster than Death&Taxes can make your life miserable?"

Five minutes later, Wulf marched back out into the Arena to face off against the AbaraTank guildmaster. Ligma spat some blood onto the sand. "Don't think that bullshit is going to work twice."

"Oh, it's totally going to work twice," Wulf lied.

"I'm going to enjoy torturing you. You're pretty much the only individual I can pin this humiliation on, aside from your friend anyways, and I've got a lot of stress to work out."

Wulf grinned. "Well, I'm sure it will burn that much more when you lose to an NPC who only knows how to fight monsters. Accept."

"Accept," Ligma echoed.

The duel interface went green, and again, Ligma threw up his hand to summon half a dozen magic sigils. Once more, Wulf sprinted in and stabbed him, except this time he activated the necklace he had on to add fire attribute to his spear attack. Twenty percent of Ligma's health vanished in the first strike, emptying out the necklace.

Wulf repeated his flurry of blows, trading damage for debuffs until Ligma was down to critical health. The fire enchantment snuffed out when Ligma added a new enchantment to the mix, [Short Circuit], which canceled all of Wulf's ongoing spells and reset their cooldowns. Had he been a caster, he could have immediately recast the fire enchant, but resetting cooldowns did nothing for item charges.

"[Greater Restoration]," Ligma shouted, dumping the last of his mana into a full heal on himself, capping his health once more and putting the biggest grin on his face possible. The knight finally hefted his sword up. "Grit those teeth."

Wulf tried to dodge back, but [Stasis Walk] grabbed onto his feet like a swamp. The sword hacked into his chest, taking out a tenth of his health. Ligma's manic laughter hurt more than the steel. Again, Wulf tried to dodge backwards, to buy himself time.

Ligma followed, slicing his arms, his legs, his shoulders, anything that wouldn't deal a critical hit to him. [Stasis Walk] affected him as well, but with the two of them moving at the same speed, he could easily keep up.

Until Wulf equipped a shield and dropped a bomb at his feet.

Ligma blinked and looked down at the item. The fixed damage wouldn't even register on his health pool. Confusion did more to him than the explosion did.

Wulf parried the explosion. [Stasis Walk] or no, the physics engine still didn't know what to do with the forced knock-back. He flew backwards in a hyper-slide and crashed into the far wall of the Arena, suddenly fifty feet away from Ligma and laughing.

"Oh, who's the cheater now, huh?" Ligma roared as he trudged over to Wulf.

Wulf chuckled and dusted himself off. "What are they going to do? Ban me?"

Ligma growled. "And what is it you think you can do over there? Wait me out?"

"This," Wulf answered, and pointed his Monastery Spear at the knight. He activated the ring on his hand and started using one charge after the next. Each burst of magic raced down the length of the spear and blasted out the end as a small fireball. The flying infernos struck Ligma in the chest one after the next.

They did pitiful damage. One percent each by the looks of it. By that metric, the item would have been useless in the Arena. However, for as little damage as it dealt, it also dealt Stagger. A close-range, surprise blast could interrupt magic sigils and swing the tide of a fight. At long-range, any Player worth their salt could dodge.

If they weren't affected by [Stasis Walk].

Ligma screamed in frustration, holding up an arm and trying to march against the tide of fire. Every blow struck like a hammer, slowing his march to a crawl. Death&Taxes had a dozen ways to deal with the magic spam, but Ligma had used up all his mana to heal and prevent a [Mana Burn] death. The moment he tried to retrieve a mana potion to top off again, Wulf just blasted it out of his hand and resumed hitting him in the face.

"God damn it, this wouldn't be possible if you hadn't cheated," Ligma shouted.

Wulf flipped him off with his free hand. "Says the guy who got revived by the dev. Eat shit and die. Hell, you're twice my level and still bitching?"

"You've got endgame equipment. Bullshit you're half my level."

"I'm just a merchant. If I was actually level one hundred, I would have just cast flame shield or something," Wulf said, continuing to pelt Ligma as the knight drew closer.

"That's it!" Ligma canceled [Stasis Walk] and sprinted forward.

The effect ended on Wulf simultaneously. He swore and turned tail to flee. The knight already had a headstart though, penning him in against the wall of the arena. Wulf swallowed the knot in his throat and stamped his foot into the ground to pivot back around. "Eat [Mana Burn]," he shouted, wheeling about on his foe.

Ligma flinched. He jerked back and threw up a guard as his eyes locked on Wulf's offhand to dodge the spell. So the spear thrust went straight through his blindspot and into his neck. Critical damage chimed, knocking the AbaraTank guildmaster down to less than five percent health and pumping him full of enough anger to kill a horse.

Wulf pulled the spear back and shot Ligma in the face with another fireball to blind the man for a moment. That bought him time to sprint to the other side of the arena. Something like a sixth sense in his gut tingled. The feeling that things had gone too well. That tension before the drop every time Cohen had screwed him in the market.

Over his shoulder, Wulf saw Ligma chugging a mana potion. He threw the brakes on and took a wild shot with a fireball, missing completely as the knight lifted up his sword once more to summon the biggest magic sigil yet. "[Summon Spirit Guardians]," he roared, triggering the trump card for the Death&Taxes Build. All around him, ethereal hands clawed up from the sand. Ghostly warriors rose up with swords and hammers, wailing barbarian war cries. Dozens of them formed ranks, marching towards Wulf. Each was flagged as a level one hundred.

Wulf activated the Diamond Rose sash and drew out Arriene's spell. "[Solar Rain]."

A direct line of artillery magic blasted from his outstretched hand and into the ranks of Spirit Guardians. It chipped away at their health a mere five percent. Five percent was all the health Ligma had left, after neglecting to heal. The magic knocked him off his feet and sent him flying into the far wall of the arena. The knight collapsed to the ground, conscious but unable to move a finger as the System asked Wulf whether he wanted to kill or spare the man.

Just because the duel ended though, and Ligma's spell effects wore off, and the Spirit Guardians vanished, didn't mean [Solar Rain] ended. The rest of the blasts started to go wild, firing off in every direction. Some blasted into the arena stands, others into the sand at his feet. With virtually zero experience casting spells, it was all he could do to thrust his hand into the sky and let the last of it fill the air like fireworks.

36

The market price of Diamond Roses skyrocketed the night after Wulf's duel. The entire Grand Central Market shut down to stop the mass liquidation of assets as people tried to buy Diamond Roses still available. City-wide riots and brawls broke out over the queue to get into the market.

Block by block, the whitecloaks began slapping down bids to buy the houses back from the Players. Just like Wulf and the others, Jeanne's people had set conservative sell prices for their first Diamond Roses. For them, conservative meant a million gold each, and they still had a hundred Buy Orders placed for as long as the System would recycle the materials.

Wulf took the celebration back to Greenhorn, to Mead's Taproom. "I brought the real elven wine!" he roared, hefting an amphora over his head to the cheers of every NPC in the tutorial zone.

Stone hands pulled him aside. "Wulf," Garry said, with an admonishing shake of his head. "How'd you go and afford that? Don't they got your trades still held up in inspection?"

Wulf winked and punched the golem in the chest. "The trades are, yeah. Did you forget though? I got that dickhead

Ligma's entire inventory before the System started liquidating them."

Ash jumped up on the bar counter, swaggering from far too much alcohol salve on his bones. "Let's get the fucking ticker up here. It's time to party. And guess what? The server is getting reset so go wild!"

On command, a menu interface appeared above the crowd. The going rate for Diamond Roses displayed like a straight, vertical line. Every few minutes, the System bought the next cheapest Diamond Rose, driving the price exponentially higher.

Wulf watched it from behind cup after cup of wine, until his head was loose and his body sweaty with booze. Arriene sat down next to him, in her usual after work attire; the same outfit he had first been smitten with. "Think it will get all the way to the top? All the way to nine hundred and ninety-nine million?"

"And nine hundred and ninety-nine thousand, nine hundred and ninety nine," Wulf said.

She rolled her eyes, but was smirking. "Can't forget the ninety nine coppers too, can we?"

"No we can't," he said, ignoring the ticker to look at her. "Maybe, maybe it will get there. I think it will at least hit sixty-nine million though."

"Oh?" she leaned her elbows on the table, drawing in close so they could hear one another. "And what makes you say that?"

"Because it's a nice number. And because Skyye told me that there were like twenty offers for that amount."

Arriene rolled her eyes. "Have you decided what you're going to do with all that money?"

"Pay off my debt first. I'm doing my best here to pretend that Sofia isn't going to flay my skin off and force me to sit on a throne of salt while I watch a hundred hours of drama channels arguing with each other over whether some popular guy cheated at a children's game."

Arriene snorted, immediately covering her mouth with a hand as she set her cup back down. "Okay, hold on, those aren't all bad. That last flareup is why Obby got a following in the aftermath."

Wulf slammed his cup down on the table. "Oh, fuck Obby. He never even logged back in after he got assassinated."

"Oh, he just switched back to his speedrun account. He had a Diamond Rose put in at the sale price cap, so he's just off doing other things. So, you still haven't answered my question. What are you going to buy with all the money?"

Wulf kicked back and put his hands behind his head. The ticker had jumped up to twenty million. "Assets, I guess. Cohen was right, I think we completely destroyed the economy. The System is going to have to generate so many gold coins we'll be able to fill lakes with them. Runaway inflation is going to be a bitch, but land will always hold its value. Maybe I'll buy up all of the Burning Aerie? Kick Players off it entirely and charge a fee to go fight the Phoenix?"

"Back to business, then?"

He grinned. "Well, it is my class. Just now, I'll be the one taking advantage of them, you know? Actually, I've got a better idea."

Arriene brushed some hair away from her face and leaned an elbow on the table. "And what's that?"

"I'm going to buy Greenhorn. It's a quaint town, and will be quiet after I force all the anonymous accounts to find somewhere else to hook up. There's this really nice tavern I like to drink at."

She smiled, her lips curling into that perfect little smirk she had. "You'll have to show me some time."

"I'd be happy to. This girl I know showed it to me once, before she taught me what an idiot I was being."

The two of them leaned in close. "And how did she do that? A slap to the face?"

"A deserved one, yeah," Wulf said, their foreheads almost touching. He could smell the wine on her breath mingled with a hint of perfume. His eyes danced between hers and down her slender nose to her lips.

She was doing the same to him, and they leaned closer and closer.

Ash screamed, "What the fuck is that?"

They both grimaced and glanced over. The ticker price had turned red and plummeted from a high of sixty-nine million back to five thousand gold. The taproom erupted into shouts just like the GCM as everyone's interfaces chimed alerts. Wulf got one himself, notifying him that his limit sale of one Diamond Rose for nine hundred and ninety-nine million gold had been canceled and refunded due to "an unexpected System error."

Garry squeezed over to the table. "Hate to interrupt."

Wulf buried his face in his hand. "We're already inter-rupted."

"What's up?" Arriene asked.

Garry pulled up his interface. He had Obby's livestream up. The speedrunner was just standing on a bridge, holding his middle finger up at the sea as he filmed. The Kraken kept swatting through the air, throwing tsunamis around like a child in a bathtub. In the sky above, a black inferno clashed with a titanic angel.

Sofia Portnim was trying to kill Lord Cohen.

"Is Obby throwing away his world record run?" Arriene asked, squinting at the screen.

Garry arched a brow. "For the amount of money on the line here? I'd throw a world record run too."

MythAndMire intruded into their conversation through the crowd. He slapped one hand on Wulf's back and said, "Oh, I wouldn't worry about that. Look at his view count. Hi guys, did you miss me?"

"How the fuck did you get in here?" Wulf demanded.

MythAndMire grinned. "I own the place. I sold my first Diamond Rose for two million gold, and bought this place. Pretty nifty, ain't it?"

Wulf tried to throw the Player's arm off of him. "You fucking dickhead. I was going to buy this!"

MythAndMire laughed. "Well, maybe you should have set your sale prices a bit lower, don't you think? Don't worry, I'll sell it to you, for a hundred million gold."

"Hey, you, the one who stabbed his way into our

operation," Arriene said as she twisted to look at the Player. "Why don't you get the hell out of my sight before I get my casting staff and blow a hole through your fancy new building?"

"Woah, easy there. I'm here on business, and it's not just the business of running a bar. The Queen of Hell herself contracted me to pick up Wulf. I'm a bounty hunter first and foremost, you know."

Wulf hooked a thumb over his shoulder at the showdown they were watching. "She seems a bit preoccupied."

"Bah," MythAndMire said with a shrug. "So what if she kills Cohen? This is just a game avatar for him anyways. I'm sure she'll be done in just a few minutes here."

Wulf stood up and shoved his chest against the Player, forcing him away from the table. "Take the hint. Get lost. I'll go see her on my own time to clear up the debt. I don't need some bastard like you dragging me away right when I'm finally getting somewhere."

MythAndMire pointedly glanced over Wulf's shoulder at Arriene and folded his hands together. He shrugged again. "Bit late for that, ain't it? I already poisoned you."

"What?"

Then the debuff hit him with paralysis. He faceplanted onto the beer-coated floor of the taproom, unable to budge a finger. His health pool began draining like someone had set fire to it. "Son of a bitch."

The crowd turned into a mob. Weapons were drawn, spells were cast, and not a single person actually cast a heal spell on

Wulf. Around the time someone summoned a demon into the room, Wulf died.

For the second time that week, a pair of psychopomps dragged him out of the River Kharon and tossed him into the infernal courtyard. Lou and Toby groaned when they recognized him. "Aww man, again? I'm sorry, Wulf," Lou said as he patted him on the back.

Wulf coughed up some blood and river water, waving them off. "I'm fine, it's fine. Fuck!" He pounded his fist. Gravel flew. "That was the perfect moment! And Cohen just had to fuck it up right then."

"Sorry, Wulfie," Sofia said as she walked over to him. She looked like a mess, still covered in burns and slashes from her fight with Cohen. He could see the way worms and shadows crawled beneath her skin to knit it all back together, pulling her once more into the towering, human form. "But don't be too upset about the timing. You'll be spending your days with me from now on, and we're going to have so much fun together. You and me, my most valuable customer."

Wulf cleared his throat and got up to his feet. "About that, actually. How much do I owe you for the God Sword?"

Sofia shook her head and held out her hand. The contract ledger appeared, tallied the interest and loss clauses, and she proclaimed, "Six hundred and sixty-six million gold. A little hard to price a priceless artifact, you know?" She winked at him.

"Okay. So, I just need to transfer that much to you?"

She grinned. "So sorry to see Cohen screwed you on the

market prices. I'm still going after him for all that, breaking the treaties and so on. But, these kinds of circumstances are just part of the risks you take when you take out a loan."

Wulf nodded. "Yeah, I completely understand. So I just have to transfer you the money?"

Sofia blinked and looked down at his calm face. "Wulf, were you not watching the ticker? Cohen shut it all down and canceled the Supply Orders. The price reset to five thousand gold."

Wulf shrugged. "Yeah, going forward. But anything that sold before then still went through. Here you go," he said, and started a trade with her through his interface. A few taps later and he confirmed it.

Sofia's eyes opened, her mouth dropped. "How did you... Weren't your sale prices all set at the gold cap?"

Wulf scratched his nose and grinned. "One was. I set the rest to one gold short of sixty-nine million. So, that's just like, half of what I made, give or take. Thankfully, AbaraTank wagered another ten Roses in our duel. So, we're all clear and good I think. I'm going to go now, if that's alright. I've got a lot of property to buy."

"But... But that's... There's a holding period on exchanges!" she protested as he started walking out of the Brass Bank.

He waved over his shoulder. "I've got a really good broker! Good luck getting the God Sword back from Cohen!" he said, and began his journey back to Arriene.

37

Epilogue

A month later, ZelCat had a new account and her streaming was still on hold while Skyye gave her business lessons on how to navigate the GCM. Her old account had been added to Amaranth's collection for fifty million gold, which she was quickly burning through trying to buy in on fluctuations in the price of micro-materials.

Skyye had been skeptical at first, but needed a hobby while Gordon was away in the Highlands chasing down rare field monsters. He had lost twenty pounds, which he credited to no longer stress drinking in the office. He still showed up to Wulf's Taproom to get drunk on the weekends though.

Garry managed to buy himself a fortress on the Burning Aerie, turning it into a training camp for the Spirit Seekers away from Hub. As it turned out, High Pope Jeanne had in her possession a glitched inventory bag, that anything could be put into but never taken out of. With his control rod locked away in that divine artifact, he was finally free of his fear of Players and began dueling his way up to level one hundred.

Ash The Reborn only sold one Diamond Rose before the market collapsed, and that was his safety sale at one million, so he couldn't quite afford resurrecting himself. He was, however, able to buy a holiday event skin off ZelCat for a few hundred thousand gold. When equipped, it turned him into a her, but she had internal organs again. She was able to drink and fuck as much as she wanted.

Arriene saved her money. It was enough to live off of without working at the GCM, so long as she rented a room at Wulf's Taproom, and she said she wanted to save it for buying level one hundred gear. While she didn't admit it to anyone outright, she had put almost all of her sale prices at the price cap, and walked away with barely anything.

Which was fine by Wulf. After buying all of Greenhorn's inner district, he was still happy to offer her a loan for half. Payback period, the rest of their lives.

About The Author

James likes to think about worlds that don't exist. Growing up on a diet of video games, anime, and the internet, ending up as an engineer was accidental. At least it helps write about computer systems and robots. The covid pandemic re-ignited his childhood dream of being an author, dating back to when he was a child sitting on his grandfather's knee making up stories. Now, he has a head full of stories he wants to tell, and the freedom to do so.

You can find more on his website, jameskrake.com

If you enjoyed this novel, please consider leaving a review, telling a friend, posting about it on social media, or otherwise getting the word out.

More From The Author
Ship of Fuls, by James Krake

Chapter 0 - To Win The War

Marcus sat beneath the shadow of a gas giant, surrounded by metal skulls. He held a gun in his hands, ripped from the arm of one of the enemy war machines. The thing fired needles, or maybe they were micro-flechettes. From the spare magazine, he couldn't tell if they were a metal alloy or some kind of nano-material. The munitions cracked between his trembling fingers, but he had seen them pierce body armor. The man inside had burst into blood like a balloon.

Marcus squeezed his hand into a fist as tight as he could, until it felt like he would rip the environmental suit. When the shakes subsided, he put his mind back to the gun. It had no trigger that he could find. The firing mechanism was entirely digital, which explained why it had locked up under the assault of the attack scripts. They had been lucky the ship's defenses were out of date. Luckier than the dead Camrians strewn across the hangar bay. He tried not to look at his own handiwork.

Marcus felt only one step removed from the corpses as he sat upon a collapsed bulkhead. He had been hit by bullets, tossed by explosions, and singed by fire; but, that hadn't been enough to put him in the ground. His armor sat heavy upon him, and he couldn't even take off his helmet. The internal systems warned of unidentified neurotoxins in the air, which left him rebreathing his own sweat.

Ranger Levy whooped as he got the flood lights to power on. Beams of artificial daylight blasted across the battlefield, painting the walls with shadows. He leapt down from the control booth, landing on the smoking ruin of some kind of fighter plane. Marcus didn't know whether it was a manned craft, or just an elaborate way of launching missiles. What he did know was that something inside it had caught fire, and the smoke ate the paint from Levy's armor. His comrade had to scrape it off as he said, "And here I was starting to think the locals were blind."

Marcus tossed the gun back to the metal goliath he had taken it from. The steel face grimaced back at him. "Would have been easier for us had they been."

"We're never that lucky though, are we? Come on, we have to keep moving." Levy said, turning his head up. The charge field overhead kept crackling and flickering, letting the moon's hydrocarbon atmosphere leak in. Eventually, the fuel to air mixture would be just right and the whole place would explode. Not even corpses would be left.

Marcus turned his head up too. He could only see the planet by how he couldn't see the stars. The huge mass had seemed so important on the star charts, and he still couldn't see it. The local star may as well have not existed. None of its light reached so far out.

The burning trails of ships crossed the void like shooting stars. The Camrians had given up on the moon, but he didn't let himself hope that they were retreating. There was no way they were that lucky. It would be some other battlefield, some other star, some other year. For once though, Marcus knew where that would be. "Does it feel like we're getting to the end of the war?"

Levy shrugged. "We have to be, by now. Earth has been working to break the stasis for centuries now. Got that Manhattan Project Two coming along."

"Weren't we that project?"

"Project Three then. Pretty soon Earth is going to retaliate and put an end to the war. We just have to keep buying them time."

"We've been buying them time for centuries."

Levy slapped him in the shoulder. "Means we're good at it. We're experts. The best there is at all things warfare. Now come on. We've got ships to catch. I'm thinking the old boarding rocket special. What about you?"

"Levy, those ships have nuclear missiles headed for Earth. How many of us are even left? Do we have enough?"

Levy turned his head up, counted the ships, and said, "Enough for one each, I reckon. Won't be our first time. Good thing we've had practice at it." The other Ranger laughed.

Marcus sighed and got to his feet. He felt heavy despite the low gravity. For a moment, he was reminded of the myth of Atlas holding up the heavens. The ancients could never of known how weighty the heavens were with the trillions of people needing protection. "I guess we don't have much of a choice."

"You could always run away. Get yourself a girl, ditch the armor, settle down..."

Marcus put his hand on Levy's shoulder. "You know that's not an option for us," he said, and headed off to the next in a long line of battlefields.